Violet Ghosts

Also by Leah Thomas

Because You'll Never Meet Me
Nowhere Near You
When Light Left Us
Wild and Crooked

Violet Ghosts

LEAH THOMAS

BLOOMSBURY

NEW YORK LONDON OXFORD NEW DELHI SYDNEY

BLOOMSBURY YA
Bloomsbury Publishing Inc., part of Bloomsbury Publishing Plc
1385 Broadway, New York, NY 10018

BLOOMSBURY and the Diana logo are trademarks of Bloomsbury Publishing Plc

First published in the United States of America in June 2021 by Bloomsbury YA

Bloomsbury books may be purchased for business or promotional use. For information on
bulk purchases please contact Macmillan Corporate and Premium Sales Department at
specialmarkets@macmillan.com

Library of Congress Cataloging-in-Publication Data
Names: Thomas, Leah, author.
Title: Violet ghosts / by Leah Thomas.
Description: New York : Bloomsbury Children's Books, 2021.
Summary: Loner Dani and his best friend Sarah, the ghost of a teen murdered decades
earlier, team up to help other murdered women who are still tethered to this life.
Identifiers: LCCN 2020040635 (print) | LCCN 2020040636 (e-book)
ISBN 978-1-5476-0463-0 (hardcover) • ISBN 978-1-5476-0464-7 (e-book)
Subjects: CYAC: Ghosts—Fiction. | Future life—Fiction. | Murder—Fiction.
Classification: LCC PZ7.1.T463 Vio 2021 (print) | LCC PZ7.1.T463 (e-book) | DDC [Fic]—dc23
LC record available at https://lccn.loc.gov/2020040635

Book design by Jeanette Levy
Typeset by Westchester Publishing Services
Printed and bound in the U.S.A. by Berryville Graphics Inc., Berryville, Virginia
2 4 6 8 10 9 7 5 3 1

To find out more about our authors and books visit
www.bloomsbury.com and sign up for our newsletters.

To every queer kid stuck in a small town:
This isn't forever. Hang in there.

Violet Ghosts

JANUARY 1998

SARAH

LISA FRANK

By the time I met Sarah, she'd already been dead for two decades.

It was the winter of 1998, and I was just barely eleven. My classmates were obsessed with *Titanic*, but Pokémon was becoming a thing with the younger kids. I knew I should be fawning over Leo, but if I'd had any friends apart from my GigaPet, I'd have sheepishly traded two of my cold lunches for a Meowth card.

I was just barely eleven, and I was already learning to hate the things I loved.

Sarah was lying supine beneath my bed in the exact place where she'd died. My fingers brushed against her tangled hair as I reached for the Lisa Frank folder that held my hidden stash of magazine cutouts.

I felt the prickling clench of a ghostly hand around my wrist. "Need something?" she asked dryly.

I don't know why I didn't scream.

Maybe it was because her grip was lukewarm, not cold. Maybe I really didn't want to wake my mother. Or maybe I didn't scream because living dead girls weren't the scariest thing I'd ever encountered.

Sarah sounded like the older sister I'd always wanted: sarcastic and funny and cool. And I was so desperate for company that a family of rabid opossums could have bitten my hand and I'd have offered them lemonade.

"Um, yeah. Do you see my folder?"

"There's a *ton* of stationery and such under here. Be more specific."

"It has a panda on it. And, um, the panda's painting a picture?"

"Well, that's weird." I could hear her smirking. "Okay. Give me a minute."

Sarah's ghost let go and I withdrew my hand, rubbing my tingling skin. I heard the shuffling of paper and boxes, and a stuffed animal was ejected from the darkness.

"Wow, you weren't kidding. A panda painting a picture."

I peered over the edge of my mattress and watched the colorful folder slide out from beneath, propelled by a pale brown hand with bloodied, broken fingernails.

If Sarah were a corpse, the flesh and blood of her murderer might have been scraped from under those nails. But Sarah was only a ghost. There was nothing forensics could do for her now.

"Yeah." I plucked it from the floor. "Thank you."

"It's casual."

"What?"

She sighed. "*It's casual.* It means don't worry about it. So. What kind of secrets do you keep in there?"

"Not secrets. Just . . . things I like, I guess." I pulled a crumpled photograph from the pocket of my robe and flattened it against the folder. The picture showed five members of a boy band standing on an airport runway, arms aloft or bodies lean-ing, hair meticulously styled and faces brightly lit.

"Why should the things you like be kept in a weird panda folder under the bed?" Sarah asked. "Believe me, it's *not* a pleasant place to be."

I tucked the photo into a pocket filled with dozens of similar pictures: boys in cars, boys in fashionable clothing, images of fishing trips and EXTREME!! hiking from a copy of *Boys' Life* magazine that I'd stolen from the school library.

"Can you hide it—I mean, put it away again?"

"Sure, Daniela."

I cringed. "Can you call me something else?"

"But Daniela's your name, right?"

Doubtless Sarah's ghost had heard Mom yelling, just as she'd felt the bed rattle as I sobbed atop it, had heard me scribbling notebooks black until I poked holes through the pages.

"I don't like my name. Can you call me Dani?"

"Fine. Hi, Dani. I'm Sarah."

"Sarah." It tasted sugary on my tongue.

"So? Hand me the folder, then."

I set the folder in her palm. In the glare of the streetlight outside my window, I noticed that her chipped fingernails had once been painted yellow, and she wore a mood ring around her middle finger. "Daniel—Dani. You should really clean up down here. It's like living in a junkyard."

"Sorry, I didn't know."

"It's casual," Sarah repeated.

———

In the morning, I peered under my bed. There was no sign of Sarah. Somehow that made sense to me. Everyone knows ghosts and nighttime go hand in hand.

Sarah's absence carved a little ache in my chest.

And she was absolutely right. It was a real pigsty under there.

BOO BERRY

Before January 1998—*before* Sarah—my knowledge of ghostly encounters was limited to watching *Ghostbusters* on a battered old VHS recording and eating Boo Berry cereal in December after it went on sale. That was about it, apart from a single cherished memory of telling ghost stories around a fire at Girl Scout camp. I must have been like eight or nine, because this was right before Mom and I fled West Branch to live in the Rochdale women's shelter.

I'm sure that night's been forgotten by the rest of the troop. Those girls probably had a dozen more nights just like it. I'm pretty sure they only tolerated me because Scouts can earn badges for being nice to social lepers, or something. Our leader, Mrs. Stenley, saw me as some kind of charity case.

Still, around that fire, for several minutes or more, I felt like I actually belonged to something.

The stories all had death and a certain random chaos in common. This girl named Elaine told the tale of a hook-handed man who *really* didn't like teens who engaged in PDA. And Tammy Carlson spoke of "the hag," an elderly woman who broke out of an insane asylum (or maybe a retirement home?) and attacked a babysitter for no good reason.

Sure, these stories were fun, but even then I thought they were unrealistic. Mom and I had watched the first dozen episodes of *Forensic Files* religiously. I knew that statistically, *most* monsters were middle-aged white husbands, and not senile, neglected women or piratical amputees.

Chelsea Lyttle was almost in hysterics by the end of the hag story, so I tried to ease her mind: "Don't worry, Chelsea, some random old lady won't kill you."

"I *know*, but . . ."

"Strangers aren't so bad. Almost half of murders are committed by an acquaintance," I recited, "but almost a quarter are committed by a spouse, parent, or other male family member."

Mrs. Stenley gasped, and Elaine's marshmallow fell into the fire. Chelsea burst into tears.

"You're such a creep, Daniela," Tammy said, wrapping an arm around Chelsea's shoulder. "That's *not* funny."

"Why would you *say* something like that, Winky?" Elaine demanded.

I winced at the nickname; my right eye had always been an easy target, because my pupil and iris were always pointed inward toward my nose. The doctor called it "strabismus," and said it was caused by injury, and that we might be able to fix it with surgery. But my classmates called it "lazy" and said, "You can't fix ugly."

"I wasn't being funny," I protested. "It's important to know!"

"Important for *you*," Chelsea spat. "Your dad's always trying to kill your mom."

The other girls fell silent. Meanwhile, my heart collapsed inside me.

Mrs. Stenley cleared her throat. "*Girls.* That's enough for tonight."

It *was* enough. It was enough to make me realize that most people enjoyed horror because it was far removed from their reality, while I enjoyed it because it showed me I didn't have it so bad, not really. Maybe Mom and I had to file restraining orders against Dad. Maybe we had to run away from home. But it could have been worse, right?

I could have been left to bleed out under a bed.

SCARY STORIES TO TELL IN THE DARK

"Thanks for tidying up under here, Dani."

"Sarah?" It had been a week since our first meeting, and the night was cloudless, and I was beyond relieved to hear her voice, relieved she existed. "Is that really you?"

"I mean, unless you've got other dead girls under here, then yeah, it's just me. You're not losing it, are you?"

"It's *casual*," I told Sarah, when it was anything but.

So far the Winky nickname had not followed me to Rochdale, and neither had Dad. But the gloss of being a new student had lasted all of one hour before girls started sneering at my stained clothes and boys began teasing me about the botched bangs of my self-inflicted haircut. Nobody bothered talking to me now, unless snickering counts.

Sarah's voice was the farthest thing from casual to me.

She snorted. "Well, we can *say* it's casual, sure. But *I'm* dead and you seem downright miserable, so I'd say it's not *totally* casual, Dani."

I swallowed. "Sarah. Will you . . . I mean, are you going to tell me how you died?"

"Nope."

"Oh."

Sarah sighed, long and heavy. "Is that all you wanted to ask me? Typical. That's all anyone wants to know about a murdered girl, right?"

"No! No, it's not!" I was terrified she'd go quiet again, so I blurted the very next thing that came to mind. "Sarah—did you have any brothers or sisters?"

"I did, but I don't want to talk about them, either. Siblings are overrated. I had three of them and I wouldn't wish them on anyone else. And my parents were another can of worms."

"I get it. My parents are like . . . a can of snakes."

"Right? So let's talk about *anything* else apart from death and family."

It was hard to think about what else there was, except—

"Sarah. Do you like ghost stories?"

One of her bloodied hands took hold of my comforter. The fabric barely wrinkled under her transparent weight, hardly shifted when she hoisted herself above the edge. "Sure I do. Why wouldn't I?"

"Well . . . *because.*"

"What, you think a ghost can't like ghost stories?" Sarah pulled her torso up and onto the bed. I noticed dark stains on her forget-me-not-patterned nightgown. "You're still breathing, but don't *you* like stories about living people?"

"I guess I never thought about it that way."

"I've had a lot of time to think things over under there."

Sarah, exposed by the moonlight, knelt at the end of my bed. Her hair was long and black and braided into the loose, messy pigtails I imagined real girls—girls who *knew* what to do with their hair and their bodies—might wear to bed. Sarah's ghost existed in color, but she was faded like photographs left in the sunlight too long. Her skin was darker than mine, but I couldn't decide what color her eyes had been, because now they were entirely black with no irises to speak of. Insubstantial though she was, I *felt* her, like those breezes that rustled the shortest hairs on my legs and arms.

"You're staring." Sarah cocked an eyebrow. "What, are you scared?"

I shook my head. "No. I'm not scared of you."

Ghosts were not the things to be afraid of. Ghosts hadn't murdered Sarah.

"Then quit it." She placed her hand over one of the many stab wounds that marred the fabric across her chest. "I'm self-conscious. No one wants to be trapped in pj's for eternity."

"You're so *pretty*." Warmth blossomed in my chest. Would I have said those words in daylight? Would I have dared sound so envious?

"You think so? Well. See where being pretty got me?" Sarah looked away. "Being pretty is a curse."

"Being ugly sucks more," I snapped. "Pretty people have no clue."

"*Hey*." Sarah leaned forward, eyes gleaming. "Did you just get angry? I've seen you cry and all, but I've never seen you *mad*. Now *that's* a good look, sis."

I blushed furiously but I would not lower my gaze. I had never looked at someone for so long, and no one had ever looked back at me for so long either.

Sarah's grin faded. "But you're right. It's *bogus* being pretty, *and* it's bogus being ugly. Girls suffer either way, you know? Besides, who says what's pretty or ugly anyways? Probably some creepy old pervert decided what pretty was a thousand years ago and taught everyone else to believe it."

"Oh. I guess . . . yeah, maybe."

"Definitely. Pretty doesn't *mean* anything. Say it enough and it stops being a word that means anything."

So what if Sarah had eyes that looked like shining marbles? So what if she was brutally sarcastic and incurably deceased? It wasn't like I had room to judge. In stories, ghosts were always sad and defeated, but Sarah wasn't. She was a wall, unbeaten and resolute, more real in my room than I had ever been and I already loved her.

Sarah said things I'd never dared think of.

"Why won't you tell me *your* ghost story?"

"My ghost story's not the kind *anyone* likes, all right?" Sarah wrapped her arms around her knees. "No one wants to be known for what someone else *did* to them."

I didn't think I'd ever heard truer words, not in my classes or outside them. And I knew then how she might feel. I knew the value of secrets. People like to say secrets are bad for you, but sometimes secrets are the only things that keep you warm.

"Okay, Sarah. I won't ask."

She smirked. "Never again, no matter how long we're friends?"

I held up three fingers, the Girl Scout Promise. "Never again."

"Fine." Her posture unwound a bit, and she lay back on my

bed with her arms behind her head. "Because if you ask me about my family or my death again, I'll vanish, and you'll never see me again."

The air grew chill and I shivered. "I won't ask. Not ever."

"Good."

"But did you know," I added carefully, "that the majority of murder victims are killed by acquaintances or family members?"

Sarah paused, just as the girls around the campfire had. But before I finally closed my eyes, I heard her whisper, "Yeah, I *definitely* know that."

SHARPIE FINE POINT

On a Monday in February 1998 I walked into my sixth-grade classroom to find the word "whore" written on my desk in bright blue Sharpie. The word was as long and wide as my forefinger, just big enough not to ignore.

"Whore" was a word I had sometimes heard my dad call my mom, not long enough ago. It was one of a dozen words my Rochdale classmates used on the regular without seeming to care about its actual meaning. "Whore" didn't suit someone like me. Loser? Yes. Freak—oh, definitely.

"Whore" didn't describe me at all.

For a minute or longer I stared at the blocky, uneven letters. The snickers of boys in the back of the room pinged off my eardrums. Tiny bullets. Dad used to lay his hands on me whenever he wanted to see me cry. But sometimes, if I refused to cry, he'd take his hands off again, because where was the fun in that?

The best thing to do would be to smirk like Sarah, to pretend "whore" was a compliment.

Finally I sat down, eyes tingling, breathing heavily through my nose, *not crying*.

But I was not good at pretending, and I wasn't Sarah, and it wasn't a compliment.

Despite my best efforts, several double-crossing tears dampened my desk as the bell rang. I shoved my chair back and ran from the classroom before Ms. Peele could see me go. The boys at the back pulled grisly faces as I passed.

I'd almost reached the bathroom when I realized that someone had followed me out. The ghost of his heavy footsteps, an echo after mine, made me turn.

Seiji Grayson, a hulking boy with broad shoulders and big ears, glared at me through the strands of black hair that perpetually hid his eyes. He was one of a dozen bullies who plagued the back of my classroom, maybe the backs of all classrooms. He only stood apart because he was tan in a field of white. Otherwise he was interchangeable with the rest of them, just as heartless and removed.

"Why are you crying?" Seiji demanded.

"You *know* why!" I could almost smell the Sharpie wafting off him.

His expression didn't change. "But it's a dumb reason to cry."

"Shut up." I pressed my back against the bathroom door.

"*Are* you a whore?"

"Obviously I'm not!"

"So why cry about it, if it isn't true?"

I slipped backward into the restroom. Seiji didn't take his eyes off me as the door closed. By the time I'd locked myself in a stall like a middle school cliché, my breath was coming in high-pitched wheezes.

I knew this was a panic attack, and I knew I needed to focus on my breathing, and I *knew* I wasn't a whore, but I couldn't understand why some asshole like Seiji Grayson could decide that a word shouldn't hurt simply because it was untrue.

FORENSIC FILES

The day felt eternal. When I got home, Mom was on the couch watching *Forensic Files*. If I seemed miserable and puffy-eyed, so did she.

"You want macaroni tonight?" She tapped her cigarette against the rim of a mother-of-pearl ashtray. On the screen, a private detective described the way he'd used gas station security footage to track a "perp" all the way from Idaho to a cabin in Colorado. "With ketchup and hot dogs?"

"Sure." She didn't ask me how I was, and I didn't ask her. This was about as close as we got.

"I picked up some Bugles." Her smile was always a little uncertain. "If you want a snack later."

"Thanks," I said, eyes on the screen. I wondered if there was an episode about Sarah in the series. I wondered whether Mom knew that a girl had died in my bedroom, or if we were in a part of town where that might be a fair assumption no matter which bedroom I slept in.

———

After dinner, I crawled into the space under my bed, relishing the darkness, being unseen and unheard. I placed my folder of secrets under my head, even though my frizzy hair clung to the gloss. I must have dozed off. When I came to, Sarah lay beside me in the darkness.

"Welcome to my neck of the woods," she whispered. "What's up, chicken-butt?"

I told her about my day, about Seiji and the others.

"Boys are such assholes."

I knew I should agree with her. I had no reason not to, but something in me ached at the finality of her words. "Not *all* of them are assholes . . ."

"Believe me, I'd love to be proven wrong," Sarah said, with the saddest laugh.

For a moment or many, the air under my bed fell still. We listened to the hazy murmur of the television from the living room. I hoped Mom had put out her cigarette before conking out. I hoped she'd set down her shot glass, too.

"Sarah. You asleep?"

"Sleep's not really my thing."

I took a deep breath. "Can I ask you another question?"

"I'm not the one who has school tomorrow. And I like talking to something other than dust bunnies for a change."

The idea that anyone would feel anything other than annoyed by my presence made me teary. "Have you ever talked to anyone else? I mean, before me?"

"I've been dead awhile. A lot of families have passed through here. This isn't the kind of house where anyone stays for long, you know? It's a real shithole."

This so-called shithole was better than the trailer we'd left behind. The linoleum here was peeling, sure, but the ceiling wasn't leaking and the air smelled less sour. And I'd never had my own bedroom before. I'd never had a door I could lock, or walls I could put between myself and violence.

"But you know what? In all that time, I never thought to talk to anyone. I mean, why would they listen? No one ever has before. Time sort of passed like I wasn't part of it. I thought I'd 'move on' or whatever, like ghosts do in movies. But I never did."

"Do you . . . do you want to?"

"No. I'm too stubborn, I guess. And too angry." She paused. "Every time someone moved out and took their bed away—that was the worst. I made myself as small as a spider and hid in the closet. I can't stand the sunlight."

"I thought vampires were the ones who hated sunlight."

"I used to think that, too. But I don't think I'd last a minute in sunlight."

"Why not? Does it burn?"

"Not really. But in the sunlight, I can't ignore the holes in me, and I'm pretty sure they'd grow big enough to swallow me up."

I felt ghostly fingers on my cheek. My eyes shot open. Sarah was warm like a summer breeze, soft like cotton.

"So why did you start talking to *me*, Sarah?" I did not ask, *Am I special?* I think she sensed how much I longed for answers, to matter. What child doesn't want to be a wizard? Who doesn't want to escape a life of insults and bruises for one of magic and wonder?

Her fingers left me. "I'm not sure. Maybe it's because you're on the same trajectory I was. Tragic girl, shitty family, bad vibes. We're the same."

This was very far from being special, and we both knew it.

"You mean someone's gonna murder me, too?" I thought of Seiji's shoulders, Dad's dull-eyed boozy stare. "That's what you think?"

"Not while I'm around." I felt a great rustling beside me, as if Sarah had become a swarm of winding strings. "What happened to me—I don't want it to happen to anyone else. I think that's why I can't just . . . go."

"If you're waiting for the world to be safe, you'll be waiting forever," I whispered. Mom had told me that my eye hadn't always been lazy, but a punch or seven got it there. "You're stuck under this bed, and I'm . . . I'm stuck, too."

"I'd resent the comparison if I didn't know how much the world sucks," Sarah said. "Fine, so we're stuck. Let's start local. This Sam-gee guy. I've got some ideas on how we can deal."

"Seiji," I corrected.

"Who cares? He called you a whore. He's Joe Schmo to me."

Somehow, I actually laughed. But Sarah's eyes were darker than ever, and her mouth was a grim line. "Sarah. I don't want to hurt him. I don't ever want to hurt *anyone*."

"*Fine*. We won't, not *physically*." Sarah looked right into me. "Trust me, okay?"

"I do." I did then, and I still would years later.

SPACEMAKER

On Tuesday, minutes before the first bell, I hurried across the courtyard, past meandering classmates and teachers, up the stairs, and into the semi-vacant school hallways.

I'd have to be quick about it.

"Joe Schmo can't accuse you of swapping desks with him unless he admits he knew what was written on yours," Sarah told me. "He'll be stuck looking at the word for a day at least. His friends will give him endless shit for it, if nothing else."

Each time Sarah swore, a little trill hummed in my rib cage. Dad always said girls were ugly when they swore, but Sarah was never ugly. That helped me think maybe I wasn't, either, and maybe girls who acted like boys were beautiful, or maybe ugly existed even less than pretty did. Her "shits" and "damns" lit a wick in me, and those flames fueled me as I snuck into the classroom.

I made a beeline for my desk and began yanking my stuff from the front slot. It would take at least a minute to clear out mine and then Seiji's, and even empty desks weren't the easiest things to move—

"Jeez, Daniela, you scared me!"

I dropped my pencil box, scattering erasers and gel pens across the floor. Sarah and I hadn't considered Ms. Peele might already be in the windowless classroom, sitting at her desk in the dark.

"Sorry—did I scare you back?" She turned on the overhead projector, illuminating a square of the wall and ceiling, adding lines to her bespectacled face. "You know, sometimes I close my eyes for a bit before the chaos begins." She frowned. "Daniela? Everything okay?"

I nodded and then shook my head. Ms. Peele stepped closer. "I know it can be hard starting at a new school."

"I've been here since September."

"Even so. This is a small town, and things stay new for ages. If you need a friend to talk to . . ."

"I have friends," I snapped.

"Oh, of course you do. I didn't mean to imply—"

"No." I looked away. "I mean. I have one friend. Just one."

"Oh? I'm glad to hear that, Daniela." She smiled a real smile, and I thought we were done, but then her gaze fell to my desk. "What's this?"

I sat down, crushed and tired.

"Daniela. Do you *know* who wrote this?"

I shook my head. Snitching wouldn't help.

Ms. Peele pulled a black dry-erase marker from the front pocket of her denim dress and proffered it to me. "The easiest way to remove permanent marker from plastic is to trace over it with an impermanent one. Go on."

Because she was watching, I did as I was asked. I outlined

every hateful letter. Ms. Peele pulled a whiteboard eraser from the same massive pocket and handed it to me.

"You do the rest."

Whore vanished in a few swipes, leaving an unmarred patch of desk behind.

"There's no word in the world that can't be overwritten." Ms. Peele returned to her desk. "You can come here early whenever you feel like it, Daniela."

"*Dani.*"

"Sorry?"

She and I had almost cleaned the mess up when the bell sounded. The boys, Seiji among them, stumbled into the classroom, laughing and jostling one another.

Halfway through first hour, a spit wad struck the back of my neck.

I spun around. Seiji held his Game Boy under the desk, pretending to be fixated on *Mario Bros.* But I saw the red flush in his cheeks and the cafeteria straw tucked in one of his big hands.

One of the others whispered, "What you lookin' at, whore?"

Ms. Peele had her back to us, busy with the board and equivalent fractions. No matter her kindness, she couldn't overwrite these cruelties. She wasn't the one with saliva dribbling down her neck.

And clean as my desk was, their hands were still dirty.

POP ROCKS

Sarah paced without ever touching the floor, unshod feet dangling inches above the ragged carpet so that only her toes brushed the fibers. "Look, we'll just have to think of something else."

"It won't change anything. It'll only make it worse."

"Not if you put a *real* stop to him," she said, baring her teeth. "There are a thousand ways you could take revenge on those dumbass boys!"

"I don't want to hurt anyone," I reiterated.

"You keep saying that! But *they've* hurt you, haven't they?"

I shrugged. "What else is new."

Just like that, a windstorm began.

"Dani—no. *No.* Don't sit there and take it!" Like a sponge filling with water, Sarah expanded. Her shoulders scraped the ceiling, and her braids split apart and rose as if she were floating in the sea. The blinds rattled and my bangs blew back. "How can you sit there and *take* it?"

"Sarah. You're freaking out."

"I—I know." The wind died. "I know, all right?"

"Are you okay?"

"God, I wish *I* hadn't *taken* it." Sarah's ghost shrank to smaller than a cat. She sank to the floor with her arms around her knees. I climbed down off the bed and sat beside her. After a moment, she raised her head and her shoulders until she was girl size again.

"What I wouldn't give for some Pop Rocks," she murmured.

"They still make those," I told her, wiping my eyes.

"No way. Can you bring me some?"

"Yeah. But . . . can you eat them?"

Sarah snorted. "Nah. Dead girls can't eat a thing. But I can watch *you* eat them. Do you know the meaning of the word 'vicarious'?"

"No."

Her eyes looked faraway and her outline turned a bit fuzzy. "When you're living vicariously, it means you're living life through someone else. Like, those dads who used to play football but got injured or weren't good enough for college teams, who go crazy if their kids aren't good at sports?"

"I get the idea."

"Well, it's like that."

"You want me to play football," I joked, and she rolled her eyes.

"Oh, ha. I'm saying, because . . . because *I'm* dead and stuck in darkness and everything, I have to get my kicks through the things you do. The boys who hurt me are probably as long gone as I am, god willing. But I'm still so dang *angry*, and I have to—to put it somewhere. Helping you school Schmo will have to do. Vicariously."

I couldn't help it—a laugh built inside me and burst from my throat. I clapped my hand over my mouth to capture the sound.

Her expression went jagged. "What's so funny?"

"It's just . . . I think I'm living through you, too."

"*God*, Dani. You must be desperate trying to live through a dead teenager." When Sarah tried to hug me, her weightless arms encompassed all of me, wrapping me in velvet.

My bedroom door burst open. Light pierced the room like a blade, and Sarah hissed and vanished like dissipating steam.

My heart was already racing, my throat already closing up—

Then I recognized Mom's silhouette, not Dad's, and began breathing again.

"What's with all the racket?" Mom demanded, the slur of Jack Daniel's on her tongue. "Get to bed. Big day tomorrow."

"Big day?"

Mom leaned against the doorframe. "We're moving."

"Moving?"

"Yes. Moving."

"*Why?*"

"*Why?* The new place is cheaper, and hopefully the landlord's less of a creep." Her voice softened. "Don't worry. It's not about your father. He's still got no idea where we are, okay?"

"Okay."

"We'll start packing after you get home from school tomorrow."

I could do little more than nod as she kissed me on the head and left me alone with the door open. I closed it and put my back to it.

". . . Sarah?"

"Told you," whispered the smallest voice, from deep within the closet. "No one but me stays in this shithole for long."

27

GAME BOY COLOR

Blood rushed in my ears. If this random Wednesday was to be my last day at Rochdale Middle, my last day living with Sarah, I would live for her as best I could.

Once again, I left the bus and hurried across the courtyard. Before I reached the steps, my eyes slipped to a gaggle gathered beside the play tunnel—Aaron Walker, Billy Williams, and yes, there—Seiji Grayson.

Our eyes met. I waved him closer.

Seiji's expression was as unreadable as ever. He muttered something to his friends, shoved his Game Boy into his backpack, and lumbered toward me.

"What do you want?" Though Seiji loomed, my father had loomed taller. And I knew something Seiji didn't:

Soon I'd be a ghost, too. After today, I'd never have to face Seiji Grayson again.

No matter what I did to him, he couldn't take revenge.

"You're not going to bully me anymore, Seiji."

He blinked. "Is that all you wanted to say?"

I steeled myself. "I know you're only shitty to me because you hate yourself."

He stiffened. "*That's* what you think?"

"That's what I *know*."

At last he showed some expression, his scowl as jagged as the cracks in the sidewalk. "Am I supposed to be afraid of you?"

Of course not. I was supposed to be afraid of him. I wondered if I would always be a little wary around big shoulders and large hands and unreadable expressions. Boys like Seiji were not what I thought boys should be, and not what I longed to be. I loathed him for wasting what I'd never been allowed to have.

I turned and left him there.

———

Outside Ms. Peele's classroom, I looked left and right to ensure the coast was clear. I took a deep, steadying breath, pulled my sixth-grade science textbook from my backpack, and held it horizontal, level with my lazy eye.

I thought about Sarah's outburst the night before, about the infinite power of appearing helpless but blossoming into anything but.

I tilted my face to the side and thrust the hardcover once, twice, three times against my eye socket, until my cheekbone throbbed and my face began puffing up, tender and broken. The swollen skin tore just above my eyelid. I could already feel bruises darkening my cheek, spreading like puddles in a storm.

Perhaps this would have been harder for someone who hadn't been struck a dozen times by fatherly fists. But it was as familiar as sleep to me, as familiar as pizza.

After a minute, I took another breath and burst through the classroom door, clutching my eye and shrieking.

Ms. Peele stood quickly in the lamplight, knocking over a heap of paper.

"Daniela! What's wrong? What's happened? Are you *bleeding?*"

"The courtyard," I gasped. "Seiji hit me. He hit me *so hard.*"

"*Seiji* did? Seiji Grayson?" She tilted my face toward the light. "Oh my god! Where is he now?"

"Outside," I whimpered, as she led me to my desk. "By the steps."

"Wait here a moment, sweetie," she told me, and she called the office from the phone beside the door. I settled into my seat, head throbbing. Minutes later, she reappeared with a cold CapriSun in her hand. "Press this to your eye. The office is going to call your parents."

My heart stopped. "My parents?"

"Sorry, it's just your mother, isn't it? She's on her way."

I exhaled, staring at my feet. "What will happen to Seiji?"

"Principal Hardisty has gone to fetch him. He'll be suspended, most likely, depending on his side of the story."

"His side of the story?" Again, my chest tightened, my ears burned. "He's not the one with a black eye!"

"I know how you must feel, but we still have to hear it."

"People always want to hear what *boys* have to say."

She sighed. "Daniela. Did anyone see him hit you?"

I shook my aching head. "I pulled him aside to ask him to apologize for writing on my desk. He hit me instead."

I could not understand how that seemed to register in Ms. Peele's expression.

"Seiji was the one who wrote on your desk? Are you sure?"

I nodded.

"Okay. I just—I'm so, so *sorry*, sweetie. Thank you for confiding in me. We'll get this sorted out, all right? We'll all sit down and talk it out, once your mother and Seiji's aunt get here."

I grabbed her hands and shook my head. "Please. Don't make me see Seiji again."

"Daniela. I'll be there, we'll *all* be there, and we can figure out why this happened."

"Why this happened?" I repeated. "He *hurt* me."

"I never thought—but you and Seiji—both of you have had a tough year." She opened her mouth and closed it again. "I'll have a word with Principal Hardisty."

Behind us, the door opened. It was too early to be the other students—or had I not heard the sound of the bell over my screeching, glaring lies?

Ms. Peele placed herself slightly in front of me. "Seiji. What is it?"

There he stood, my sometime torturer, pale and breathless. He must have scraped the hair from his forehead while Principal Hardisty reamed him out. Seiji's eyes, usually obscured, were made more striking by their sudden exposure, spooked and glossy black. My breath caught at the prospect of that gaze falling on me, calling me the liar I was, cutting me to my hollow center.

But Seiji looked right past me. "Principal Hardisty told me to come get my stuff. I'm suspended. For a week. He says I have to clear my desk."

Ms. Peele's posture softened, but her expression did not.

"Okay. I'll gather your assignments, Seiji. Don't forget that your planetarium project is due in two weeks."

"I won't forget." His eyes flickered to me.

I watched Seiji bury his hands in his desk, blood pulsing in my swelling cheek. I waited for the truth to leave him, for him to point the finger of accusation at me. But Seiji only swept the contents of his desk—loose papers and pencils and pens—into his backpack.

Seiji didn't have to speak for me to hear what he must have been thinking. The words projected from his big eyes: *You're as bad as I am.*

He zipped up his bag and accepted a folder of homework from Ms. Peele. The bell rang, and the phone on the wall rang, too.

"Yes, he's on his way back down." Ms. Peele cupped the mouthpiece with her palm. "Seiji, your aunt's waiting for you in the office."

Seiji flinched and sped to the door. His green Game Boy was dislodged in his hurry, and fell on the floor near my feet. I picked it up and held it out to him.

Seiji met my eyes at last. "Keep it. I hope it makes you feel better."

My arm fell, all of me fell, as he stepped into the hallway.

BEETLEJUICE

They sent me home with Mom before third block began.

She didn't speak as we crossed the school parking lot. I didn't expect her to, exactly, but my anger was growing along with the bump on my forehead, made itchier by her indifference. She had barely reacted when Ms. Peele relayed the tragedy of Seiji's supposed attack, hardly blinked when the teacher recommended I see a doctor and maybe even a *doctor*, as in a *therapist*. Mom just stood in the office in her sweatpants and winter coat and let Ms. Peele's impassioned words drift past her like cigarette smoke.

The truth we knew that Ms. Peele didn't was:

Mom expected me to get beaten up, just like she'd been beaten up. For us, bruises were as much a reality as dust on dashboards, as black ice in winter.

As I climbed into the passenger seat, Mom scanned me from head to toe. "You don't need a doctor, do you?"

I shook my head and we hit the road.

Even then, even at eleven freaking years old, I was deeply aware that this interaction was wrong. Mom didn't ask me what happened. Questioning bruises didn't make them fade any faster.

Once we were standing in our dim, cluttered living room, she said, "Well, we can get a head start on packing now. Can probably move a few carloads over tonight."

I froze. "Tonight? We aren't moving to a new town, like last time?"

"Not this time, Dani. It's a little apartment complex in downtown Rochdale that's twice as clean as this place. I've agreed to manage the property, so we'll live there for cheap so long as we keep the tenants in line."

"Rochdale," I echoed. "We're *staying* in Rochdale."

"The new place is only ten minutes away. You'll be able to walk to school, and I'm gonna look for part-time work on Main Street. That'll be good, won't it? Less of a do-over, more of an improvement?"

Wordlessly, I left the living room and dragged my feet up the creaking stairs.

I made it to my bedroom and shut the door before all the air left me.

I crumpled into a breathless coil on the bed. Something rectangular dug into my stomach—I yanked Seiji's Game Boy from my hoodie pocket and tossed it to the floor.

I was going to be *closer* to school. This wasn't going to be another false start in a new place. I'd have to face Seiji and the others again, and again, and again.

Today I had buried myself alive.

And once we left this house, I'd have to face my fate without Sarah's nighttime pep talks, without her sarcasm to buoy or build me. And she'd have to face the long dark alone.

I could hear Mom shifting furniture and clearing cupboards. A pickup's engine revved somewhere down the block, and a stranger hollered junkie nonsense in the street, but mostly what I heard was Seiji's voice:

I hope it makes you feel better.

My fear became another sound, a dull whining in my ears and chest. I switched off the bedroom lights and pulled my blinds closed. They went crooked as they descended; I whimpered as I fought them into submission.

Stubborn daylight continued to creep between the slats. I cursed and tore the red comforter from my bed. I stood on my mattress, stretched toward the top of the window frame, and wedged the blanket between the wall and siding.

The room was lit in orange but empty of real daylight.

Finally I could breathe again, and I could call out her name. "Sarah?"

She didn't appear. And I wondered whether I'd imagined her after all. I wondered how pathetic I must be, to delude myself into thinking that a ghost would want to befriend a twisted, lying freak like me.

I yanked the pillows from my bed and attacked the tiny beam of light beneath the bedroom door, rug-burning my knees in my hustle, determined to shut that light out, too—

"What the hell *is* this thing?" Sarah sat on my bed in her eternal nightgown, bathed in diffused auburn light. Her broken fingernails hovered above Seiji's Game Boy. "I've never seen anything like it. Is it some kind of robot?"

I slumped back against the door, limbs leaden with relief. "Sarah. It's a Game Boy."

"Doesn't look like a boy to me."

I winced. Lots of things don't look like boys.

"No. A Game Boy . . . a computer . . . a video-game player for rich kids."

"Don't be ridiculous." Sarah shook her head. "Computers are huge. They take up whole *rooms*. Computers help send people to the moon."

"Not anymore." I sank onto the mattress beside her, close as I dared. "This one's only a toy. It can help you catch some Pokémon, but it can't send anyone to the moon."

"A *toy*? Computers are *toys* now? Christ." Sarah seemed so much deader whenever she was sad. "The world's really changed, huh? Man, sometimes I forget. Or maybe I *try* to forget." She glanced at my black eye. "Then again, some things don't change. You okay, Dani?"

I bit my lip, eyes welling. Sarah had asked the question my mother hadn't.

So I told her what I'd done.

After, Sarah whistled. "You're kind of terrifying, you know." *"Don't."*

Sarah rested her hand on my cheek; summer breezes found me. "Hey, it's not a judgment, you know. I'm a ghost. *Terrifying* is a compliment."

"You're not terrifying," I blurted. "You're lovely."

Her grin faded along with her fingertips. "That's what *he* said, too, before he killed me."

I'd promised never to ask more, but every glimpse into her reality, every glancing mention of the man who'd ended her, infected me with her fury and sadness.

"I'm sorry."

She shrugged. "Say what you want, but if I'd been less lovely and more terrifying, things might have ended differently when he came at me. Just . . . never get too lovely, okay? Follow my advice and maybe you'll live to see college."

"But Sarah . . . we're moving *away*." A sob shattered my words.

Sarah put her palm to the back of her neck, suddenly shy. "Well, I mean, I didn't want to just up and *say* it . . . but can I come with you, Dani?"

I gaped at her. "Come with us?"

She stared at her knees, voice tight. "Dani, give me a break. This isn't easy to ask."

I grabbed both her hands, or tried to—I mostly passed through them, but I tried all the same. "No—Sarah, I mean, can you *really* come with us? You're not stuck haunting this bedroom for forever or something?"

Her face became less shy and more sarcastic, more her own. "What, did you think I was doomed to live under a bed for eternity? Come on, Dani. That'd be dull as hell."

"But in stories, ghosts get stuck where they died. Like in *Beetlejuice*! The ghosts can't leave the house."

"Betelgeuse?"

"It's a movie."

"It's part of a constellation, actually."

"Whatever. In the movie, there's a handbook of, um, ghost rules."

"Gee, that'd be convenient."

"And when the ghosts try to leave home, giant sand snakes attack them."

Sarah rolled her eyes. "That's so freaking stupid, Dani."

I laughed. "Yeah, I guess it is. But a lot of stories go that way."

"Do I *look* like a story to you?" Sarah drew herself upright. She caught fire in the orange light, or close enough. She lit up my everything. "I mean, maybe people say dead girls have to haunt the places where they died. Come on, Dani. Isn't that just one more way to dictate where a woman should be, where she belongs? Fuck that. I'll go anywhere I want, so long as I don't catch too much sun. I'm over reliving my tragic demise here."

I savored that "fuck," that entire speech. I wanted to put her words on my tongue. "If you could have left all along, why *haven't* you?"

"At first I thought I couldn't. Not because of some movie, or any 'ghost rules'—I mean, come on, how would I know any ghost rules? But . . . the light leaves me holey, like I've said. I've thought a lot about sunlight." Sarah shuddered. "I wonder how many ghosts have stepped outside and disappeared. Like maybe in some ghostly *handbook* that's what dead girls are *supposed* to do. Straighten our shirts, fix our hair, step into the sun, smile, and evaporate." She rubbed her hands together, then let them separate and fall to her lap, slow like feathers. "Spick-and-span."

"People aren't spick-and-span," I said, thinking of Seiji, of the shame burning a hole in my heart. "We're all a train wreck. And ghosts are people, too."

"*Exactly.* Fuck the rules. We'll write our own. I refuse to tidy up my act! I refuse to be scrubbed away or told what to be."

"I don't want to be told what to be, either," I admitted, for the first time, and though she couldn't know what I was really saying, couldn't know the betrayal in the core of me, Sarah's grin was every confirmation I needed.

"But . . . that's not the only reason I've stayed here." Sarah looked away, tinged by a spectral blush. "I never seriously thought about leaving, until I met you."

My cheeks flushed. "Never?"

"Time passed differently when I was alone. I didn't always know what time of day it was, whether I even existed. It was like I was living in a constant fever, until you started talking to me." Sarah cleared her throat. "I don't know how, but . . . I think you made me realer, Dani."

"You made me realer, too," I breathed. "Definitely."

"Christ, just give me an answer," Sarah blurted, covering her face with her hands. "You're killing me here! Will you take me with you or not?"

I threw myself around her. "Please haunt me forever, Sarah."

"Sure thing, Dani."

TOY STORY

Moving house took all of nine trips, since we'd only been in Sarah's old place for a few months. Mom didn't think any of the furniture was worth keeping, apart from a claw-foot side table she'd inherited from Oma. She said the thing was a priceless antique. I doubted it; that table was scratched to pieces, and one of the feet constantly fell off. But this weird table was a hill Mom wanted to die on.

"It's the only nice thing my family ever gave me." That was obvious, since her family had given Mom virtually nothing. You could probably argue it was more creepy than nice, this table that might crawl around the house whenever you weren't looking, some monstrous adult escapee from *Toy Story*.

I had no room to talk, considering the last thing I had left to pack.

"You ready?" I asked, peering under the bed.

My lazy eye had swollen right up, so I couldn't see her. Sarah's voice rang out, tremulous but determined. "I'm ready. Get me the devil away from these dust bunnies."

I pushed a battered fanny pack into the darkness. "Are you sure you'll fit?"

"One way to find out." A moment later, I heard the zipper jangle.

"How *do* you make yourself smaller, Sarah?" I asked, as the fabric rustled. "Do you just wish you would shrink and—ta-da! You're pint-size?"

"The worse you feel, the smaller you get. So I think of really awful stuff until I want to vanish."

"Well. That sucks."

"Give me a second. Hey—your panda folder with those magazine pages of pretty and ugly boys is still under here."

I flinched. "Oh. That's fine. I don't have to take it."

Sarah paused. "But do you *want* to take it, Dani?"

I thought of what she might say if I admitted I *did*. I thought of all she'd said about the shittiness of boys, and how much I wanted her approval, wanted never to see her disappointed in me. "No. I . . . I don't need it anymore."

"Of course you don't," Sarah agreed, triumphant. "Can you zip me up?"

I felt for the fanny pack zipper. When I brushed the space inside with my fingers, it felt full and soft, like a heated water bottle.

"I'm not even gonna ask what you're up to," Mom said, as I backed out from under the bed on all fours.

"You never do," I grumbled, but she didn't hear me.

I pulled my hoodie down over the fanny pack and followed her through the doorway. If Sarah felt any loss as I put distance between her ghost and the place where she'd died, she didn't say so.

———

41

Downtown Rochdale was mostly indistinguishable from other downtowns of small-town America, but because this was Michigan, there was probably a higher ratio of pine trees within its boundaries. Rochdale was a hunting and snowmobiling town, more a place for cabins and campgrounds than apartments. It wasn't all that surprising to learn we weren't moving into an actual apartment complex, but some defunct old motel a few potholed roads away from Main Street, backed by a dark line of trees.

The motel had once been called the Teepee, which seemed about as tactful as it was accurate. The first thing we threw into the dumpster after we arrived was an offensive statue of an Indian chief selling cigars. The tin roof of the distended lobby at one end of the mono-level strip of rooms *had* been shaped to look like some approximation of a tepee, but the tin was filthy and rusted. Mom warned me that the lobby was locked up and out of bounds, because the roof could cave in any day.

The "apartments" themselves were a tragedy. The walls between every other room had been knocked in when the place was converted; twenty-four ragged and rustic motel rooms had become twelve oddball lodgings, of which only four were occupied—well, five, after we showed up. Ours consisted of a living room, two bedrooms, a bathroom, and horror beyond horrors: a *carpeted kitchen*.

"Your bedroom doesn't have a window," Mom told me. "Sorry about that."

"It's fine." It was better than fine. The moment I got away from Mom and the boxes, I closed my new bedroom door and let Sarah stretch out in the dim, grungy space.

"I've always wondered what a coffin feels like," she joked.

I didn't want to sound defensive. "You told me you wanted to come."

She placed a hand on my shoulder. "Calm down, Dani. I wasn't talking about the room—I'm *psyched* about the room. The *fanny pack* was a coffin."

"Oh."

"It's casual. You couldn't even hear me when I was in there, could you?"

I shook my head. "No. But I thought I . . . um, felt you."

"God, I hope you did. I was pounding my fists on the vinyl the whole time. We're gonna have to try some other way of getting me around. Seen any movies featuring rules about ghost transportation? Should I get a bike?"

"Transportation? But . . . there are no windows here, and there's a closet."

Again, her shyness came as a surprise. "Well, yeah. But . . . I was thinking I might start going to school with you, too. I don't want you facing Asshole Schmo alone, not after I've just made things worse. Get a little more vicarious, you know?"

"Really? You wanna go to middle school?"

"You're frowning." Sarah folded her arms. "What is it? You worried you'll be seen talking to yourself?"

That hadn't even occurred to me. The truth was, selfishly, that I wanted Sarah to remain my secret.

"Just trust me, Dani."

And I did trust her, like I'd never trusted anyone else.

That realization should have frightened me more.

TAMAGOTCHI

"Going somewhere?" Mom asked, poking her head out from heaps of boxes. "You need to start unpacking. We won't be living like hoarders here."

"I'm going for a walk. I wanna check out the neighborhood."

"Not much neighborhood to it," she observed. "But fine. Be back before dark."

The sun was already sinking, but I didn't say so. I pulled up my hood and walked out into the empty parking lot. It was a chilly winter evening, and the forest of pines behind the motel didn't make the place feel more welcoming. I doubted summer sunshine or a marching band could make this place feel more welcoming.

I reached the end of the lot, looked both ways down the vacant road, and pulled a pair of battered headphones from my pocket, shoving them over my ears. "This is crazy."

"YOU SAY THAT, BUT WHAT *ISN'T* CRAZY?" Sarah asked.

I yelped and yanked off the headphones. It took me a moment to find the tiny volume switch on the Game Boy, and by the time I managed to put the headphones back on, I realized my terrible mistake:

I'd been holding the Game Boy directly in the red light of the sunset.

"Oh my god, Sarah. Sarah! Are you all right?"

"I'm fine." Sarah's voice was tinny, but no longer ear-shattering. The Game Boy weighed heavier in my pocket now that she'd slipped inside it. "Better than fine. That was the first sunset I've seen in . . . well, you know. Never thought that would happen."

"*Could* you see it?" There was no lens and no camera on the Game Boy. Even as Sarah spoke, the screen remained blank, although the machine felt as warm as a sleeping cat. "I mean, *how?*"

"I'm not stuck inside your deathly fanny pack, for one. But even when I was under the bed, I could always see every part of the bedroom. I never *really* have a body or eyes, so I guess it doesn't matter too much. I can probably see more than you can."

"Then why am I hearing you through the headphones, and not just in general?"

"Huh. No idea. Ghosts don't make a ton of sense, Dani. Those rules of yours don't exist, remember?"

"That's true." A giddy laugh escaped me. "Oh my god."

"What?"

"Sarah. You're like the world's weirdest Tamagotchi."

"That's not a real word. There's no *way* it's a real word."

"It's like a portable electronic pet." I explained the difference between GigaPets and Tamagotchis, tiny artificial creatures that rely on the whims of children to exist.

"Again with the stupid computers! And I thought computers would save the world one day. Man, was I wrong."

I laughed and pressed the Game Boy close to my chest. "And I haven't even mentioned Furbys. You sure you're okay in there?"

"You mother me more than my own mother ever did."

"Rightbackatcha."

"Well, Mom. Let's take that walk. I'd dig that for sure."

There weren't any sidewalks on Iroquois, but once we crossed onto Main Street, there were a few. The neon orange and green of a 7-Eleven illuminated one side of the road, and sparse streetlights helped us walk all five blocks of town.

We passed what looked like a public library, and a more familiar sight: the Green House Women's Shelter. Midway down the strip, a furniture store crammed between a pizzeria and a video rental place declared that it was going out of business: 75% OFF ALL RUSTIC FURNITURE!

Sarah and I spotted two other souls downtown: A drunk man smoked a cigarette outside the Big Anchor Bar and Grill (I hurried past, avoiding his eyes). Another man stood inside the most inexplicable business on the sad little strip: Murphy's Flower Shoppe.

Rochdale was the kind of town where probably no one was ever in love, let alone wealthy enough to waste money on floral arrangements. Later, it occurred to me that the shop's business was likely funeral and church functions. But that night, my first night as a townie, the shop felt as improbable as being besties with a ghost girl.

The man in the window was bent over window boxes filled

with flowers I couldn't name—I mean, *could* I name any, other than violets and pansies and tulips? Other than roses?

I paused to watch him, and he offered me a small smile.

I wanted to wave at him, but I didn't.

"Dani?" Sarah's voice was weaker. I felt a chill and turned from the window.

"Sarah?"

"You don't really think I'm like a computer or a toy or something, do you? Because I'm not. Or I didn't use to be, even if people treated me that way."

"No, sorry, it was a bad joke. I shouldn't have said it."

"I know you didn't mean it." Her sigh grazed the smallest hairs inside my ear. "Let's head back, Dani. I don't feel well."

I tried to imagine how overwhelming a sunset walk might be after decades of darkness.

And I would not realize for almost five years that opening up my heart to Sarah somehow meant welcoming a whole world of dead things, that Sarah was right about ghosts not being computers, and I was right about people, ghosts included, being messy.

Sarah said I made her realer, and she made me realer, too.

Turns out getting too real can be dangerous.

PATRICIA

ADIDAS

It was 2002 before Sarah and I met another ghost. I was almost sixteen, *The Lord of the Rings* movies were pretty great, and you couldn't escape *The Eminem Show* if you tried.

I was running laps in the woods behind Holland Park with the rest of the junior cross-country team. As the sun slipped behind the pines, the wind turned frigid cold, but we kept at it all the same. Late as it was, we were practicing hard for district finals the following week, tackling the longest trails, taking advantage of all those winding paths before the snow could smother them.

The October air pricked at the cords of my throat, left my fingertips needled and numb, and adhered clumps of hair to my forehead. I'd cut my hair as short as Mom would let me, but since I was determined to hide my lazy eye, I'd ended up with awkward bangs and a bob too short for a ponytail. Despite my headphones, my ears were freezing, and a stomachache had plagued me since lunchtime.

My feet beat the uneven earth. Inevitably I would lose the cadence that had put me ahead of my teammates. The boys' and girls' teams practiced together, and usually broke into smaller groups. In a mile or so, I'd be overtaken by slower runners because I could never pace myself.

I knew this but knowing didn't seem to change anything.

"Honestly, want me to clap my hands to keep tempo?" Sarah's voice shook my eardrums. The Game Boy that held her was pressed against my chest beneath my shirt, secured by a strap and my sports bra. "Coach Ma is gonna be *pissed* if you're last again."

I was too breathless to answer. Sarah probably didn't expect me to. Her voice was as much a constant in my head as my own thoughts were. Speech was hardly necessary between us these days.

"*Christ*, Dani! Slow down!"

A sharp, strange pain pierced my abdomen. I caught my foot on a tree root and toppled forward. My knees grazed the dirt. My hands scraped the earth.

"Dani—*Dani*. I feel *sick*." I'd heard a lot of cussing from Sarah over the years, but I'd rarely heard her sound so scared.

"You too?" I wheezed, rubbing my bloodied knees. The ache in my stomach lessened. "Sorry. What do you *mean* by sick?"

"It's . . . like something's *earthquaking* through me. I'm seeing double, or somehow I'm not as real, like *I'm* a double? And I'm cold. Christ. Really, extremely cold."

I placed my hand over the Game Boy, as if that could help.

Every so often, I had this one, specific nightmare: Sarah left me. She achieved the sort of catharsis Patrick Swayze reached in *Ghost* and abandoned me for some higher plane, heaven or an ethereal nothingness. I always woke up a mess, worried I'd revert to that scared kid who punched himself in the face, ashamed that I didn't *want* catharsis for her.

I'd promised Sarah years ago not to ask about her death, but that wasn't the real reason I didn't ask. Close as we were, she didn't know the selfish heart of me. I didn't want to know her secrets, because what if that would release her somehow?

What if she stepped into the sun one day?

Anyone's stomach would hurt if they were full of thoughts like these.

"*Dani.* Up ahead. What *is* that?"

"What? I don't see anything."

"*Look.*" Her voice sharpened, popped in my icy ears.

Once again, Sarah made it realer, made me see what I had missed.

As the trees swallowed the last of the sunlight, the dead woman appeared on the trail. At least, her feet appeared. The bulk of her body remained obscured by the ferns and tree trunks that lined the path.

I approached slowly, almost on tiptoe. The vision didn't fade.

The woman's shins were blue.

"Look," Sarah said again.

Carefully, I parted the ferns and peered down at her prostrate form.

"Please don't step on me," the dead woman rasped, without much conviction. Glassy blue eyes stared skyward above pronounced cheekbones. Her crow's-feet made me think she was Mom's age, but maybe she wasn't. Maybe she was only exhausted. Blood stained her lips, her chin. "I'm so *tired* of being stepped on."

Her neck was red with bruises, and her head was askew, twisted to the side at a disturbing angle, jammed against the trunk of a tree. She wore Under Armour with Adidas trainers. Striped track pants had been pulled down to her knees with her department store underwear still inside them, and strands of her graying hair had been torn loose from her scrunchie.

I looked away to spare her, or maybe to spare myself.

Sarah said, "She's like *me*, Dani."

Even though Sarah was the only ghost I knew at the time, I didn't doubt that for a minute. If life had taught me anything, it was this: every place is haunted by something, and most people just pretend otherwise.

Maybe that was why Sarah felt so ill as we approached, shaking like we'd struck a note on a tuning fork, like we were forcing two negative magnets together.

The woman blinked and repeated herself:

"Please don't step on me. I'm *tired* of being stepped on."

She seemed no less tangible to me than Sarah, but her gaze was distant.

"I don't think she knows we're here." In the twilight, Sarah could leave the Game Boy behind. Now she stood beside me, holding her stomach. She padded forward and knelt before the woman. "She's probably really confused . . . I mean. Who *knows* how long she's been stuck here."

Judging by her clothes, I thought she must have been dead at least a decade.

I could hear footsteps rapidly nearing, voices filling the trail behind us.

"Sarah, the others are coming."

Sarah placed her palm on the woman's forehead. "We won't leave you here."

"Sarah . . ."

"Dani. We *can't* leave her. We'd have to be monsters."

The plaintive note in Sarah's voice pierced me. I knew she was right. Leaving this woman here, half-naked and alone and trod upon, would be monstrous.

But this ghost was *not* Sarah. She was not the girl beneath my bed. This was a stranger, who looked right through us. And maybe, just maybe, I *was* a monster.

"*Dani*. Help me help her."

"I don't know *how* we can help her . . ."

Sarah's eyes flashed, humming with upset. "This isn't a *choice*."

The footsteps were close now—not one pair, but a dozen—so I hushed her, knelt over my shoes, and put my back to both ghosts.

Charley Meyer came around the bend in the dimming light, followed by a boy I didn't know and a girl named Leann. Not surprisingly, none of them seemed to see the dead woman, but they could see me, crouched on the path like a weirdo.

"You burn yourself out already, Dani?" Leann called, as she and the other boy plowed on by. Charley slowed to jog in place beside me, grinning beneath his freckles. He was tall and 90 percent Adam's apple, and about as cheesy as stuffed-crust pizza.

"Dan the Man! What's up? Charley horse? My bad!"

It was an awful joke, and a nickname that rankled. Still, Charley wasn't a bad guy, despite Sarah's derisive snort. "Nah, I just tripped. I'm fine."

"Want me to hang back with you? Need help getting up?"

"I'm good, thanks." It still surprised me, how easily kindness came to kids like him.

In the years since we'd moved downtown, something unexpected had happened: I'd gotten by *okay* at school. Maybe Sarah's presence, that conscience in my pocket, had something to do with it.

But honestly?

My self-inflicted black eye in middle school had been the start of it. That twisted incident had garnered me a lot of sympathy, especially because I refused to talk about it. By the time Seiji returned from his suspension, most of the class had blacklisted him for unspeakable horrors he'd never committed. Several girls sat beside me during lunch, an unexpected line of defense, and walked with me between classes. Because Seiji never said a word to defend himself, the kindness of those girls stuck.

They didn't know what I was, and I didn't tell them. Because, dream of dreams, I had *friends* at school, or at least people who didn't sneer at me.

Maybe Sarah couldn't see the appeal of guys like Charley, but I could.

"Dani? Do you need help?" he asked again.

"Don't step on me," the dead woman said.

To my horror, Charley was jogging in place directly on top of her spectral ankles.

I stood so abruptly that Charley took one merciful step back. "Or you know what, hey—I'll get ahead of the others and tell Coach Ma what happened, all right?"

"Thanks, Charley."

56

Charley clapped me on the back and moved on, running backward with both thumbs up.

"Stop mooning after him, Dani, let's get her out of here!"

"Not yet." I shook my head. "Let's wait for the rest of the team to pass first."

"Are you *serious*?"

"It shouldn't take more than five minutes."

"Dani!"

I didn't answer, but I crouched on the path to prevent anyone else from treading on the woman. As the remainder of the team passed by, I stared at her legs. There was mud on her calves, but her shoes were still tied. One of her socks was shorter than the other, an off-white mismatch.

There were only a few more kids to go. One or two asked if I needed help, but I smiled and waved them on. They were as fearful of Coach Ma's retribution as I was, and none other than Charley offered to go down with me.

Sarah pinched my cheek in frustration, but I ignored her until Kylie Waters, the slowest among us, huffed by with a half-hearted nod.

"*Really*, Dani? You care that much what those breathers think?" Sarah demanded. "This woman needs us, but you're worried about them?"

I swatted her hand away. "Come on, Sarah! What difference did five more minutes make?"

Even as I said it, I regretted it.

"It makes a difference," Sarah said hollowly. "Every *second* makes a difference."

"Okay. Yeah, okay. Sorry."

Sarah stared at the woman. "Let's help her up."

Sarah helped the dead woman to her feet. The ache in my stomach intensified as the woman stood. I could only watch, awkward and useless, as Sarah held her steady, pulled the woman's pants back up, and plucked phantom twigs from her tangled hair. Later those twigs might reappear, like Sarah's bloodstains did when she was unhappy. But for the moment, the dead woman was returned some small part of her dignity.

Being upright seemed to rouse her, or maybe Sarah's touch made her more alert, because the dead woman met my eyes for the first time. "They kept stepping on me. Can you believe that?"

"What's your name?" Sarah asked.

"It doesn't matter," she said. "I just don't want to be stepped on."

"You won't be," Sarah said, drawing the woman's arm over her shoulders. "Never again. I promise."

Sarah caught my eye over the woman's shoulder. As usual, I read her mind.

I nodded, powerless against her eyes. "You're coming home with us."

SLURPEE

I led them down the path, back the way we'd come. Somewhere at the opposite end of the trail, I knew Coach Ma was checking her watch and rolling up her sleeves, ready to dig into me. I might get kicked off the team for ditching practice, but the longer I walked beside Sarah and the woman, the less I doubted my decision.

The woman was quiet, trembling as we walked the path out of the woods.

Twigs cracked under only my feet, and the starlight and occasional high beams that pierced the woods rendered my companions luminous. It occurred to me that the dead woman had good reason to tremble. A murderer had passed through these woods at least once before, as she was testament. The branches seemed like veins inching toward the sky, and the trees muffled the wind too much, their branches crossing like capillaries over our head, trapping us beneath them.

My stomach knotted again.

Had I been alone, I might have started sprinting.

But Sarah was beside me. She always was, now.

And with Sarah riffing in my pocket, I was braver. I cared less about saying something stupid in class, less about whether people were looking at my good eye or my lazy one. And she softened bigger fears, too. Last month I overheard Mom talking with Dad on the phone. I had my first panic attack in years at the possibility they might get back together. Sarah climbed in bed beside me and pressed her hands over my ears in our coffin of a room so I wouldn't have to hear Mom laughing at his stupid, disarming jokes. Sarah sang Joni Mitchell songs until I fell asleep.

Sarah and her loose braids exuded a soft white glow as we led the nameless woman out of the woods. Sarah was another moon, a star to see by. Again the ache in my belly spiked, as if punishing me for disappointing her, even for a moment.

At last we reached a clearing and semi-civilization once again: the barren excuse of a park known as Holland. No one was walking a dog as we crossed the lawn. In small towns, visiting a park at night is sinister as hell. Autumn leaves crunched under my tennis shoes. The cool night beaded the sweat on my neck and back, but the ghosts kept the shivers at bay.

We reached the road and paused on the curb beneath a flickering streetlight. I'm not sure what stopped first: me, feeling another inexplicable pang in my stomach, or the woman, taken aback by the sight of the faded water tower and the streetlamps stretching above the tiny houses.

Sarah urged us forward until we were walking along Main Street. I glanced left and right, up and down.

"You can walk ahead of us," Sarah told me, "if you're so worried about someone seeing you walking the streets at night, talking to yourself."

I winced. "No. I'm not—I'm just—"

"Look, I get it." Sarah turned away. "I go to school with you, you know? Those idiots'll use any damn excuse to alienate a girl."

I looked at the woman's face, her reflective glassy eyes and the trees that still seemed caught in them.

"No one's around to see us," I said finally, and I stayed beside them.

Sarah nodded. "Fine."

As we passed the 7-Eleven, mere blocks from home, the woman halted again. Her head sat a little less crookedly on her neck as she stared at the orange-and-green sign above the entrance.

"Come on, now," Sarah said. "We're almost there."

"I want a Slurpee." The woman's voice was as clear as water.

"You *what?*"

She put a hand on her stomach; her pants were slipping again, but she tugged them up herself. "I really, *really* want a raspberry Slurpee."

"What the hell is that?"

"It's a drink, Sarah." I broke the news to the trembling woman. "You won't be able to drink it."

She frowned. "Please. Please don't step—I mean. No, that's not it. *Please* get me a Slurpee."

"But there's no point." I wanted to go home and lie down; my stomach felt like the aftermath of running it through a garbage disposal.

Sarah folded her arms. "Dani, if a slurp-thing is what she wants, let her have it. When do you think she last got *anything* she wanted?"

And just like that, Sarah had silenced me once again. The prospect of a raspberry Slurpee seemed to break the newcomer from the loop she'd been stuck in. Against all odds, she seemed *present*.

"Okay," I muttered.

The ghost smiled, and I looked away, face on fire.

SOBE

Buzzing fluorescent lights shredded my vision to sparks and lines. Behind the counter, an elderly cashier craned his neck, watching a TV in the back room. He didn't look at me as I crossed the linoleum.

The Slurpee machine had clearly seen better days, but whatever; who hadn't?

As I filled a medium cup with glooping liquid, a door slammed behind me, scaring me out of my skin. You wouldn't think anything would spook me anymore. But honestly, most things do, when I'm alone.

I spun around.

Seiji Grayson knelt on the peeling tiles, midway through restocking a cooler with orange SoBe. He held my gaze before dropping his eyes. I cursed as my cup overflowed and flicked the sticky blue ice from my hand before popping a lid on as quickly as possible.

The old man still wouldn't look at me, even after I put my money on the counter.

"Um. Excuse me?"

"Grayson!" the man barked. "Take care of it, won't you? It's the last inning."

To my dismay, Seiji lumbered his way to the register. These days he was so much bigger than he'd been in sixth grade. His shoulders were always rounded and hunched, as if he were made of hills, and his hair had grown longer. His eyes were deep glimmers beneath reeds of black. His work polo didn't fit him.

But there I was in my track uniform, covered in pine needles and sweat, and nothing ever fit me either.

"That'll be $1.19, please."

The softness of his voice was jarring. I slid the fiver toward him.

Our history aside, Seiji had earned a real reputation over the past few years. He'd been kicked off the soccer team for punching both an opponent and a teammate, and rumor had it that he spent every single day in after-school detention. There were whispers, probably racist, that Seiji was involved with the yakuza (because being Asian in northern Michigan meant people had to come up with some ludicrous excuse for your presence, right?).

Then again, as he took the money from my fingers, I noticed tattoos—actual tattoos!—between each of his knuckles. Who has tats at sixteen, other than gangsters?

"Blood." Seiji spoke not to me, but to the counter.

"What?" I snapped.

"You're bleeding." Seiji gestured with a limp hand.

For a wild moment, I thought that the dead woman's blood might have stained me somehow.

But when I looked down at myself, the blood in question was a terrifying patch staining the fabric between my legs.

64

Just like that, I was looking down at a stranger's body, and though suddenly it made sense—the restlessness and sadness and bellyache—I wanted to sob, for reasons beyond lost childhood and beyond Seiji fucking Grayson.

This could not be happening. I had hoped it never would, and after so many years dreading it, I'd almost believed it wouldn't, thought I'd wished away this curse. I thought in this small instance, some heavenly bastard had taken pity on me, and maybe, maybe, that bastard knew what I was and wasn't.

But here I was, bleeding in 7-Eleven.

Seiji shoved a small box my way—pads. He must have pulled it from the shelf when I was getting the Slurpee. He must have seen the blood, while I was still oblivious.

"Here," he said, as if that fixed everything.

"I don't need that," I sputtered. "Put it away."

He was as expressionless as ever.

"Seriously, get rid of it. I don't want those!"

"I live with my aunt," he said cryptically.

"That's nice. But I'm not your *fucking* aunt."

I felt his stare trail me as I grabbed my change and hurried out the door, wishing I could hide all of me, wishing for hilly shoulders of my own, for *anything* but the blood.

Sarah and the dead woman stood right where I'd left them, staring at the sky. I set the Slurpee on the ground below their levitating feet and crouched on the pavement, trying to breathe, trying to be any other boy.

"Whoa there, is that *Windex*?" Sarah asked, peering at the drink while the woman knelt before it as if it were holy. Then Sarah saw my face. She put her hand on my back. "What is it? Dani? What the hell happened?"

I shook my head.

Mom hadn't bothered talking to me about puberty, but I'd learned all about it from school and living in general. Ostensibly, I'd *known* this was coming. But some part of me had hoped my body would not betray me more than it already had. Because I always knew what I was, even if no one else did.

I always knew that I *wasn't* a girl.

This heat between my legs felt like another death, one that I couldn't discuss with Sarah. She'd never understood my panda folder of boy photos, and she couldn't understand why I fought so hard not to wear bras, why I refused to wear dresses or makeup. Maybe she wouldn't understand this, either. Maybe Sarah had welcomed her period.

I could not relate.

"I just got my first period," I said dully.

"You think?" Sarah glanced me up and down, then let loose a whistle. "Yeah, I'd say so. Wow. Guess you're a woman now."

At that, I lost it.

"Whoa, h-hey, it's not that big a deal, Dani—" Sarah began, clearly shaken by my sobs. Before she could question the scale of my reaction, we were interrupted.

"I can't even pick it up!" the dead woman hollered, as her hands passed through the sticky cup of ice. She aimed a doomed kick at the cup and swung with all her might.

The Slurpee didn't even tremble as her foot passed through it.

"I can't drink the damn thing!"

"Wow, Windex must taste good, huh?" Sarah joked, but humor didn't touch her voice. She knew better than I that the woman's rage had little to do with the Slurpee.

"After all of this, I can't even enjoy a fucking Slurpee? What *right* did he have? Who the hell was he? Some stranger! Some creep! Who told him he could take anything—no, *everything*—away from me? As if I had anything left? What *fucking* right?"

She collapsed as I had, but with far more reason to.

I stood and wiped my eyes. I may not have been grateful for my body, but at least I had one. No one had taken it from me yet.

"Fuck him, truly and forever," the woman whispered.

"Yeah, fuck that guy," I agreed. "Let's get you home."

"My name's Patricia," the woman said.

Sarah smiled. "Nice to meet you, Patricia."

We walked home, leaving the Slurpee behind.

ALWAYS

Mom worked late-night shifts at the Big Anchor, serving the locals their Natty Ices and Long Islands, so there was no chance of colliding with her as we crossed the Teepee parking lot. There were only seven occupied apartments in the building, and virtually everyone minded their own business. Probably no one saw me arrive, and of course no one saw my companions.

I wanted to put a few doors between me and every part of this night so far.

Once me, Sarah, and Patricia got inside, I ran straight to Mom's bathroom. At the bottom of the cupboard I found a pack of pads wrapped in strange soft plastic. Pulling down my shorts proved that the damage had already been done; there was no salvaging them. I crumpled my clothes and resolved to toss them in the dumpster ASAP, and then I climbed under the showerhead and tried to erase myself beneath it.

By the time I reemerged, still cramping and bleeding, Sarah and Patricia were sitting on Mom's bed, watching MTV with the volume all the way up. Sometimes lights turned on when Sarah was around, but this was the first time she'd switched on the TV.

"Music's gotten worse again," Patricia observed. Sarah was

sprawling, but Patricia sat primly on the edge of the bed. "What-ever happened to Pearl Jam?"

"I can actually change the channel, if you want." These days, Sarah was pretty damn good with technology. At least in her case, the ability to manipulate machines was one aspect of ghosthood that *Poltergeist* got right.

Sarah couldn't move physical objects as a rule, but electric-ity was different. She rationalized it with a shrug, arguing what were ghosts, if not concentrations of energy, much like electric-ity? After a few months in the Game Boy, Sarah could operate the electric mixer on a whim, and turning on lights was as easy as blinking for her.

"Good god, a shower would feel amazing." Patricia stared at me, envious. She seemed calmer and the bruises on her neck had faded, but there was no denying her deadness.

"I say that every time, too," Sarah told her. That wasn't quite true, but I didn't call her out on it. Clearly Sarah was pleased as punch to have another dead person around. I told myself the jealousy I felt was misplaced.

"Mom will be home soon."

"I used to be a mom," Patricia said, silencing us.

After another Avril Lavigne video petered out on *TRL*, I tried again.

"Mom will be home soon. We probably shouldn't stay here." If Mom had ever noticed me whispering to Sarah, she'd never said so, but then, she hardly noticed anything. Still, keeping two ghosts secret might be harder than one.

"Fine," Sarah said. "I have something in mind."

The motel lobby beneath remained decrepit as ever, its windows blacked out, doors chained shut and boarded up by a landlord we hadn't heard from in months.

"My grandmother was Chippewa." Patricia stared up at the rusted tepee facade, frowning a little.

I winced. "Oh. Um. Sorry."

"It's not as though you built it," Patricia said gently.

Sarah was all summer heat, but Patricia felt like rain.

"Over here." Sarah led us around to the back of the building, where the petroleum pig blocked most of the wall from view. The curves of the tepee guttered out here, staining the building orange and brown.

"There's a way in through the cellar." Sarah gestured with her eyebrows raised. I craned over the damp tank. Beyond it was a broken basement window. Whatever glass had been there was all but cleared away.

"In we go."

I stared at the rectangle of black. "When did you find out about this, Sarah?"

"Saw some kids creeping in here to smoke dope. They covered the place in graffiti, but the upstairs was mostly left alone."

I frowned. "Do those boys still come here?"

"Nah, not likely. I spooked 'em pretty good." Her nonchalance was jarring; I hadn't known she haunted anyone but me. I hadn't known she *could*. "I'd bet they won't be back. Probably won't be smoking dope again anytime soon, either." She grinned wickedly. "They thought I was the worst trip ever."

I followed Sarah and Patricia carefully through the broken window—they couldn't get splinters, but I could—and all three of us dropped into the dank cellar. It seemed like it had served as a storage or maintenance area, and maybe also as the motel laundry, based on the pipes draping the brick walls like forlorn snakes. Sarah was right about the graffiti—I spotted obligatory dicks and swear words on the wall. The boys had left other evidence behind, too: tattered couch cushions arranged around a dubious ashtray, the glass of a shattered bong.

"I'm not fond of the damp," Patricia admitted. "It rained too much in the woods."

"We'll go upstairs. Come on." Sarah led us up a narrow set of concrete stairs and we emerged in a mildewed, beige lobby beneath the tepee's peak. There was the check-in counter, coated in dust and adorned with a tasteless taxidermied raccoon. The remains of a few ugly sofas were tipped over here and there.

"Here's home, Trish," Sarah declared. "It's a mess, but no daylight gets in here, and there are still some chairs and good cubbies under the desk where the room keys were kept. I don't know about you, Patricia, but I feel safer when I sleep in small dark places these days.

"I don't know about me yet," Patricia said, "but thank you."

"Nah, don't thank me." Sarah locked eyes with me. "You should thank Dani. I wouldn't be here to help you if she hadn't helped me first." That comment felt barbed to me—Sarah and I both knew I'd almost left Patricia alone in the woods.

"Thank you, Dani." Patricia nodded at me, unaware of my shame. She sat down on a deflated cushion and stared at the pointed ceiling.

"Well," I said, "we'll let you get some rest."

I made my way toward the stairs. Sarah hung back.

71

"I think I'll spend the night here with her," she said. "You don't mind, right?"

It would be selfish to mind. "No, it's cool. Good night."

———

Mom had returned from work. She glanced up from the television when I came in, eyes glossy with drink. "You're home late."

"Track practice." It was only half a lie.

She must have seen some part of it in my face. "You okay?"

Once, I would have cherished that question coming from her. There was a bloody pair of shorts in my bedroom closet, an emptiness in my ears, an ache in my belly, my best friend and a murdered woman shivering in the motel lobby. I felt a sadness I couldn't express. "Yeah, I'm fine."

"Okay. I'm clocking out. There are leftover chicken strips in the fridge."

For the first night in years, I slept without Sarah's warmth beneath or beside me, and I dreamed of rain that wasn't really falling. Patricia needed Sarah, I knew that. And it really would be selfish of me to mind.

I guess that made me pretty damn selfish.

FUNYUNS

The next morning, I woke up lying in my own blood.

My cramps worsened during the walk to school, these small and constant kicks to my abdomen. Sarah stayed back at the motel to help Patricia settle into the lobby. Being alone wasn't *that* unusual—Sarah didn't come to school with me *every* day. But her absence didn't usually feel like another unbearable cramp.

Coach Ma found me in the hall before homeroom, pulled me aside, and reprimanded me loudly enough that passersby stared.

"Do you *know* that I spent an hour alone on that trail, searching for you? And then, when I couldn't find any sign of you, I had to call your mother to tell her I'd lost her daughter? She said you were home sleeping, safe and sound. Do you know how worried I was?"

Her words hit me hard. Coach Ma was stocky and strong, but she'd still walked those woods alone.

"I'm sorry. Really, Coach Ma."

"That's not an explanation." She folded her arms.

I could pull the period card for the first time in my life. Maybe I'd avoid punishment if I cried. But this was Coach Ma. She'd probably tell me to man up.

God, if only I *could* man up. I wish people who said that actually thought about what they were saying.

"I'm really sorry," I repeated, then pinched my mouth shut.

Coach Ma shook her head. "You're gonna be. You'll be doing double the blood and guts of your teammates tomorrow. Got it?"

"Um, yeah. Got it."

I couldn't believe she was letting me off so lightly. I thought the day might be turning around, until I felt a sudden warmth between my legs. I ran to the bathroom, breath wild and heavy. I hadn't bled through, but the pad seemed like another kind of victim.

It wasn't that I thought menstruating was gross. Women's bodies are *not* gross, periods are not gross—Sarah had drilled that into me pretty well, and I agreed it was bullshit that girls ever felt *gross* at all, or like they were worthless when they bled.

What was gross to me was how my body didn't feel like mine.

I wouldn't mind if it was anyone else's blood. But my body was staining me, screaming, *You're what people call a woman, and there's no changing that. No buts. It's been decided for you.*

It felt like a life sentence.

———

I avoided the cafeteria. I didn't feel up to smiling and putting on a bubbly face for the girls I usually sat with. Instead I sat down in front of my locker, tucked out of sight, and ate my sad salami sandwich and FUNYUNS there. Soon I felt too queasy and achy to eat, so I pulled out the Game Boy and caught some Tentacools in Pokemon Blue. The games never worked when Sarah was in there, which meant I hardly ever played, and I was still stuck on, like, the third gym.

A few minutes before lunch ended, I tucked the Game Boy under my arm, stood, and walked to the trash can to dump my grease-stained lunch bag. When I turned, Seiji was there, leaning against the window with a chocolate milk carton in his oversize fist.

He was beginning to haunt me in his own way, or maybe he always had. I fought the self-conscious urge to look at my lap to check for blood. He was staring not at my legs, but at the battered old Game Boy tucked beneath my arm.

Oh.

His battered old Game Boy.

"Does it still work?" he asked, but I'd started for the bathroom.

For Christ's sake.

HBO

Patricia got to be a lot older than Sarah ever was, around as old as my mom, before a stranger strangled her while she was out jogging early one January morning. Before the sound of her killer's footsteps broke the snow on the trail behind her, the sunrise gave her hope that spring was coming soon, that the future might be brighter. She told us that hope took her mind off her aching joints and the difficult holiday season. Patricia told us she was already dead before her killer raped her.

"There's no mystery to solve," she told us.

She was right about that. Searching online articles revealed that Patricia's murderer was caught months after her body was discovered, in the summer of 1993. His wife called in a tip after finding a bag of women's hair in his glove compartment. The man stood trial for the murder of three Michigan women, each one strangled, then raped. Each one abandoned in a forest. His fate in court was sealed when his wife attested to years of abuse, and numerous women came forward to claim he had tried to attack them or had offered them rides while masturbating or worse. Patricia's killer was killed in a prison brawl.

He wasn't anyone Patricia had known, and his name mattered less than dirt.

What mattered then, and now, was Patricia. She'd started talking more, and within a week, she wasn't as jumpy as she'd been when we first helped her in from the cold. She was never as brash as Sarah (no one was). Patricia was thoughtful and experienced, and had this acerbic sense of humor that made our lobby conversations more meaningful.

Two weeks or so after she moved in, Patricia was watching Sarah and me trying to rearrange the couches in the lobby to make the space more comfortable. She said, "So long as I won't be stepped on, it'll feel like a luxury to me." When Sarah pondered whether we should save up for an old TV from St. Vincent DePaul, Patricia joked, "That's very kind, but don't bother unless you can arrange for HBO. I need to watch *Ghost* on repeat for weeks straight, thank you very much."

"I don't know what HBO is," Sarah said, holding aloft a finger, "but I'm going to 'Ask Jeeves' about it later." Sarah had come along with me to the library, nestled in my pocket while I looked up Patricia's story. Her newfound internet prowess was going to her head, but who could blame her? Sarah had spent years beneath a bed, unable to interact with anything or anyone. Once she realized that her electrical aptitude applied to computers and search engines, there was no stopping her.

With Patricia settled in, Sarah began slipping away alone at night to spend hours at the library, relishing the internet and all the injustices it exposed. She'd come a long way from when I met her, when she couldn't even grasp the existence of handheld games. Now she was something of a cybernaut, at least when it came to true-crime research. She said the forests of Rochdale had their fair share of ghosts. Sarah was collecting the names and photos of local victims in an online folder, a strange echo of the Lisa Frank one I'd left behind at our old apartment.

According to Sarah, running into someone like Patricia was bound to happen. Small as Rochdale was, it was part of rural America, and statistics claim that three women are killed in small-town America each day. Girls go missing all the time, too, and half the time they're just called runaways and ignored until months have passed.

"There isn't a square mile in the world that isn't haunted by a dead girl, you know."

Sarah shared her findings with me and Patricia, who began spending the whole of her time inside the hexagonal lobby.

"I've had enough of the outdoors," she said. "I'm old, or trying to be. I wanted to be a grandmother, you know." Her posture collapsed a little, brambles grew through her hair. "I don't know what my children are doing now."

"I can 'Ask Jeeves,' if you want," Sarah offered, but Patricia shook her head.

It was the one rule of our lobby: we didn't ask questions that one of us might not want the answers to. I knew how unwilling Sarah was to talk about her life before death, and how unwilling I was to talk about my life before I knew her. It became instinctive not to pry. But when Patricia told us more about her life, she became alive.

First she told us she adored reading, so Sarah had an idea. I started "borrowing" library books and tearing out the pages, stapling them to the bulletin board and walls so she could walk around the room to read them. I could barely keep up with her voracious bookworming, and of course she missed every other page because she couldn't flip the pages over, so I began tacking crossword puzzles to the walls, too. Eventually the entire lobby was wallpapered. It felt cluttered, more like a bird's nest than a home, but all those words seemed to reassure Patricia.

To my surprise, her favorite books were epic fantasy and science-fiction novels. The wall behind the check-in counter was soon smothered in maps torn from the front matter of books. Sometimes I caught Patricia squinting at them, readjusting her track pants, which tended to slip down when she was a little low or distracted. Other times, Sarah would float just above her head, staring at them with her, asking questions like, *Where's the McDonald's?* and *What makes a mountain lonely?* and *Excuse me, miss, but where are the toilets?* until Patricia could not help but chuckle and shoo her away.

Sometimes they touched each other—little nudges or hugs, like real sisters, and I felt a twist of envy in my gut.

"Have you always liked books this much?" I asked Patricia once, while I tacked the pages of Octavia Butler's *Parable of the Sower* to the wall. By then it was almost November. Patricia had started requesting specific books. I didn't have the heart to tell her that the library would soon get wise to my antics and she'd be cut off.

"Oh, absolutely. I loved reading when I was your age. I used to come home from school and read an entire book before bed. Have you ever done that? It's exhilarating."

I shook my head and frowned; the stapler was out of staples.

"No. I'm not a big reader. The effort never seemed worth it to me."

"That's a shame. Escapism is humanity's best invention." Patricia had her back to me. "Every page is precious as *mithril*," she'd told me, whatever that meant.

"But when I got older, I sort of . . . stopped reading. I don't know why. I think maybe I stopped seeing myself in the characters."

I looked at the back of her head. The brambles had grown long and thorny, but she hardly looked bruised anymore.

"Maybe that's my issue," I admitted. "I've *never* seen myself in characters."

Patricia turned and met my gaze, eyebrows raised. "Really? I suspect you haven't found the right book yet. I used to do really well with reluctant readers, back in my teaching days. Give me some time to get to know you better, Dani, and I'll think of a good one for you."

"Really, you don't have to," I protested. "It's a waste of time."

"I *want* to do it. And I've got nothing but time." She smiled, eyes mischievous. "As you and Sarah seem intent on giving me what I want, Slurpees and all, you'll have to accept this home-work assignment."

I threw up my hands. "Yes, Patricia."

She turned away from me again. "Get back to work! Those pages won't staple themselves, will they? I need to know what happens to the intergalactic necromancers."

I returned to the wall, face flushed, happy to be parented for once.

GATORADE

Patricia had been living with us for a month—it had to have been a month, because I was bleeding again. Coach Ma hadn't kicked me off the team after I left her worrying, but she *had* made good on her promise to punish me with exercise; I had to do twice the push-ups and crunches as everyone else.

Usually that was fine, but usually I wasn't a gory mess. It infuriated me that this was a problem I'd have until menopause, a recurring, violent battle. On the second day of my second period, my cramps left me lagging behind the other runners, bent double on the track. Charley passed by with an encouraging "You can do it!" His two thumbs up felt really damn condescending.

By the time I got home, I was in a vile mood. Sarah had enough of my muttering, and asked me to tuck her in my backpack so she could get a break from my dramatics.

"As if you aren't dramatic," I snapped, pulling my shoes off.

She sighed in my ears. "I'll go check on Patricia. In the meantime, chill."

"People don't *actually* say chill," I said.

"How would you know? You don't talk to other people."

I yanked off my headphones and pushed the Game Boy to the bottom of my bag.

I stomped to my bedroom to find Mom digging through my drawers.

"Why are you in my room?"

She looked up at me. "Why didn't you tell me?"

"Tell you what?"

"I do your laundry, hon, and suddenly you've got no underwear. And funny thing, *I* ran out of pads, but I haven't been using them." She frowned and sat down on my bed. "Why didn't you tell me?"

"It wasn't about you," I said, because the truth was *I* was angry.

We flinched in unison. We were so unused to talking to each other.

"Why . . . why don't I treat us to dinner tonight, sweetie?" Mom suggested. It sounded like the last thing she really wanted to do. "We can go to China 1 Buffet, catch up."

"It's not my birthday. There's literally nothing to celebrate."

"Well, you might feel like that now, but this *is* a wonderful thing, and I know it was late in coming. I'm . . . well, I'm proud of you, Daniela."

I cringed at the name. "*Proud?* What the hell is there to be proud of?"

She looked at me. Heavy as her mascara was, the bags beneath her eyes outweighed it. "He told me I couldn't raise you alone, but here we are. We're doing okay, and you're growing up fine."

"I'm not," I blurted, before I could stop myself.

"Of course you are! Sure, puberty's no pleasure cruise, but you'll get through it. And I know you probably don't want to hear this from me, but you're looking older, too. Boys are probably interested in you. You're plenty good lookin', sweetie, even with your eye, and—"

"Stop. Mom." I knew she was trying, in her ass-backward way, to be a parent. To give me *the talk*. But she was terrible at it, and so was I. I couldn't express how deeply I hated the basic premise of this conversation: that I was a woman, and soon I'd fuck men.

I didn't believe either of those things. Why did she?

"What about that cute boy on your track team?" She'd gone to all of one meet, but Mom'd noticed Charley and his stupid grin. "I think he likes you."

"Mom, *stop*." Why wouldn't she? Hadn't we both had to tell Dad to stop? Didn't she know how *vital* it was to honor that word? How terrifying the world was when that word stopped working?

"I'm sure other girls your age are dating. It's natural—"

"Stop."

"Sweetie, first we need to set some ground rules. Some boys might have other *intentions*, and you need to be careful—"

Blood roared in my ears. "*Stop*."

"You need to be prepared to defend yourself, or say no—"

"I'm *not* you, Mom! I don't feel the need to screw every dirtbag I meet!"

If I could have bottled those words inside me again, maybe I would have. Instead, I tore my gaze from her shattered face and fled our ugly little apartment.

THE LEFT HAND
OF DARKNESS

By the time I crawled through the window and up the stairs to the lobby, I was heaving. This wasn't quite a panic attack, but it wasn't great, either. "Sarah? Sarah!"

"She's not here." Patricia was floating near the ceiling, feet dangling as she perused the pages posted highest.

"Not here?" I gasped. "She said she was going to check on you."

If Sarah wasn't here, then where was she?

Patricia frowned down at me. "Is everything okay?"

"No," I said, slumping into one of the chairs. "It's never going to be okay."

"Never say never." Patricia floated to the ground and perched on the chair across from me. It was still a bit sad, but we'd put some embroidered throw pillows on it. "Although what does 'okay' mean, anyhow?"

I shrugged, abdomen aching.

"Maybe there's no such thing, and there's only better or worse. I suppose the more important question would be, is there any way I can help you, Dani?"

Sarah's absence made me more honest. "No one can help me with this."

"Hmm. That may be the case, but it may not be. I didn't think anyone would ever help me out of the woods, until you came along."

I threw up my hands. "It's really unfair when you guys do that! I mean, how can I complain about my dumb eleventh-grade problems when y'all were murdered and stuff! It makes me feel like my issues are stupid and petty."

Patricia patted me on the arm; she felt like cool water. "You can only be where you are."

I narrowed my eyes. "Were you a therapist?"

She laughed, suddenly seeming younger in the face. "I told you: I was a teacher, but sometimes there are parallels, I guess. So let's try it. What's on your mind, Dani?"

I looked at her. Patricia wasn't angry like Sarah, and she didn't seem as sad anymore. Something about her seniority and stillness slowed my heartbeat. Mom's words were still pinging off my eardrums.

"What do you think of men?" I asked.

Patricia considered this. "That's a pretty broad question. Help me out?"

I tried to put words to thoughts I'd always had, but never dared to voice. "I mean, Sarah *hates* boys, and a lot of men do evil things. I *know* that. God, do I ever know that. And it's not like I've met many boys that I trust or even *like*, and obviously I shouldn't, because . . . well."

"You spend your time with people who have been victimized by men," Patricia said bluntly. "You've seen my reality, and Sarah's reality."

"And mine. Dad used to hit us." I spoke as quickly as I could. "Me and my mom, I mean. All the time, when he was angry or drunk or sober or tired, whenever. That's why—well, that's partly why we came to Rochdale. I still dream about him sometimes, and it makes it hard to breathe. When I wake up, I wish men didn't exist. But at the same time . . ."

"Again, you can only be where you are." Patricia adjusted her glasses. "I don't hate *all* men, because I have to believe that individuals can outweigh the negative norms of the patriarchy, and that all the evils the patriarchy has proliferated in our culture for centuries won't be eternal, and men can be allies to the women and minorities they've subjugated for so long to use their privilege for the good of humanity."

"Um." I gawked at her.

She stared at the ceiling, gathering her thoughts. "Let me say this: I have a son, and I love him dearly. I raised him alone. And I tried to raise him to treat people—all people—with kindness. I taught him to listen before speaking. But when he was seven, I got a call from one of his teachers saying that he had hit another child, a little girl, and called her a 'stupid bitch.'"

I thought of Seiji and the angry word scrawled on the surface of my desk.

"I *know* my son didn't hear those words from me. When I asked him why he would ever say such an awful thing, he told me 'All the boys do that kind of stuff.' It broke my heart to hear that, and even more to know that I couldn't change what others taught him. He'd lowered his expectations of himself."

"So what did you do?"

"I made him read," Patricia said with a little smile. "And I told him to promise me that for a year he would only read books written by people who were *not* like him. Women, people of color, queer people."

"Queer people," I echoed and the words resonated deep inside me.

"I told him if he was surrounded by white boys at school, he'd better not surround himself with them at home. Maybe it was sentimental, but it helped. I believe my son grew up to be a decent person, for the most part. So to answer your question: I don't think all men are bad, or at least they don't have to be. What do *you* think?"

"I think . . . I think they're lucky. I don't want to be a girl." I shocked myself by going further. "I don't feel like I *am* a girl, and I never want to be a woman."

I couldn't meet Patricia's eyes but I felt the soft weight of her gaze on me. Finally she said, "Well. Maybe you're *not* a girl, then."

I glanced up so quickly my neck cracked, expecting to see her smirking. But she looked matter-of-fact. I could only stammer, "B-but th-that's crazy, right?" I laughed at myself, chest aching. "I've got to be crazy. I mean, I'm a girl. I'm on my stupid period, and I'm starting to get boobs and . . ."

"Those are just body parts, not who you are. And you know what?"

"What?"

"I taught my kids to treat people kindly, and that included themselves. Don't call yourself names. You're *not* crazy."

"But everyone *knows* I'm a girl."

"Everyone but *you*," she amended, "and *you're* the only one that gets to say."

I couldn't even respond to her words, but I clung to them like a buoy. I wanted to hug her, or at least hug her words close and hold them in my heart until I believed them.

But I didn't hug her, and she didn't hug me, and I wiped my eyes.

"Don't tell Sarah," I said, after my voice returned. "She won't get it."

"Are you sure that's true?" Patricia asked. "She's pretty understanding."

I shook my head. "Not about this."

"It's not my secret to tell. But you know what?"

"What?"

Patricia's smile was the warmest glow. "I think I finally have some book recommendations for you."

BONE DANCE

At around midnight, Sarah appeared beside me in bed. I rolled over and her face was three inches away. If she still breathed, we would have been sharing the same air. Her hair was always tearing free of its braids, and looking at her stilled something in me.

I thought she looked beautiful, not because she *was* beautiful in any specific way, but because she was Sarah. But she looked sad, as if she was carrying some heavy new weight.

I put my hand to her cheek, close as I could, so the fuzzy warmth of her seemed to bounce off my skin. "Sorry I was so angry today."

"Pah. Don't apologize for feeling emotions," Sarah said, her eyes crinkling.

"Where've you been?"

"The library." I was relieved she didn't try to lie and say the lobby, but I was worried about what had left her so unhappy. I felt I couldn't ask, as if asking her what was wrong might encourage her to ask the same of me.

"Did you see any of these books there?" I pulled a sticky note from my nightstand.

She frowned at the titles I'd scribbled on it. "*The Left Hand of Darkness?* Sounds familiar-ish. *Bone Dance?* Never heard of it, but maybe it was written after I died. *Triton?* Sounds like a toothpaste brand. More aliens, right? Gosh, Trish likes some trashy stuff."

Patricia's words still warmed me. "These books aren't for her. They're for me."

Sarah laughed. "But you hate reading, Dani."

My cheeks flushed. "Maybe I haven't read the right books."

Sarah didn't reply. Clearly something was on her mind. And I knew I would hear about whatever it was. No matter our secrets, we had more truths in common. Like clockwork Sarah sat upright, levitating above the bedspread. "Did Patricia seem okay to you today?"

I wanted to say that she had seemed wonderful, like the family I never thought I could have, but Sarah's expression was lined with worry.

"As okay as ever. She was in a good mood, almost. Why?"

"Well, I know she asked us not to look into her family . . ."

"Curiosity got the better of you. Honestly, I figured you looked her up the day she told you not to."

Sarah punched my shoulder. "Gimme some credit. But fine. Yeah, today I looked into her family. On Patricia's obituary page her family was mentioned, so I looked them up and found an article about her son."

The son Patricia had spoken of an hour ago? "Oh really? What about him?"

Was he in jail? Had he hurt someone, called another woman a bitch and gone a few steps further? Or—

"Oh god. Is he dead?"

Sarah sighed. "No, he's not dead. He lives a few towns over, in Faylind. He seems like an okay person. He's a teacher like Patricia was. His students seem to like him, or at least that's what they told the papers. You know how Patricia mentioned grandkids?"

"Yeah?"

"Apparently her son and his wife had a baby girl about two years ago."

"Wow, so she's a grandma after all? Cool."

But Sarah shook her head and lowered her eyes. "The baby's got brain cancer. So the whole town's doing a fundraiser, but if I'm reading between the lines correctly, the doctors think she'll be dead by Christmas."

"Oh," I said hollowly, because there were no words for this. And I thought how Patricia had had such kind words for me when I didn't think they existed. It didn't seem right.

"Yeah. The town's doing this thing where they bring Christmas to the kid early, you know? Like so she can get presents from Santa and whatnot. It's so fucking sentimental."

"You mean it's so fucking *sad*." Maybe my shoulders trembled at the thought, because Sarah placed her velvet hands on them.

"How are we . . . I mean, what do we tell Patricia?"

Sarah shook her head, her touch fading. "We can't tell her any of this, obviously."

"What?" I sat up. "We *have* to tell her. She might want to meet the baby, or check on her son, or go . . . go say goodbye. She might want to visit the hospital or something."

"Believe me, she won't want to visit."

"How do you know if you haven't asked her?"

Sarah seemed surprised that I would argue with her. "You wouldn't understand."

"Aren't we supposed to *help* her? Isn't that why we took her in?"

"You think *that* would be helpful? You think anyone wants to see their loved ones living and dying, and not be part of it? Why the hell should we suffer more? Christ. I don't want to know what happened to *any* of my family."

"But you're not Patricia," I said slowly. "It's not okay for us to know about this when she doesn't. That's absolutely not okay."

"Again, you wouldn't get it." Sarah looked away from me. "There's too much life in you for you to get it."

"But *you* understand everything? About the living and the dead, about everyone?"

Sarah bristled. "I've been around long enough to know pretty well, kid."

"*Kid?* You don't even understand *me*."

That comment looked like it stung, but she bit her tongue. The color in her skin faded.

I backtracked. "Look, I'm sorry. You know me better than anyone."

"It's fine, I get it. But it's not like *that* says a lot."

"What do you mean?" I asked, cheeks flushing, because I suspected I knew precisely what she meant, and didn't actually want to hear her say it. I was friendly with people at school, but no one really knew me. No one knew my insides, my past, my ghosts. Not my Mom, and now not even Sarah.

But Patricia was trying to understand me.

"Sarah. Seriously. I think Patricia deserves to know this."

"Remember when we found her out there on that trail? She asked us *not* to tell her anything about her family. Are you really okay with taking that decision away from her?"

"As if you researching her behind her back is any better?"

Sarah's skin became fully translucent, her face a distant star though she remained beside me. "What I do with my time is not Patricia's business. And maybe . . . I don't know, Dani. Maybe it's not yours, either."

"Sarah . . ."

"Honestly? I don't know why I told you this. I guess sometimes I forget that we're separate people. Because I don't *belong* to you, you know? Half the time I live in your stupid Game Boy, but I'm not your accessory!"

I stared at her, silenced by the sudden grief in her expression. I wondered if it was mirrored in mine. After all, I *did* belong to Sarah. Whatever bravery I had in me, whatever fearless confidence—they had once been hers.

If it weren't for meeting Sarah, would I even know how to argue?

"Please don't tell her," Sarah whispered. "Promise me you won't."

Thing is, the lesson couldn't be unlearned now.

"I can't promise that. I won't."

Sarah shook her head. "Fine. You win. I really don't understand you."

She shrank to a pinprick, then wafted into nothingness.

THE CRUCIBLE

The following morning, Sarah wasn't in my room.

Had I really treated her like an accessory? And maybe she was right—I could be wrong about what was right for Patricia. But even so, this felt, in my gut, like information Patricia should know.

I needed a third opinion, and realized, with a hollow thump in my ribs, there was literally *no one* in the world who I was close with to give me one.

Sarah's words echoed in my mind: *You don't talk to other people.*

There was Mom, but regardless of me being vaguely furious with her, I'd never been able to turn to her for advice. She was as afraid of giving it as I was of getting it.

And let's say I had friends, actual living, breathing friends. What had become mundane to me—living with ghosts—would sound batshit to them. Over the years with Sarah, ghost rules made more sense than social cues; telekinesis was infinitely easier for me to comprehend than asking someone out on a date. Maybe somewhere down the line, I'd become a story told around the fire.

Even if I had friends, I'd only have secrets from them, too.

———

At school, I was so jittery that I probably looked high. During silent reading in American lit—a class that's already stressful enough because (a) I hate reading and (b) Seiji fucking Grayson sits at the table behind mine—I sort of lost it.

Anne Blumenthal tapped me in the arm with her gel pen. "Hey, Dani, did you do the Algebra II homework?" she whispered.

And I blurted aloud for the entire class to hear: "If someone in your family was dying, would you want to know about it?"

Anne flinched before snickers erupted near the back, prompting Mr. Hammond to say, "*Silent* reading, folks. *Silent*."

I was pretty damn silent after that. Anne didn't speak to me again, but stared intently at her book with her hand over her mouth to hide her expression. I guess that was a fair response; my question didn't have a lot to do with what we were reading in *The Crucible*.

When the bell rang, she said, "See you!" and caught up with some other friends. They glanced back without any subtlety at all before hurrying away without me.

I waited a long moment before standing, and by the time I got all my stuff together, I was alone with Mr. Hammond and his outdated moustache.

"Everything okay at home, Daniela?"

I'd asked Mr. Hammond not to call me Daniela at *least* seven times. "Same old."

He nodded, seeming relieved to disengage. "Okay. Well, get to your next class."

Seiji Grayson loomed in the hall, blocking the doorway and scowling beneath his bangs as always.

"The answer is yes," he said.

"Sorry?"

"If someone I loved was dying, I would want to know."

He turned and left me there without another word, but the conviction in his voice left my ears and mind ringing.

STAR TREK

I stopped by the public library on my walk home from school to ask about the books Patricia had recommended. The librarian told me that *The Left Hand of Darkness* was definitely in the stacks, but she'd have to request the other two from the library system. For that, I'd need an interlibrary membership, so she showed me to a row of old desktop computers where I could sign up for one.

I felt a little guilty, listening to her explain how to make an account, showing me a brochure and everything, as if I were another one of the elderly patrons sitting at the back table swapping church stories. I'd already stolen more than a dozen books from the place, tossing them over the sensor at the door, and subsequently torn them to shreds. I wondered if this librarian was trawling the shelves at night, hunting for them like missing persons.

The desktop computers were pretty clunky and slow, but we had no internet at home. I set up my account and requested my books, then followed in Sarah's footsteps and searched for information on Patricia's family.

When I searched for Patricia's name—Patricia Lyttle—I mostly got articles about her death. How she was missing for months, buried in a snowbank. How once she was found, it took a week to identify her because her body had deteriorated so much.

All of this was exactly as Patricia had said, but her words hadn't quite conveyed the poignancy of seeing Patricia's obituary photo, which featured her visiting a sci-fi convention with her son. Her Vulcan ears were striking, but more striking was her smile mirrored on his round face.

I found his name in the caption under that photo, and that led to the articles Sarah had relayed. Once again, the visuals stole my breath. Hundreds of messages of support littered the comments section of a public fundraiser that had already reached $12,000. Again and again, my stare was snagged by the same picture: a bald, grinning toddler with tubes in her nose.

Against my better judgment, I clicked on a video file and waited five minutes for it to load on the dial-up. The video featured an interview with Patricia's son and daughter-in-law.

"We're humbled by all the support." Gary Lyttle didn't look too much like Patricia, but his voice had the same cadence and his glasses made me think he'd been a bookworm for decades. "We've had difficult days before, but this is . . . this is . . ."

His wife, holding the baby close, placed her hand on his arm. "Gary lost his mother to violent crime. We named Patty after her."

"We're grateful to the community." His eyes were exhausted and his smile was forced. But no amount of fundraising or gratitude would shake the tumors from his kid.

A little old lady at the computer beside me offered me a tissue. I took it and said thank you.

It cost five cents per page to use the library printer. I printed two dozen pages, and paid for the articles with my lunch money. I thought at the very least Patricia might want to read the transcript of her son's interview or see a photo of Patty Jr.

I felt light-headed as I left the warm glow of the library and trod down Main Street in the cold. For some reason I felt compelled to walk past the Rochdale Women's Shelter, aka The Green House.

When Mom and I arrived in Rochdale on a rainy night years ago, the Green House was our first home. They took us in on the recommendation of a kind, tired social worker, Kathy Myers, who reassured us both that Dad wouldn't find us, not here, not if she could help it, and even if he could, that's what their security was for. We stayed there for a month or so while Dad broke parole and went missing, and in that time, the staff of equally tired and helpful women ensured Mom got a part-time job, I got school supplies, and we both got fed and clothed and counseled.

One of the counselors, a woman named Raquela, told me something I won't forget: "Don't ever let someone else, *especially* someone you love, decide who you are."

Sarah had shaped much of who I was, but she wasn't all of me.

The Green House windows were curtained for privacy, but the porch light was on. The earliest snow of the year had started falling. I couldn't help but think that Patricia's granddaughter might get her white Christmas early, after all, and I didn't care if Sarah would call that sentimental.

NATIONAL GEOGRAPHIC

"Did you get the books?" Patricia asked, when I climbed the stairs to the lobby, stomping fresh slush from my boots.

"One of them," I said, and pulled the old laminated hardcover from my bag.

She smiled, sitting up straighter. "That's the best one! You'll have to let me know what you think."

"Oh, she'll *definitely* let you know what she thinks," someone muttered.

Sarah was lying just above the check-in counter, staring at the ceiling with her arms folded behind her head, as if she were lounging in a spectral hammock.

I felt the tension in the room rise, as perceptible as my clouded breath on the air.

"Hey," I said, awkwardly.

"Hey," Sarah told the ceiling.

I couldn't stand her impassive expression, and glanced around the space instead, trembling with cold. The calamity of the wallpaper aside, the lobby was much neater than it had been. I'd brought a few flashlights and blankets, and there were broken book bindings and pillows on most surfaces. I'd even dragged out my old boom box, and the low buzz of a classical radio station colored the air. The lobby felt a bit like a living room or den, the mad study of some eccentric old person.

Perhaps it was. Patricia sat in her favorite battered armchair beside the blacked-out windows, leaning over a side table to peer at the glossy pages of a *National Geographic* magazine. She couldn't flip the pages on her own, but we three had all puzzled that one out together weeks ago.

I'd placed a fan on the floor, angled upward. Every day, I taped the back and front covers of a new magazine to the surface of the table. Whenever Patricia wanted the pages turned, she clicked her tongue at Sarah, who simply pointed her finger, switching on the fan blades with her electric expertise. It was a haphazard method, as a lot of pages got skipped or clung together. Still, the three of us were so proud that Patricia applauded and gave Sarah a massive hug.

It felt like years ago. The printed pages in my backpack were heavy like an anchor.

"Do you need something, Dani?" Patricia asked, and I realized I had kept a noticeable distance between us.

"Um." I hesitated. "Sarah . . . ?"

"I'm taking no part in this." Sarah looked at Patricia. "I'm sorry, Trish."

"Sorry? What for?"

But Sarah shook her head and sank downward through the floor.

"What was that about?"

Patricia appeared before me, her weary face only a foot

away—sometimes ghosts moved in a flicker, a bending of light that had long ceased to scare me.

"I have something for you," I said, unzipping my backpack.

"Something new to read?" This close, the traces of blood around her mouth were visible, the twigs in her hair suddenly impossible to ignore, the hollows of her skull peeping through her skin.

"Yeah." I swallowed.

She was already holding out her hand.

"But the thing is, this isn't a book. It's true."

"We still call those books, Dani. They're nonfiction." Her teacher voice slipped at the sight of my face. "Go on, then."

"The pages are about your family," I blurted.

"My family," she said, and suddenly she was yards away again, as if she'd never left the chair. "I told you. I don't want to know about my family."

"I know. I'm sorry."

She looked at me sharply. "Is that why Sarah's upset with you?"

"Sort of. I mean, yes."

Patricia's posture stiffened. "You two have trouble with honesty. I suppose she told you that it's futile for the dead to care about the living."

"More or less." I couldn't tell whether she agreed. "But . . ."

"But what?"

"But you bring them up all the time. Just yesterday, you told me about your son, and . . . before that, you talked about . . ."

Her stare silenced me. "I told you about my son because I thought it might make you feel better. Is what you want to show me going to make me feel better?"

I inhaled. "No."

"I didn't think so," she said, staring at the *National Geographic* again. "You know, according to this article, there's a cemetery in Mexico full of naturally mummified corpses. It seems they died in a cholera outbreak, but the soil preserved them perfectly."

I knew a change of subject when I heard one. But after all I'd shared with her the day before, I couldn't bear the walls she'd put up now. I couldn't shake the shame or self-righteousness I felt, vying against each other in my chest.

"That's interesting."

She vanished and reappeared in front of me, blocking the doorway. "Do you really think I should know about it, whatever it is?"

Seiji's words ran through my head. "I do."

Patricia softened, flickered in and out of sight. "Will you— could you read it with me, then, whatever it is?"

"Yeah. Yeah, of course."

We sat together in the armchair. It shouldn't have been big enough, but Patricia made herself small and almost invisible, a haze-like steam in the air. I held aloft the first page, and after a few minutes, she said, "Next page." When she'd scanned the second page, her voice even smaller, she said, "Next page."

Finally, we'd read through all the pages. She'd read about her granddaughter, her son, the fundraiser, the plans for an early Christmas at the Knights of Columbus hall. The comments of people who knew her son and his family and strangers who had posted on the site. She was entirely invisible now, but I could sense her cool presence. I set the pages on the table.

When a few minutes had passed, silent apart from the wind outside, I realized she wasn't going to speak. I felt the trembling of her unseen shoulders beside mine.

"Do you want to talk, Patricia?"

She didn't answer, but held my hand for a long, long time.

POLTERGEIST

The next day was Saturday. I woke up almost frozen solid in the lobby. I couldn't feel my fingers or my nose or ears, and my breath was more a storm than a cloud. But the bulk of me was warmer than it should have been, as if a blanket had been draped across my torso.

"Patricia?" I said aloud.

"You *idiot*," Sarah said, appearing before me. She was lying atop me with her arms around my waist and her cheek on my chest, the only thing keeping me from turning blue. "Why the hell are you sleeping out here in the cold? You wanna be a ghost that bad? Don't believe the hype."

I was so glad to be near Sarah again, so glad she didn't hate me enough to let me freeze to death. No matter what came between us, there was that. I sat up and threw my arms around her and she put her arms around my neck, her cheek against mine.

"Calm down, Dani. You need to get yourself indoors, all right?"

"I know." My teeth chattered. "But . . . P-Patricia?"

"She's here, but keeping quiet. She came to get me last night after you fell asleep. You know how hard it is for her to leave this room, but she did. You really must have scared her half to life."

"Ha ha." I wiped my nose on my hand. "Did she seem okay?"

"She seemed like . . . well, *herself*, I guess, and that's as okay as she can be. Can't stop a geek from geeking, you know?"

I nodded, sniffling like a sad puppy.

Sarah stared at me, then sighed heavily.

"Look. Maybe you weren't *totally* wrong to tell her." Sarah felt so like and unlike a real person atop me, like a down comforter or something. "She didn't look like she was going to go all poltergeist on us, anyhow."

"I don't see how that would help." The voice startled even Sarah, who jerked out of my arms. "Losing myself wouldn't help me, my son, or my dying granddaughter."

Patricia leaned against the counter with her eyes closed.

"Yeah." Sarah sank away from the ceiling. "I mean, nothing can help, you know? Which is why I didn't want to tell you."

"Knowledge is power." Patricia said it like she was lecturing a class. Her eyes remained closed, her face placid. "But I'm not powerful. I'm a coward. I was so afraid to know what I might be missing."

"You don't have to miss it," I breathed, finding my feet. "Do you . . . I mean, we can try to see her. Patty Jr. Before she—we can go to the fundraiser. I can get Mom to drive us, or maybe there's a bus, or something. Or . . ."

"I could teach you how to get cozy in something electronic," Sarah added. "Pockets aren't so bad when there's a buffer. I'll go, too, if you want."

106

I squeezed Sarah's shoulder.

"Thank you." Patricia opened tearful eyes. "Really, thank you. But you know, I am a coward. I *can't* leave this place."

"We'll help you."

"I *can't*," Patricia said again. "I'm afraid of the woods. I'm afraid of the world. Being here with these books has been nice, and being with the pair of you . . . but it's only made that fear worse. I've got something to lose again. I'm trying to build an unlife. But I don't want . . . I *can't* be hurt again."

"But nothing can hurt you anymore," I said.

"That's not exactly true," Sarah murmured.

"The dead are not exempt from suffering," Patricia said.

"Emotionally I get that, but we'll be there to—"

"She's not talking about hurt feelings, Dani!"

The knowing glance Sarah shared with Patricia, so impenetrable to me, clearly meant something special to my dead friends.

"But you're incorporeal. Nothing can *physically* hurt you, right?"

I felt the divide between us grow wider.

"Please, Patricia. Tell me. What are you afraid of?"

"It's not as though fear *needs* an identity to exist," Patricia whispered. "But mine has one. I hate to admit it, but I'm still afraid of that creep."

"What creep?"

"Come on, Dani. You *know* who she means."

And I did, or at least I thought I did. But it didn't make sense. "Even if you weren't already—I mean, your murderer died in prison."

"Yes," Patricia said. "He died in prison. And what do you think happened next?"

Sarah's voice was heavy. "Your killer came back to haunt the woods, didn't he?"

Patricia put a hand over her eyes. "He found me again."

Sarah nodded. "I wondered about that."

I felt nauseated at the implications of this conversation. "Wait—you mean—but that's *so* fucked up! It can't be like that. It can't be."

Sarah stared at me. "Why, because you don't want it to be? Join the club."

I fell back into Patricia's shoddy recliner. If what they were saying was true, how many violent ghosts stalked the world? For all the victims who haunted the earth, could there really be as many victimizers, haunting the haunted? Had Patricia's rapist really followed her into the afterlife?

"Where's the fucking justice in that?" I thought aloud. "Where?"

I wasn't religious, but where was the fucking *heaven* in it? I was trembling for so many reasons now.

"You wonder why I don't trust men," Sarah said, with a grim smile. "You think the sexism stops at death? You think the cycles of violence end? Nope. There are as many shitty living people as good ones, and that goes for the dead, too."

"That's too awful."

Patricia almost smirked. "Only as awful as people can be, sometimes."

But I thought it must be worse. Because both the ghosts I knew, both these women I admired, had mentioned that in the years before I met them, they spent a lot of time confused and lost, aimless and unanchored. At least in life there were moments of okay-ness, sunlight through leaves and laughter and Halloween. At least bruises would heal, and sometimes bad people were punished for their crimes.

But in the finality of death, where was the good to balance out the bad?

"Hey, you're turning blue," Sarah said. "Get your butt inside where there's heat."

I nodded, numb, and left my friends to grapple with a burden I couldn't fathom.

LIME JELL-O

I didn't catch my death from the cold, but I did come down with a nasty flu. I spent most of the weekend feverish and pukey, and by Sunday evening I was still so irredeemably phlegmy that Mom even offered to stay home from work with me. I protested, and finally she left me with a kiss on my sweaty scalp, a two-liter of Sprite, and two packets of Jell-O I didn't have the energy to make.

She closed the front door and I felt a warm wind settled beside me. Sarah tucked her skinny legs under my blanket and put her hand on my forehead.

"Jesus. Death warmed over, etcetera."

"Pretty much. How's Patricia?"

Sarah frowned at my red eyes. "You sap. You should be thinking about feeling better, but you're still thinking about the tragic doom of the dead, huh?"

I stared glassy-eyed at the television, where a bright and obnoxious sitcom cast made bad jokes inside a cardboard living room. "Yeah, I am. I repeat: How's Patricia?"

"Stubborn." Sarah leaned her head back on the cushions.

She was a little translucent in the light of the television, and I could see blocks of color through her skin, the sitcom picture through her torso and face. "She's sad, you know, and probably really *fucking* annoyed."

I flushed. "I wouldn't have told her, if I'd known she couldn't leave . . ."

"Don't give yourself so much credit." Sarah cuffed my ear and let her hand rest on my cheek. "She's probably not mad that you told her about her grandkid. She's annoyed at feeling helpless. God, feeling helpless is painful, but it's also just so annoying."

"Annoying." When my father used to pull me to my bedroom by my hair, or when he used to knock Mom to the floor and smack her, it hadn't occurred to me to feel annoyed. I'd never been anything but scared.

"Yes, annoying!" Sarah had that fire back in her eyes. "Look, it's bad enough that someone hurts you and you're expected to carry the word *victim* like a scar, whether you want to or not. But sometimes the world is so bogus that no matter how you try to avoid it, you end up being a victim *again*."

As usual, her words rang true. "The world's so freaking scary."

"Sure. But scared's not all you feel when this shit keeps happening. When someone tries to make you feel helpless again when you know you're not, fuck them for putting that on you. I'd rather be annoyed than afraid. At least anger is something I can throw back at 'em."

"Sarah, you're amazing."

"Don't you snot on me," she said gruffly.

"Sarah?"

"What?"

I'd thought through my words, hampered slightly by my stuffy sinuses. "If there are as many bad ghosts as good ghosts, why haven't I met any of them?"

"You've only met two ghosts total, to be fair," she said, "and not everyone who dies ends up haunting the world. Most people don't, you know? Otherwise this tepee would be a lot more crowded, don't you think?"

That notion had occurred to me. I thought about asking whether it was only people who died at the hands of others who stayed. I also wanted to ask whether there were ghosts she saw that I didn't, and why that might be so.

But those were conversations we should have had years earlier. I couldn't decide how to begin them now. They were like picks that might shatter the ice we stood on.

"Does your murderer haunt you, too?"

I felt her temperature plummet. As my fingers turned numb in hers, she said, "No, he doesn't."

"But . . . did he ever?"

She was barely visible, a girl made of glass. Her chin dipped only once.

My heart fragmented. "Did you . . . I mean, did you stop him?"

When I couldn't feel her presence, I thought I was alone. I thought she was angry. but then I felt a peck on my cheek and heard her whisper, "Get some rest, you turkey."

TIDY CATS

Rest didn't come easy, but by Monday I was itching to leave the couch. I dragged my sorry self out of the apartment. The first snow had stuck around and become a sheet of ice. I almost had to skate to school, moving so sluggishly that I almost slipped twice on the back road. I made for Main Street, hoping it might have been salted.

Main Street's Halloween decorations—the flour-painted ghosts and skeletons in shop windows—seemed incongruous against the flecks of falling snow. I made my way down the sidewalk. It *hadn't* been salted, but a few townies had dumped kitty litter on the pavement to counteract the slipperiness.

As I passed the flower shop, I heard the ringing of a bell in the doorway. Looking up too quickly, I lost my footing with spectacular aplomb and collided with a small giant. I cursed and caught myself on a display window filled with autumnal flower arrangements and a painted illustration of a pumpkin latte.

Seiji stood before me in his duffel coat, a satchel slung over his shoulder. Of course it was Seiji, again and always. Seiji was like a splinter I couldn't remove. He looked about as glad to see me as I was to see him. Although who knew really, with that blank face of his.

"What the hell are you doing here?" I gasped, drawing myself upright.

"I'm walking to school."

"I've never seen you walk this way before."

He shrugged and began walking away. "Not my problem."

No, of course it wasn't his problem. But his turn of phrase riled me. Maybe it was the fever or exhaustion, or maybe it was my exchange with Sarah, but hearing Seiji discount me like a piece of trash irked me to no end.

None of *my* problems were anyone's but mine, but I also had a dozen problems that *weren't* mine but were the problems of the ghosts I lived with, not to mention a thousand problems that had nothing to do with my choices. I didn't know any "girls" who *didn't* take on problems that didn't belong to them: the woes of siblings or friends, the weight of a stranger's stares, the doors held open unasked for.

And here was Seiji, carefree and callous, broad-shouldered and indifferent. Was that what it felt like, being a *real* man? Like you didn't have to bother with anyone but yourself? That everyone else's problems were simply irrelevant?

I hated him. And how I *envied* him.

"Hey," I blurted, stomping after him, ignoring the ice, "why is it that you're everywhere I am, all the damn time?"

Seiji didn't slow his pace. "You're the one following me."

"I don't mean now. I mean lately. At the 7-Eleven—"

"I work there."

"Okay, fine. But last Friday, at school—"

114

"I want nothing to do with you at school." For the first time emotion colored his voice. "I don't want any more suspensions, thanks."

My face burned. I grabbed Seiji's arm and finally he stopped moving. He scowled at my fingers as if they were spider legs.

"You brought that on yourself!"

"I don't remember hitting you in the face."

I cringed. "But do you remember calling me a whore?"

"No," he said firmly. "I've *never* called anyone that, and I never will."

His denial was infuriating. "Oh, right. You didn't *call* me that, you just wrote it on my desk in permanent marker."

"Clearly there's no point in denying it," Seiji said, with another shrug.

"You are *such* an asshole, Seiji Grayson. Do you get off on hurting people?"

He spun, black eyes glinting. "Do *you?*"

"*Excuse* me?"

"You are so angry all the time. That must be exhausting."

"I'm *not* angry!" I shouted, and I knew that was ridiculous, because god, was I ever angry, and god, did his calm demeanor upset me more.

Very seriously, Seiji said, "Maybe you should see a counselor."

I had no idea what to make of him. I wanted to think he was devoid of empathy, because that would justify what I'd done to and thought about him. But I also wanted boys not to suck, to think that people like Seiji could grow from being bullies into decent people. If there was anything redeemable about Seiji, I wanted to know about it.

"A counselor," I echoed.

"Yeah." His face remained deadpan. "Counseling has helped me a lot."

For a moment, we both huffed on cold air.

"That thing you said, on Friday," I said, staring at my shoes. "About loved ones? You said if someone in your family were dying, you'd want to know about it. Why?"

He stared at me. I couldn't tell whether he was playing dumb, so I stood up straight, wishing I had broad shoulders and a stoic, handsome face like his.

Then he said, "Because I wish I'd known. My mom was dying, and I didn't know. I wish she'd *told* me. Now please, leave me the hell alone."

He pulled himself free of my limp grip and left me on the sloppy sidewalk.

"NO SCRUBS"

I made it through school and to cross-country practice. Coach Ma eyeballed my wan face and tired eyes, but didn't let up on my prescribed double dose of crunches. This was our second-to-last week before regional finals, so she was pretty fired up. Only four of our runners had placed high enough in districts to compete, but my teammates had decided to practice alongside them, to cheer them on and hope that someone might slip through to state finals, too.

To my dismay, after warm-ups, Coach Ma announced we'd be busing over to the trails behind Holland Park again.

"I don't want you getting lost again, Dani," she added, "so you'll be running with Charley, buddy-system style."

I was frustrated, but also a bit relieved. I loved Patricia, but I wasn't eager to stumble across another dead woman today, especially without Sarah around.

Charley chatted my ears off as we hit the frosted trail. His endless gossip about weekend bonfires and comic book movies did a lot to ease the crisp quiet of the darkening woods. I tried not to think about what had happened to Patricia out here, and

I tried not to think about the murderer who might still haunt these paths, or the number of clouded breaths that may have ended here.

Charley's inane chatter had a grounding effect. I smiled and laughed as we jogged. In the first few minutes we fell behind the others because we were wasting our breath on talk, but eventually we were too winded for conversation.

As the sky darkened, the trees became more like hands. Was Patricia's killer really among those fingers, spectral and grinning?

I used to see my father's face in the half-darkness, even when he wasn't there.

I stumbled, almost fell.

"Let's rest," Charley gasped as we rounded a bend. He slowed to a stop, his hands on his knees. "I need a breather."

"We should keep going." I jogged in place, wiping damp hair from my forehead. "Coach Ma . . ."

He flapped one of his hands. "No worries, Dani. Not like either of us is competing this weekend. She'll cut us some slack."

I doubted Coach Ma knew the meaning of the word "slack," but Charley seemed determined to linger. I stopped moving my feet, rubbed at the aches in my legs and neck, and plopped down beside him on a fallen log.

"Just for a second."

"Well, it *might* take a little longer than that." Charley laughed, and the next thing I knew, he was pressed against me with his lips on mine, clutching my hair with his sweaty hands, shoving his tongue between my teeth.

I shoved back. Charley recoiled and laughed his happy-go-lucky laugh. "*Damn*, Dani, you almost made me bite my tongue!"

"The *fuck?*" I gasped, clambering to my feet. He grabbed my waist and pulled me back down atop him. His mouth was on mine again with this nasty sluggish pressure, an invasive parasitic *thing.*

This time *I* bit his tongue.

"Fuck!" he cursed, shoving me away. "What the hell, Dani? What's wrong?"

"You just forced yourself on me!"

"What? You didn't say no," Charley protested, climbing to his feet.

I shook my head in disbelief. "I guess saying 'what the fuck' and trying to shove you away wasn't clear enough? Fuck you, Charley."

"Jesus, Dani! You've been flirting with me for months. Don't look at me like I'm a creep for picking up on that."

"I have *not* been flirting with you," I snapped, stumbling down the path, trying to put Charley and his stupid smile far behind me. "Believe me."

"You talk to me all the time! And you always laugh at my jokes. I've *seen* how you look at me."

I felt absolutely sick. I looked at Charley like I looked at everyone else with my uneven gaze, and I laughed at his bad jokes because we were teammates. If I was ever admiring him, it was only because I wished I had shoulders like his. If I wanted anything, I wanted to look like him.

"I'm not interested," I repeated. "Charley, *never* touch me again."

His smile crumpled into hurt. "Fine, Dani. Whatever."

"*Not* 'whatever.' I mean it."

He threw up his hands. "I guess I felt sorry for you, you know?"

I knew I shouldn't ask. "Why?"

"Well." He gestured at me. "Just because. But hey, if you're a lesbo, just say so." He plastered on a grin, as if nothing broken had occurred between us.

"You go ahead," I said numbly.

"But Coach Ma said we should run to—"

"Get away from me, Charley!"

He blinked at me, all wounded-puppy like, and ran on.

I spent ten minutes spitting into the dirt, trying to shake the taste of him.

When I finally reached the clearing where the others were waiting, Coach Ma raised her eyebrows. On the bus, when he spotted me near the back, Charley sat with his friends near the front. Then he cheerfully instigated a bus-wide sing-along, and the whole team belted out an old TLC song.

I don't think Charley thought he'd done anything wrong, even after I'd explained how I felt. I don't think he questioned his instincts for one second. He saw the world, saw *me*, in a way that I did not. Unfortunately, the world tended to agree with people like him.

I'd been afraid of the woods, but what made the woods sinister was not confined to trees and shadows. It grew wherever there were people.

How deep did those bloody roots go?

POP ROCKS (REPRISE)

Sarah and Patricia were waiting for me in the brown-carpeted apartment, sitting at the makeshift coffee table. Whatever they'd been talking about, the conversation ended when I walked in.

"Wish I could brew you some tea," Patricia said. "You look like you could use a cup."

"I can do it myself."

"Of course you can. But sometimes it's nice to be looked after."

I wouldn't really know about that, but didn't say as much. I slumped in my seat, trying to process the horrors of the day.

"I take it school was less than spectacular," Sarah hazarded.

I didn't know where to start, and I didn't want to talk about the worst of it, especially in front of Patricia. "Seiji Grayson told me I'm an angry person."

I waited for them to laugh.

"You are," Sarah said, "and good thing, too. Being angry is a good look. We could use more angry women in the world."

I'm pretty sure I didn't react, but Patricia corrected quietly, "Angry *people.*"

I smiled at her a little. "He told me to get counseling. Seiji, I mean."

"There's nothing wrong with counseling," Patricia said. "It helped me through my divorce. It helps a lot of people through all kinds of things. Having someone to listen is vital."

"Yeah, I know." I thought back on our days at the Green House. Mom might have spoken to Dad on the phone a few times since we left him, but he hadn't been welcomed back into our lives, and in the interim, Mom had held a job and become a landlady. I don't think she'd have gotten there without some help.

"Honestly," Sarah pondered, "even I wouldn't mind a bit of counseling."

I thought she might be taking the piss, but her face was serious.

"Counseling," I said. "Counseling for ghosts."

"Is that funny to you?" Sarah asked defensively.

"No," I said. "It isn't funny."

Patricia's face crinkled up. "My mother always said that all one needs in life is a roof over your head and a good shoulder to lean on."

"Well, that and some Pop Rocks," Sarah joked.

"It makes sense. Maybe we all need the same thing. Maybe we all need a Green House." I sat up straight, my heart pounding. "That's it, isn't it?

Sarah frowned at me. "You still feverish?"

But Patricia held up a hand. "What do you mean, Dani?"

"Patricia—you said, last weekend, that even though you're scared all the time, you feel *safe* in the lobby, right?"

Patricia nodded. "I feel *safer*. It's the walls, but mostly the company."

"Right." I fought the urge to stand and pace. "So here's what I'm thinking. The living world has a lot of rules, right? There are courts and prisons to hold murderers and monsters responsible, but there are also places to hold and help victims. Rehab, hospitals, clinics, schools, foster care. *Shelters*. But are there resources like that in the afterlife? I mean, there are victims and victimizers, but are there, I don't know, ghost cops?"

"*Ghost Cop* sounds like a B-movie starring Steven Seagal," Sarah said.

"I doubt it." Patricia frowned thoughtfully. "I don't think it's feasible, considering the state most ghosts find themselves in. When I was in the woods, perhaps I saw other ghosts, but they were probably wandering lost, too. I can't imagine ghosts being organized enough to help each other like the living do."

I nodded. "Not without a safe place to do so, or a *reason* to organize, or someone to help them with the basic logistics. If ghosts are in trauma, they need the same things that other traumatized people need! They need people to listen to them, to talk to them."

"I know what they need." Sarah's eyes shone. "They need *you*, Dani."

"I'm being serious," I snap.

"Me too!" Sarah replied. "All that you said? Company, someone who listens, provides shelter? That's what you were to me. That's what you *are* to me."

"And to me," Patricia agreed. "The pair of you brought me back to myself."

Their compliments pained me, and my cheeks flushed. I refused to be distracted by the admiration in Sarah's eyes.

Sometimes, Sarah looked at me as if I were beautiful.

"You too," I said. "You've helped me, too."

Patricia smiled. "I always tell—told—my students: Helping is contagious."

Many of the staff in the Green House shelter had once been victims of one kind or another themselves. Perhaps it took being wounded to understand how to help others.

"So let's do it," I said. "Let's make this old motel a sanctuary. We can take in other ghosts who might be haunted. We can befriend them, help them, and keep them safe. If there's any killers, dead or alive, out there bothering them—we'll keep them out. We give them the wrong fucking address, or something."

"Or," Sarah said, face grim, "we could exorcise them. The murderous ghosts, I mean."

Patricia started coughing, and I nearly slid off my seat.

"Is that an actual *thing*, Sarah? Exorcism?"

"I mean, it's *probably* a thing. Haven't you seen movies?"

"You told me never to believe the movies!"

"Except *Poltergeist*," she said, finger aloft. "I told you, *Poltergeist* knew what was up, probably because the set was so freaking haunted."

I was almost sputtering. "Exorcisms might be real, and you never thought to mention it?"

"Why, did you want to exorcise me?" Sarah showed her gapped teeth.

"No, but doesn't it seem, I dunno, *relevant*?"

"Not to me." Sarah shrugs. "My killer is still alive. Exorcism won't do a damned thing for me."

I opened my mouth and closed it again. This was the most Sarah had ever said about her death, and the casual way she said it left me lost.

"Don't ask, Dani. I'm only saying, exorcism wouldn't have helped me." Sarah turned to Patricia. "But it's not just me anymore, right, Trish?"

Patricia grimaced. "I suppose it isn't."

"So it can't hurt to look into getting rid of the evil dead."

It was a terrifying and exciting notion.

But all I could hear were the echoes of Sarah's cool tone, the brusque warning: *Don't ask.*

Patricia raised her hand. "I'm all for the spirit shelter, but less enthused about the ghost-cop-exorcism operation. There are some dangerous souls out there."

"That's true," Sarah agreed, "but wouldn't it be great to walk in the woods without feeling afraid, Trish?"

"It would," she conceded. "To walk to where you once were needed."

"Or to walk to someplace new."

Hopeful quiet fell in the apartment, an unbearable, beautiful thread-like spider silk of stillness. I thought it would slip away without our help. I thought I needed to be part of it, to grab hold as well.

"Okay. So let's try it. Let's shelter the dead."

Sarah put her chin on her hands. "You're not developing a savior complex, are you, Dani? What's gotten you so riled?"

"I don't know. A hundred things."

Maybe it was Patricia, when she told me only I could choose what I was. Or maybe I'd gotten to myself. Maybe if I could become the kind of person—the kind of *man*—who was an ally to women, perhaps Sarah would accept that not all men were terrible. Perhaps she could accept *me*, or the me I knew I was.

It wasn't selflessness that fueled my crusade. It wasn't goodness. This was an act of desperation. This was the final leap from one cliff to another.

Maybe then we both could stop keeping so many secrets.

This shelter might be my shelter, too.

"It won't be easy. But I *do* think it's a beautiful idea," Patricia said.

"Patricia," I said, "you told me stories start from beautiful ideas."

Sarah gave me a genuine smile. "I love you, you know, Dani."

There were ten million ways I could've responded to that, because who knew which kind of love Sarah meant, or what kind I felt, but I knew I didn't know how to exist without her, and I thought she might feel the same.

"Rightbackatcha."

SPONGEBOB SQUAREPANTS

"So do we have to splash the undead murderers with holy water?"
I asked Sarah. That night, lying in bed after she'd spent hours at
the library, Sarah rattled off the things she'd read online about
exorcisms and doing away with nasty spirits.

"Maybe? Personally, I don't totally buy into the religious
nonsense." Sarah waved dismissively. "If murderers didn't give
a shit about following the teachings of God or Allah or anyone
else in life, why the hell would muttering Latin do anything
to them in death? Sure, the research leans that way, but I
don't."

"So . . . what *should* we do, then?"

"Well, do I have an answer for you!" Sarah chirped.

". . . yes . . . ?"

She flashed a smile and waggled spirit fingers. "I have no
idea!"

"Wow. That's it?"

"Seriously, do you *realize* how many different theories there
are? How many different methods have been written about?
Every culture has its own tactics. So I think our best bet is to

create a sort of kit—a backpack filled with different exorcism supplies. So yeah, that'd be holy water, but also shit like candles, amulets, and Ouija boards. A ram's horn. And maybe a conch shell."

"A conch shell. All hail the magic conch!"

"It's a Hindu thing."

"It's a SpongeBob thing."

Sarah had become excellent at ignoring my pop culture references. "Also, maybe some strong perfume? I think that's a Muslim tradition. And some noodle soup, so you don't get possessed?"

"That's gonna have to be one big backpack."

She laughed. "Look, we've gotta start somewhere. You're gonna have to learn some dances and chants, too."

"I can do the Macarena, if that helps."

"We'll have you memorize some mantras. That seems like a big part of it."

"Good thing I'm not busy studying for the ACT," I said dryly. "Oh. Wait."

"Sit on it. To begin with, start hoarding your mom's salt."

I imagined myself lobbing a canister of Morton salt at some spectral psychopath. "Right. And if none of this stuff works?"

She snickered. "Well, lucky you're good at running."

The silence shifted between us, weighted by what I dared not ask. "Sarah?"

She sighed. "Seriously, Dani. Don't ask."

"You don't know what I'm going to say!"

She sighed beside me. "Of course I do. I know everything about you."

"And if you didn't?" I inhale, then exhale. "If there was something about me that I'd never told you? Would you . . . would we still . . . Sarah?"

I waited for her to reply, but the silence grew bigger, and Sarah grew smaller, and I knew that no matter what I told her, she could never truly sleep beside me, and I could never truly hold her, but I couldn't stop trying.

NOVEMBER 2002

ADDY

ORAL-B

Maybe I *was* good at running, but I quit the cross-country team about a week after we decided to open a shelter for ghosts. I told myself it had nothing to do with Charley, and everything to do with being busy with the afterlife.

But there was no denying that the team didn't feel like home anymore.

I don't know what Charley told people, exactly, but most of the other runners stopped talking to me. Because I'd always kept a firm distance between myself and my not-quite friends, there was no one invested enough to ask what had really happened, or to doubt his side of the story. Charley was beloved, a ball of sunshine that was impossible to eclipse. Gloomy moon that I was, I didn't have the will to try.

For some reason I couldn't explain to myself, I didn't tell a soul about Charley forcing his mouth on me. Sarah would go on a rampage; Coach Ma would get our parents involved. Charley would call me a cross-eyed, lying lesbian.

So what if I used to love running? These days, I couldn't shake the vision of Patricia lying on the trails, and the idea that her rapist's ghost was still there in the woods. Some dangers you can't run from.

I broke the news to Coach Ma in her office before practice on Wednesday. She folded her hands and stared at me as I explained my situation. I told her I was needed around the apartments. I said that my mom would never say so, and she cared a lot about my extracurriculars, but she needed help because she was a single mother, etcetera. I pushed a note toward Coach Ma. She raised her eyebrows at the inky signature; Mom had sleepily signed it that morning.

"I can't stop you from quitting," Coach Ma said. "But I'm not sure I buy your reasons. I've seen your mom at the Big Anchor, but I've *never* seen her at any of our meets."

I managed a shrug and an awkward smile. "Sorry for letting you down."

"Mmm." Coach Ma set down the note and leaned in, elbows on her spotless desk. "No, Dani. I'm worried I've let *you* down. I pick up on things, you know. Tell me the truth: Did something happen between you and the other runners?"

I didn't answer.

"Look." She sighed and hesitated, as if chewing through a difficult thought. "I *know* what kids are like—and yes, I know you're teens, not *kids*, blah blah, but I'm an old lady and you're all very young to me. Kids say and do some awful things to each other, and are the quickest to insult what they don't understand. You get me?"

"Um, not really."

"I'm saying—I'm saying, sometimes kids are afraid of what's different. And scared dogs bite. So you wanna tell me what's really going on?"

It was clear she didn't know what had happened between me and Charley. But obviously Coach Ma had her own theories about why I was quitting. I suspected Charley was being *very* specific in the story he was telling: *But hey, if you're a lesbo, just say so.*

The pickle of it was, it was an open secret in Rochdale that Coach Ma was gay. No one ever talked about it, but she'd adopted two kids with her partner, a dentist named Sheila, and the four of them had been a family for as long as anyone could remember. Coach Ma never said a word about it, and no one else did, either. It was like there was a quiet agreement that so long as she kept getting runners to regionals, her sex life was fine.

But it was also understood that if she ever talked about being gay, ever validated kids who were, too, she might have to find work elsewhere.

There were so many ways to be trapped.

"Dani? I'm waiting."

I couldn't look at her. Coach Ma thought I was quitting because I was gay and fed up, which wasn't exactly *untrue*. I was grateful for her concern. But this wasn't a conversation she felt entirely comfortable having, based on the lines in her face. Coach Ma was gruff and grizzled, firm in her convictions. I'd never seen her uncertain.

And I *wasn't* a lesbian. I still couldn't bring myself to say aloud what I thought I was, because it seemed impossible.

I shook my head. "Sorry, Coach."

"Fine," Coach Ma said, disappointed. "My door is always open, Dani. Except when I'm at practice, where you should be."

I left with my heart in my throat.

MOD PODGE

While Sarah was preoccupied with exorcisms and ghost hunting, Patricia fixated on her own darling: the shelter aspect of our cockamamie plan.

Patricia still couldn't touch anything physical. While she'd begun to turn the lights on and off, she didn't have Sarah's knack for manipulating technology. And she needed a lot of help when it came to redecorating. Now that I didn't have cross-country practice, I spent many hours in the lobby with her while Sarah worked at the library.

I convinced Patricia to leave most of the book pages on the walls, partly because they looked neat, but mostly because I didn't want to peel them away. We added splashes of color by pasting photographs wherever there were gaps or blank spaces. We must have gone through gallons of sloppy homemade papiermâché by the time the walls were finished, but the end result looked like modern art. The leftover pages we placed carefully in order and stacked in a drawer beneath the counter, bound together with my old shoelaces.

"Who knows," Patricia said. "Some of the new girls might be bookworms, too."

I didn't say what we were both thinking: Who knew when we'd even get any new ghosts? Across five years, the three of us had only found one another. No matter what Sarah said about the prevalence of other ghosts, there might be those we'd never meet because they were lying perpetually in gutters, haunting dry creeks or the narrow spaces under porches. They were forgotten, or nearly so, and who knew if we'd stepped through them on a bad day?

"It's good to be prepared," I agreed.

Patricia smiled. "Now that reminds me of my days at Faylind Middle: Prepare for the worst, and hope for the best."

I suspected seeking out dead women would amount to both.

Soon we managed to scrounge up a bit more decor and furniture. I stole enough of Mom's singles from her tip jar to buy a few Dollar Tree pillows, picture frames, and candles. I asked for a new comforter for my sixteenth birthday, then moved my old one to the lobby, where Patricia instructed me to drape it across the sorriest sofa.

All of these additions, the rugs and the tiny vacuum we'd found in the basement that Sarah could operate and Patricia *almost* could (she could turn it on but it refused to move across the carpet), had finally made a home of that hexagonal room. I hardly smelled the mildew anymore.

Patricia had endless ideas.

"I used to love teaching history," she said, "because it was an easy excuse to ask for dioramas. Dioramas are fantastic, don't you think? An entire world within a box."

If I'd ever been assigned a diorama at school, I sure as hell hadn't made one, let alone turned one in for a grade.

But there *was* something fantastic about Patricia's dioramas.

Behind the counter, in each of those little mailbox cubbies, Patricia designed homes in miniature and used my hands to execute her visions, guiding my clumsy fingers with gentle words and suggestions. As Sarah always said, ghosts felt safer in small, dark spaces, but Patricia insisted that people felt most comfortable when they were surrounded by books, chairs, blankets, and beds. People felt better, she said, with walls around them.

"Let's not forget that ghosts are people," she trilled, as I strung golden Christmas lights along the bottoms of the boxes, illuminating each cubby in a warm glow. I'd found some dollhouse furniture at the Goodwill, and Patricia had asked me to check out a few oddball books from the library about making minuscule furniture from recycled materials like jars, spools, milk cartons, bottles, and bottle caps.

I had never been good at art, but Patricia was an amazing teacher. With her help, I turned each mailbox into a bedroom or living room. I cut one of my old wool sweaters into tiny squares that served as blankets, I folded cardboard toilet paper rolls into tables and chairs.

"I'm sure you read *The Indian in the Cupboard* in elementary school," Patricia insisted while I glued fabric to craft foam couches. "It's been required elementary reading for years, or it was when I was teaching."

I shrugged. I'd spent a lot of elementary school hiding or moving from one trailer to another.

"I hope you're reading the books I suggested, at least?"

I changed the subject. "Do you think we should make the beds softer? Do ghosts care about that kind of thing?"

"That's a familiar tactic." Patricia raised an eyebrow. "Don't forget that I was a teacher *and* a mother, and I know when someone's trying to sneak one past me. You *haven't* read those books yet, have you?"

"Sorry, *Mom*," I grumbled. To my surprise, she laughed. I plucked a tiny table made from a spool of thread from the pile of slapdash furniture on the counter.

"I never thought I'd like that name," she pondered, watching me set the table onto a tiny rug made of scrap fabric. "When I was your age, I didn't want to be a mother. Let alone a grandmother."

I stared into a tiny living room adorned with Mod Podge and tissue paper and I thought of my mother, who'd never seemed comfortable with motherhood, who couldn't cook and didn't care about meeting other moms after school. Who seemed in some ways like a child, as confused as I was.

"I thought I'd study until I reached the stars, that I might be a philosopher or even an *astronaut*, of all things. I was pretty keen on astrophysics and even, god help me, *astrology*, in my youth. That was before I decided I liked fictional monsters more than real ones."

"When did you change your mind?"

"I didn't *really* change my mind." Patricia shrank seamlessly to doll size and tested the felt bed beneath her tiny weight. "There was no reason I couldn't be *both*, if I wanted. You know, the world tells us that we can be either independent women or homemakers. And there are some people who shame you for choosing the first, and others who shame you for choosing the second. There's always one reason or another to tack a scarlet letter on us."

"You're referencing a book again," I said, leaning back against the counter.

"Not all women are destined for motherhood, and even those who choose it might regret it. But I think the important thing is not to limit the expectations of what a woman, what a *person*, can or should be."

"I've never really thought about it that way."

"A lot of boys your age don't think about motherhood. So you're not alone."

I felt a little thrill run through me and heard myself say, "Thank you for calling me—for saying that."

"I'm stating the facts, backed up by significant evidence." She drew and grew herself up, until she was leaning beside me, large as life. "Don't thank me for common decency. Just remember to give the same kind treatment to everyone else, too, no matter where you end up."

For some reason, Seiji's face appeared in my mind.

Seiji had never been especially decent to me.

But I had never been decent to him, either.

ORLANDO BLOOM

The first time I bound my chest, I accidentally cut off my circulation.

It was mid-November, and my chest had grown large enough to betray me. No matter how much I longed to look as androgynous as Sinéad O'Connor or, hell, some femme version of Orlando Bloom, my body seemed determined to be curvaceous. Even hoodies couldn't help me hide, and so on a cold morning when Sarah was preoccupied, I stopped by the Rite Aid before school, bought two large ACE bandages, and shoved them into my backpack.

I was late for second-block English because I spent the first ten minutes in a bathroom stall, wrapping the stretchy material around my diaphragm, ignoring all the advice I'd read online about ACE bandages bruising and battering rib cages, because I'd also read that it more or less *worked*. My breasts felt like tumors, parasites. I was desperate to be rid of them, and no matter the warnings, everyone knew that if you wanted to suffocate a boob and cow it into hiding, ACE bandages could do the trick.

By the time I emerged from the bathroom, my breathing was a bit labored, but my reflection looked more like *me*.

I doubt anyone noticed the change—after all, I wore hoodies almost every day, and I'd stopped talking to people in general. But to me, the difference was everything. When I looked down at my chest, I felt a release at the sight of a flattened, androgynous plane.

So what if I was a little light-headed?

I was also a little lighthearted, which was such a rare feeling. And if I'd learned anything in the past couple years of living with ghosts, I knew beautiful moments went a ways toward undoing the suffering of every ugly moment.

———

By fourth-block geometry, I sat sweating in my desk, barely listening to Mrs. Harper's droning over the sound of my breathing. I felt an ache on either side of my ribs, as if I were being squeezed by a giant hand. I'd read online that bandages got tighter as time wore on, but I hadn't taken that too seriously. I'd even *relished* the idea.

I was an idiot. A flat-chested idiot, but an idiot all the same.

"Go see the nurse," Mrs. Harper advised, staring at the sweat on my brow. Apparently she'd asked me a question or three, because everyone was looking at me.

"It's fine," I protested weakly. "I'm just hot."

"Then take off your hoodie, Dani!" Charley called. To anyone else he probably sounded genuinely concerned.

"Corina, can you take Daniela down to the nurse's office?"

I cringed. I knew that she'd chosen Corina because Corina was friendly. The walk to the office felt both very short and very long. Halfway there, with my numb arm draped over her shoulder, Corina asked, "Hey, is it that time of the month?"

"Um," I wheezed.

"I feel your pain. I get terrible cramps, too. By the way, did you know that people are spreading rumors about you?"

"Um."

"Like, people are saying you're a raging lesbian. Is it true? It's not true, right?"

"Not true," I agreed, while stars clouded my vision.

"People love gossiping, you know? Especially in redneck towns like this. Everyone's in everyone's business, don't you think? It's more a girl problem."

God, did I ever have the biggest, worst girl problem.

———

The next thing I knew I was slumped over on the chair in the nurse's office, wheezing and aching as if my ribs were on fire. I couldn't feel my fingers and my cheeks tingled like snow had fallen on them. Corina was leaning in my face while someone else held me upright by the shoulders.

I was the world's biggest trans cliché, and I knew it. It was like I'd fulfilled a tired prophecy because I had no idea what else to do.

"Sorry!" Corina cried. "I'm *so* sorry! I can't believe I dropped you!"

I hadn't realized she was supporting me. She seemed too small to have lifted me, and I realized she must not have, and the other person—

A voice shouted, "Go find the nurse!"

Seiji fucking Grayson's face displaced Corina's in my vision.

143

His hands scraped his hair from his forehead again, and he was wild-eyed and pale.

"Can you breathe?" he demanded. "Why can't you breathe?"

"My chest," I tried to say, but when I gestured at my shirt, my hand flopped like a weak, landed fish. Seiji seemed to get it, because the next thing I knew he was helping me take off my hoodie. I think he was about to do CPR, because he pressed his palms on my sternum—

"Bandages," I wheezed. "Too tight."

All I could see were his big black eyes, and then the black spread everywhere.

———

When I came to, Seiji was gone and Corina was back, loitering in the back of the small room. The school nurse held my bandages in her hands, frowning in confusion. "What on earth were you trying to do?"

"Um." I guessed from Corina's expression that she was about to tell the entire school what had happened. Hazy though my mind was, that sent a spike of fear through me. "A new exercise . . . technique?"

The nurse frowned. "You might have cracked a few ribs, if you'd waited much longer to remove it. As it is, you've got cuts and bruises all over your chest, silly girl."

Not a girl, I mouthed. *I'm not a girl.*

And then, like the worst stereotype of every high school girl ever, I started sobbing.

———

By the time the nurse let me leave, there were only twenty minutes left in the school day. Corina insisted on staying with me the whole time, and the nurse, taking her for a friend and not a salacious gossip, hadn't told her to leave.

"You scared the daylights out of Seiji Grayson," Corina said. "You should have seen his face. He looked downright traumatized."

I frowned at her. "He doesn't care about me."

"I don't think it was about you so much as, you know—the *choking* thing."

"What does that mean?" I asked, wishing she might vanish and wishing Sarah or Patricia were here with me instead, but also grateful that they weren't.

"You know, after what happened to his mom," Corina whispered.

Whatever curiosity I felt was put off by the way she treated this news like a delicious snack.

The nurse had had enough. "That's enough. Out."

"I was just explaining why—"

"I don't want to hear it."

Corina left at last, doubtless running off to share the news of all the nonsense she'd witnessed here.

"Nurse," I said, "what—"

"Mrs. Mykonos, not Nurse. I couldn't get ahold of your mother. Will you be all right if I send you home?"

"Mrs. Mykonos, what did Corina mean, about Seiji's mom?"

"I'm surprised you haven't heard. If you want to know what happened, you should talk to Seiji. And you should thank him— he likely spared you a trip to the hospital."

"Right."

"Corina might buy that lie about this being an exercise technique, but I don't."

I froze. "I don't . . ."

"If you want a number for counseling, or a hotline or . . . look, come see me. You aren't the first student I've known in your position, okay? If you want to change things, there are healthier ways to go about it. Understand?"

Mrs. Mykonos's knowing look chafed me to my center.

CAMPBELL'S

The walk home seemed to take hours, complicated by the cold air, an icy downpour of steady slush—not rain, not snow, but some evil hybrid—and the bruises under my clothes. *When had I last been warm?*

The few pedestrians on Main Street hurried through the freezing rain to their cars. The sparse streetlamps and half-hearted Christmas lights in the occasional shop windows did little to allay the encroaching darkness.

By the time I passed the library, my toes were numb. I thought about going inside. Had anyone checked on the situation with Patricia's family? The moment the shelter became our collective obsession, we'd stopped talking about Patricia Jr.

I walked past the library and neared the Green House. It really was an old house that had been some wealthy person's mansion back in the early 1900s. The house was set a little distance from the road, but its white staircase and pillared porch were welcoming. I thought maybe I should go inside and collect some pamphlets on mental health and recovery, some ideas to fuel our shelter. If the layout was the same as it used to be, I knew I'd find a whole rack of them inside the doorway.

When we lived at the Green House, Mom spent the first few days going through withdrawal in a bed upstairs, sharing her room with another woman who had a broken arm and two black eyes. There were a few other children there, too, but I didn't talk to any of them.

I didn't want to believe that we had anything in common.

I'm not sure I had begun to hate Dad, not yet. I hated the gentle voices the staff used when speaking to me, resented the helplessness I felt, until I realized those soft voices were helping that helplessness fade. After the first week, I started talking to some of the other kids, and Mom started getting out of bed and looking for a job. I cried.

Dad really wasn't coming to get us. I still don't know if I was happy or sad about that.

I approached the Green House now with a strange pressure in my chest that had nothing to do with the bruising. Mom and me—we weren't entirely all right. Our lives weren't perfect and never would be. I barely spoke to Mom, almost no one could see who I really was, and my only friends were dead girls.

But still I could say, despite all that, our lives were better than they had been.

Standing on the front step, I almost embraced one of those white pillars.

I heard footsteps on the walk behind me and turned.

This was becoming downright predictable.

Seiji stood there, looking fed up. In his arms he held a large cardboard box. He wore his duffel coat and a fluffy pair of earmuffs, incongruous as a rabbit's puffy tail on an alligator.

"I'm not following you," he growled. "It's a small town."

I bit my lip. "Thanks for . . . thanks for earlier."

"Can you move? I need to go inside."

"Oh." I remembered myself and held the door. When Seiji held the inner door open with his foot and stared at me expectantly, I scurried in after him, wincing at the spike of pain in my chest.

The old floor creaked under our feet as we neared the vacant reception desk. I readjusted my backpack on my shoulder, trying to take pressure off my diaphragm. Seiji must have noticed, because he said, "You could have hurt yourself."

"As if you care."

"Maybe someone else does."

I thought of what Corina had said. Rumors about the death of his mother, the tattoos on his knuckles. I thought about his wide, terrified eyes. About his presence here in this old house. The Green House didn't allow casual visitors as a rule, but here was Seiji, standing in the foyer as if he'd been here a dozen times.

A shuffling sound came from a back room, and an unfamiliar young woman, plump and red-faced, made her way to the counter. She beamed at Seiji.

"Oh, hey, Seiji!"

"Hey, Sophie."

"Your aunt said to expect you. What goodies have you got for us?"

He pushed the box forward. "Canned soup. Ramen noodles. Some vegetable oil."

"Ooh, that's great. People always forget to donate vegetable oil. That'll make someone's day for sure." She pulled the box to her and then looked at me. "Hi! Miss . . . ?"

"It's not Miss," I said. "I'm Dani."

"Have you also brought some goods for the Thanksgiving food drive, Dani? Or . . . do you need to speak to someone here?"

I shook my head. "No, I . . . no."

"Well, if you and your family feel like scouring your kitchen for donations, we'll be collecting right up until Turkey Day. And please tell your friends at school about it, too. I'm sure they've got some canned goods to spare." Sophie jerked her thumb at Seiji. "I've asked this guy to spread the word, but he's about as chatty as a stuffed turkey."

Seiji did not reply, although his face turned a disarming shade of red. I watched him comb his black fringe over his eyebrows and mumble, "See you later," before pivoting and pushing his way outside again.

"Careful, there," Sophie said, "he'll talk your ear off."

I nodded at her, scooped an assortment of pamphlets from a rack on the counter, shoved them in my bag, and followed Seiji out.

Darkness had well and truly fallen, and the sleet had become a curtain of white.

Seiji stood on the top step. "Do you need a ride?" he asked.

I started. "Don't you live downtown somewhere?"

"So?"

"Um, *so*? Wouldn't you have walked to school?"

"I borrowed the truck today," he explained. "So I could drop off the food. Do you want a ride?"

"Oh. I mean, I live close, too. I can walk home."

"It's pissing down," he observed, walking ahead of me, letting the rain strike his bare head and soak his earmuffs. "Just come on."

Now I really was following him.

GMC

Seiji's car turned out to be a battered old GM truck. On one side of the cabin, hand-painted in oddball calligraphy that looked like it belonged in a county fair, were the words *Murphy's Flower Shoppe—We Roses to the Occasion!*

I stared, wondering if he'd stolen a flower delivery truck, but despite my reservations, my bruises stung and the rain was really coming down.

I knew what Sarah might have said, had she seen me climbing into a car with a supposedly violent boy. Except I wasn't so certain anymore that he *was* violent, and I knew that I for one *was* violent and, at least secretly, a boy.

I climbed in and set my backpack at my feet. The sweet smell of soil and blossoms pervaded the truck, dampened by the cold. I glanced into the back and spied several bags of Miracle-Gro on the seat.

"You don't seem like a flower guy to me," I observed.

"Put on your seat belt."

"Who cares?" The back talk was instinctive.

But Seiji refused to start the engine until I clicked the seat belt into place.

The engine had seen sunnier days, but growled to life on the second try.

"My aunt runs the shop," Seiji said, about a minute later. We'd already reached the main intersection in town. "My family bought Murphy's Flowers when we moved to Rochdale."

We passed the little corner business as he spoke, and I recalled running into him on the sidewalk. "When was that?"

"Around the same time you moved here."

"You've lived downtown this whole time?"

His shrug implied a whole lot.

"I mean, fine. I *know* I'm caught up in my own shit, but I've never seen you on the way to school."

"I go to school early," he said mysteriously, "and I come home late."

Everyone knew Seiji went home late because he had daily detentions, but I had no idea why he might go in early, too. The rest of our uncomfortable trip passed in silence. After the longest minute ever, he pulled into the motel parking lot.

I eased out the door and into a sad snowbank, one hand on my ribs. "Thanks."

"Hey," Seiji said, rolling down the passenger window before I walked away. His expression seemed almost fragile. "Why did you say that?"

"Why did I say what?"

"That I don't seem like a flowers guy. What did you mean by that?"

"I don't know. I guess I was just trying to make conversation."

Seiji dipped his head. When he looked up again, a line had formed on his forehead, and his cheeks were red. "I really try to be a flowers guy, is all."

"Oh." I was at a loss. He was blushing. He looked like a different person. "I'm sorry."

He nodded. "I'm sorry I called you angry."

"Well, you weren't wrong," I said, at a slight loss for words. "I am pretty angry."

"Maybe that's how you seem, but it's not necessarily how you are."

My breath caught. Seiji's point resonated—did he know that? Being called something you're not is *not* a stupid-ass reason to cry. Like being called a girl when you're a boy. Or being called a victim when you're striving to escape the word. That's not stupid, either.

Being called a thug when you're a gardener? That's got to be upsetting, too.

"So what else do I seem like," I asked, and it was hardly a question.

Seiji pauses. "Lonely."

I flinch. "What?"

"You seem lonely. You talk to yourself a lot. Do you realize?"

I take a step away, face flushed. "Yeah, I realize, and it's none of your business."

"You asked."

"Yeah, well, I shouldn't have."

"Who do you talk to?" he asked simply.

I don't know why I answered. Maybe it was the lack of accusation in his voice, the desire to mess with him like I felt he was messing with me.

"I talk to dead people, okay?"

154

"Oh," Seiji said, nodding once. "Okay. I do that, too, sometimes."

He rolled up the window while I tried to parse him. It wasn't until he pulled away that I realized I hadn't told him where I lived—he'd just known.

POWER WHEELS

I stood outside the lobby for a few moments trying to compose myself. Seiji couldn't be serious, could he? What the hell was that conversation?

From the outside, our ghost shelter remained a sorry thing: a rusting old piece of offensive architecture, but inside I hoped it would become all that we dreamed it could be.

I wanted to think people worked the same way. But I also wished my outside would match my insides without leaving me wounded and wheezing and embarrassed. More than anything else, I felt stuck in myself, and stuck in the world. I was haunting my own life.

When I finally went inside, Patricia waved hello. She'd been practicing with the fan, I could tell, but today's magazine was facedown on the rug. She seemed frustrated.

"I thought I heard a car pull up."

"I didn't hear anything. Seen Sarah?"

"She's downstairs. She said we've had some exciting developments, if you can imagine." We'd long since arranged an entrance to the lobby on the upper level, so my visits to the cellar were rare. Sarah and Patricia might be immune to the chill, but as I descended the concrete stairs I felt goose bumps budding.

"She returns!" Sarah crooned, appearing beside me. "Finally! Come and have a look-see."

"You know, I *would*," I began, blinking in the dark. "But I'm not nocturnal, so—"

"Oh, criminy. I forgot." Sarah snapped her fingers. A bulb in the ceiling flickered on, and so did my old desk lamp. Something more priceless hummed on the floor, glowing softly.

"A laptop? Sarah, where did you get that?"

"Library. They're all sitting there on a cart, can you believe it?"

"But . . . how did you get it here?"

"Come on. You know that I can move things sometimes," she said, feigning nonchalance. "When I really feel like it."

"Yeah, but . . ." I'd seen her push things when she was upset, seen doors slam or curtains ripple. When we met, she pushed my folder out from under my bed. But that seemed like a far cry from transporting a computer across town.

Patricia looked as shocked as I was. "Telekinesis?"

"What?" I said. "How does that work?"

"Does it matter? I'll bring the laptop back one day." Sarah paused. "*Maybe.*"

Our sins against librarians would probably condemn us to hell regardless of how many girls we rescued. And it turned out Sarah had gotten her spectral hands on a lot more than a stolen laptop. An electronic projector came to life, casting a blurry map on the blank wall where the washing machines and dryers had once been. The next thing I knew, Sarah was adjusting a set of speakers.

"Yeah, okay, but seriously, Sarah—*how* did you get all this stuff here?"

Sarah shrugged. "Libraries *let* people borrow things, damn it."

"Right. But how did you *transport* all this here? Can you what, *levitate* things that far?"

"Not on my own. I used electricity."

"How cryptic," Patricia remarked. "I see who taught you to skirt questions, Dani."

Sarah folded her arms, clearly exasperated. "Look, I may have also *borrowed* transportation from a kid down the street."

"You stole a tricycle?" Patricia asked, blinking innocently.

"No, not a—come *on*! It was an electric vehicle."

"What, like a Razor scooter?" I asked.

"No, that wouldn't have been big enough," Sarah said, as if that were obvious. "It was one of those pint-size pink jeeps? The ones little kids ride in."

"A Power Wheels," Patricia supplied. "A Power Wheels Jeep. I'm familiar with them."

"You stole a *Barbie Jeep* from some toddler?" I reiterated. "So that you could rob librarians of a precious laptop and projector."

"Where's the tiny jeep now?" Patricia asked. "In case the police come looking."

"It's parked out back," Sarah said, dead serious, and Patricia burst into peals of laughter. "Look, it's not like I'll get caught. And I only use it at night!"

The vision of a tiny, driverless jeep haunting the streets

of Rochdale, buzzing down the sidewalks, spooking the squirrels, brought me to laughter, too. Unfortunately, that made my wounded ribs cry out.

"Dani. You all right?"

"Fine." Was I as transparent as Sarah? Could everyone see through me these days?

Sarah's disgruntled pout brought us back around. "Do you want to see my presentation, or not? Because if not, I have better things to do."

"Of course we do," Patricia said. "Go on."

Sarah stood to the side of the projector. She blinked and twitched her pale fingers, frowning in concentration. A series of pdfs, images, Word documents, and a PowerPoint presentation opened on the computer. I was impressed. I hadn't taught Sarah anything about computers, and they'd barely been invented when she died, but I was certain she could do better in my computer class than I ever had.

"Right. So we'll start with the maps. The first layer is a topographical map of Rochdale County, from the northern woods near Marl Lake, to the edge of I-75 and the East Branch river." She blinked, and another map appeared. "And here's a road map on top of that one."

She snapped her fingers, and an overlay of gray dots, clustered like dust in some places and scattered like individual motes in the others, appeared on the map. "And this is the distribution of the county's population. Each spot represents ten people. According to the latest census, the population of Rochdale County is approximately sixteen thousand, but only about seventeen hundred people live in the town itself."

"Hooray for us townies," I said.

"Everyone else lives closer to the lake, and there are a lot of cabins in the woods. Basically, there's a concentration of people in town, but it's not the majority of the population. No, my friends"—she tried to slam her fist dramatically on the map, but her fist passed mostly through it—"I am preoccupied with everyone else."

"Have you been watching too much *CSI*?" I asked.

"This is a *bit* maudlin," Patricia agreed, "but let's hear her out. Sarah has worked very hard on her project."

"Maybe it looks like crime television, except I'm not actually solving any crimes." Sarah blinked again, and a fourth overlay appeared. This one added dozens of red pockmarks, like acne marring the surface of our little town. Even though the spots looked like they'd been added in Microsoft Paint, there was no denying that the sight of them robbed the cellar of humor.

"The fourth map isn't about finding killers, but finding the *victims*. Each and every one of these spots marks the location where the body of a violent crime victim was found in the past one hundred years. I'm sure there are older ghosts around, but the online newspaper archive isn't all that detailed, so this is our starting point."

There weren't a *ton* of spots—less than one hundred in all. What was striking was that they were spread throughout the county in varying concentrations. Several places on the map drew my eye. There was a cluster of red spots in the woods by the park where we'd met Patricia. There was a spot that appeared to be on the grounds of Rochdale high school, and another pair of spots near the west side of town where I'd met Sarah beneath the bed.

"What's *that* place?" Patricia asked. She didn't have to point, because it was obvious what she was referring to. Near the bottom of the map, between the river and Bailey Orchard, was a cluster of a dozen or more red spots that formed a large red welt on the map.

"That's the old O'Connor Petting Zoo," Sarah said.

"*Petting zoo*," I repeated. "I never thought those words would fill me with dread."

"I'm familiar with the story," Patricia said, after a moment. "It's a famous piece of local history. But the petting zoo wasn't the scene of the crimes, simply where the bodies were discovered. Seven women, right?"

"And a child," Sarah added. "They were digging up trees to build the alpaca pens and came across a mass grave about four feet down."

I hadn't heard the history. "Do they know who killed them?"

"Not for certain," Patricia said, "although there are theories about the farmer who used to own the land, and about his teenaged son." She paused, face suddenly inscrutable. "By the time the bodies were discovered in the 1960s, scientists determined that they'd been there for at least a century. Whoever put them there is long dead."

Once, that might have been a relief.

"But if the killer is a vindictive bastard, he's almost definitely haunting the place." Sarah voiced our fears. "If we're looking to try an exorcism, Dani, we're probably gonna find a good target at the petting zoo."

Patricia shook her head. "I don't think we should start our shelter outreach there. We don't have the resources to provide for ten people, not yet."

"And we don't know how to *do* an exorcism yet, even if we find the killer there," I added.

Sarah nodded. "Yeah, I know. We'll build up to that bastard." She closed her eyes, and the cursor moved the map until we were looking at a few small spots in another, more familiar part of Rochdale.

"*Downtown*," I said, as Patricia gasped, "That's close to this motel."

"It's actually *in* the motel," Sarah said quietly. "Come on. A place this seedy, you had to know we weren't the only ones haunting it. A girl was found bound and strangled in one of the rooms back in the fifties. Her name was Adelaide Williams. She was seventeen years old."

"What happened to her?" I asked.

Patricia had her hand on her throat, rubbing old bruises in sympathy.

"A *man* happened to her." Sarah swallowed. "She was strapped to the bed for four days before anyone found her, because the *Do Not Disturb* tag was on the door. Whoever killed her had already skipped town. Motherfucker."

I stared at the red spot, so close to this supposed sanctuary. The spot was one of several in the downtown area, but it was the only one on our doorstep.

We'd been here for years, and never known someone might be suffering beside us.

"Okay," I said grimly. "Where is she?"

BUD LIGHT

After we knocked on apartment 7's door, no one answered for a good five minutes. Darkness had arrived. Despite the anger that had fueled us up the stairs and out the door and across the parking lot, in the frosted quiet, adrenaline abandoned me.

"Are you sure someone's in there?" I whispered. Sarah sat small and warm on my shoulder, kicking her skinny legs against my throbbing ribs.

"Definitely. I slipped under the door to check."

"I didn't even notice." I hadn't felt her weight leave me.

"I'm telling you, the current tenant is in there, drinking beer on the sofa."

I inhaled through my teeth. Her description triggered some visceral memories.

But whoever lived here was not my dad.

"Knock again." Sarah tugged on my earlobe.

"Fine!" I raised my fist—

The door popped open and there stood one of our half dozen sorry tenants. I'd seen this guy around, but knew nothing about him besides his name. None of our tenants seemed to last long, apart from the little old woman in apartment 3.

This man could have been anyone in Rochdale. He had a beer belly and a scruffy face, and looked like he worked too much for too little.

"You need something?"

"Yes, actually." I cleared my throat, running through what we'd rehearsed in the basement. Patricia had helped us plan, but I wished she were here to whisper the words in my ear again. She had elected to stay in the lobby to "get the place ready for the new girl." Her bruises had reappeared, as had the brambles in her hair, she was clearly nervous.

"Wait—you're the landlady's kid, huh? And here I was hoping you were selling cookies."

I didn't know how to respond to that, but Sarah let loose a derisive hiss in my ear.

The man reached a hand behind his head and rubbed the back of his neck. "Ah. Look, I know I'm late on rent, but I always pay once my check comes, so—"

"That's fine," I said, back on track with our script. "Mom—Mom says you're a good tenant, so no worries."

"Yeah? Well, yeah." He hiccuped. "I try to be, yeah. It's just tough."

I believed him, but I knew from Sarah's snort that she did not.

"Great. So, Mr. Mueller—did you get our notice about the scheduled maintenance today? We notified you three times." This was bullshit, because obviously we hadn't sent any notices. But he was clearly relieved about the rent and being in good with my mom, because he nodded.

"Yeah, yeah, of course I did."

"Great! So you know that you'll need to vacate your apartment for an hour this evening. From 8:00 p.m. to 9:00 p.m."

"Oh. Is that tonight? Can't it wait? There's a game on."

I shook my head. "It can't wait, unless you want sewage to spit from your toilet."

"I'll go to the bar."

"Thanks! I'll tell the plumber he's good to stop by, then."

Mr. Mueller closed the door. Sarah cracked her knuckles. "That's that."

"What about Adelaide?" I asked, as we shuffled across the snow toward the lobby. "Did you see any sign of her when you slipped in there?"

"Oh," she said. "I couldn't see anything, really. The guy's a pack rat. But she's definitely in there."

"How do you know?"

"I felt queasy and cold again, and I started seeing double."

"Like when we found Patricia," I recalled. Sarah seemed less disturbed this time. She appeared beside me at full height and swung an arm around my neck.

"Yeah, like that. So, Dani?"

"So?"

"Are we going to save her, or what?"

I nodded. I really thought we could.

MEOW MIX

We watched Mr. Mueller depart in his pickup at around 7:30. Under the starless night, Sarah and I made our way across the parking lot, our poor excuse for an exorcism kit slung over my shoulder, just in case.

We hadn't gathered as many mystical materials as Sarah had hoped; our kit was a bottle of Morton salt and one of the motel's crappy old Bibles. I'd found a basket of seashells intended for bathroom decor at the Dollar Tree, but I didn't think any of them would actually function as a magic conch. There were two rosaries and some garlic for good measure.

None of this felt as ridiculous as the fact that all these things were crammed into my old fanny pack.

Sarah would not be deterred. Patricia seemed wan, losing her composure and her outline slightly as we prepared to leave the lobby again.

Outside, Sarah was so wound up that she wasn't maintaining her form, either. White light escaped her silhouette in arcs like solar flares, and I could only see the black of her eyes when she nodded at me on the doorstep of the apartment.

"Here goes."

Sarah would have liked to kick in the door like some television badass—she *definitely* watched too much crime television—but she couldn't, and I wasn't the type. I turned the master key in the lock and pushed open the door. Without Mueller standing in the way, we had a clear view of the havoc inside.

I threw my hand over my nose, wincing at the sour smell of cat urine and unwashed clothes. Sarah clicked her tongue and the lights came on. She hadn't been exaggerating when she said the place was a wreck. Stacks of newspapers occupied every corner of the kitchen, and there wasn't a single inch of counter space unpopulated by cups, pizza boxes, beer bottles, or other garbage. As we passed through the kitchenette into the living room, cat litter crunched into the carpet under my tennis shoes. The apartment's air felt strangely fetid.

"Patricia would have a coronary in here," Sarah commented.

There were worse things in the world than squalor, but often enough, squalor was a symptom of something else. Of being poor, or unmedicated, or lonely. Maybe it was a symptom of being haunted. No matter what kind of person Mueller was, he wasn't alive when Adelaide was killed here. He wasn't responsible for her death.

"Are you *certain* she's here?"

"Definitely, Dani. It feels like there's a beehive in my head. If it's not her or it's not her killer, then some other ghost has moved in for sure."

Something about the filth and the temperature and the odor made it feel as though the entire place was rotting. I wasn't afraid of ghosts, but I *was* afraid of what had made them ghosts.

"This way." Sarah cocked her head to the right. "The buzzing is louder when I face the bedroom."

Considering all we knew about Adelaide's death, that wasn't surprising. I took a step forward. A floorboard creaked with stereotypical timing. I was about to comment on it, to break the quiet, when—

Something moved behind us.

"What a fucking cliché!" Sarah declared, while I spun around, my heart in my throat. "It's a cat."

My ribs ached too much to laugh. A tiny calico kitten, thin and mewling, toppled a pile of papers from the sofa to the floor. It now stood with its claws in the armrest, back arched and eyes locked on us—no, on *Sarah*.

"I've heard cats can see ghosts," I said. The kitten swiped at Sarah and hissed several times, puffing up its skinny little body.

"Oh? Well, fuck you very much, too." Sarah crouched before it. "I'm a dog person, you know."

The kitten tried and failed to scratch her and seemed utterly confounded when its tiny paw passed through her hand.

But Sarah was completely smitten.

"Who's a little asshole, then?" Sarah let her ghostly fingers extend like spaghetti and dangled them like loose strings.

I was about to remind her that we were here to look for ghosts, not pets, when a soft groan emanated from the bedroom. Sarah immediately drew closer to me, shifting in and out of focus.

Whatever distraction the kitten had offered, we refocused. The kitten leaped away to hide from us, or from whatever haunted the bedroom.

I looked at Sarah. She was bleary-eyed with pain from the nearby ghost, but she nodded.

Together we crossed the filthy living room and eased open the bedroom door.

ROPES

"Ad—Adelaide?" I called. "Adelaide Williams?"

Sarah flicked on the light, and we saw her. I couldn't stop my horrified gasp.

After the way we'd found Patricia, disheveled, half-naked, and confused, I thought we were prepared for what awaited us.

And in a way, we were.

The scene was just as horrible and senseless. Adelaide was partially exposed, lying on her stomach in a white corset with her arms and legs tied. The ghost of a sheet was draped over her brown legs. She'd turned her face toward the doorway. A wad of fabric had been jammed in her mouth, gagging her.

Unlike Patricia, Adelaide seemed completely conscious of her fate. Her gaze was clear beneath her loose curls. Her brown eyes had an awareness of her situation. Countless people must have slept in this room without ever seeing her, but I suspected she'd seen them all.

When our eyes met, she let out a muffled shout, jerking her limbs.

I couldn't leave the doorway.

Eerily, Adelaide was floating a couple feet off the ground, midway between the grungy foldout and the bathroom door.

"Someone must have moved the bed when they redid the room," Sarah managed. Now that we were so close, Sarah was clearly ill, clutching her stomach and her appearance smearing when she moved. But she wasn't a coward like me, and she approached Adelaide on steady feet.

"Dani! Get over here."

Adelaide looked barely my age.

"*Dani,*" Sarah repeated. "Come on! She needs help! She's still tied up somehow."

I forced my legs forward. When I joined Sarah, I could see what she meant. While there was no longer a bed supporting her ghost, all the fabric that had touched her in death remained, just as it had for Patricia and Sarah. But for Adelaide, this meant not only clothes, but also the ropes that had tied her wrists to the bed frame. The bed frame was gone, but still she was bound to it.

Knowing it was futile, I reached for the spectral knots— they looked so real—and watched my fingers pass through them. "You try, Sarah. I can't touch the knots. They're ghostly."

Sarah nodded, but when she put her fingers to the rope, she recoiled as if burned. She cursed under her breath.

"What's wrong?"

"It's like touching knives. Like they're made of hate." Sarah tried again and cussed, her fingers partially disappearing. Adelaide closed her eyes and let out another horrible sound.

"Can you do it?"

"I . . . I don't know. Why don't we try salting the knots?"

I couldn't see what difference that would make, but Adelaide was watching us. We couldn't do nothing. I pulled the salt from my fanny pack.

"Wait." Sarah cupped her hands around the bracelet of rope on Adelaide's wrist. "In case it burns."

Feeling foolish, I sprinkled salt on the rope. At first it made no difference, but Sarah said, "More than that, come on." So I switched the nozzle from the sprinkling side to the pouring one. To my amazement, as salt passed through the phantom fibers, they hissed and disintegrated, shrinking like slugs on pavement.

Sarah whimpered as a few grains hit her hand and fizzled, pocking her with freckles of air, but she didn't move until the first knot was disintegrated. With aching slowness, Adelaide pulled her freed arm close and held it to her chest like an infant.

When we'd freed all her limbs, she drew herself up, pulling the gag from her mouth. Adelaide coughed and gasped, eyes watering, mascara or kohl streaking her cheeks.

"You're Adelaide Williams, right? I'm Sarah, and this is Dani."

"Folks call me Addy," the ghost rasped. "Unless they're calling me a hussy."

"Well, we won't call you the second name," I said awkwardly. To my astonishment, Addy laughed. What kind of resilience would it take to maintain a sense of humor after decades of suffering?

"You know, these damn pantyhose taste of feet," she said, plucking at the gag. "I mean, of all the things to complain about after being murdered, that was the part that I never expected to hate. How long have I been here?"

"Um, around fifty years?"

"Is that all?" she said, rubbing her wrists. "Imagine chewing socks for that long. Pardon my language, but that was hell."

"I'm so sorry," Sarah said.

"A lot of folks thought I had this coming. Me being a woman of the town. You can't call it rape if you're getting paid to do it."

"Of course you can," Sarah said.

"And you can definitely call it murder," I added.

"Uh-huh," Addy said, narrowing her eyes. "Why you wanna help me, anyhow?"

"Because," Sarah said, "we're the same as you."

"Well, *that's* a laugh."

"Addy," Sarah asked, "would you like to come with us?"

"What, you gonna rescue me from my life of sin? He said the same thing, or maybe one of the others did. You wanna take me far, far away from here? No, no."

"You can't stay here."

"I can't, but I must," Adelaide said softly. Already her limbs were stretching, the knots reappearing around her wrists as she lay back down. "This is how things are, see."

Sarah frowned, and a chill went up my spine. "It doesn't have to be like that, Addy."

Before Addy put the gag back in her mouth, she said, "He won't like it if I leave."

"You mean, the man who did this to you? Do you still see him here sometimes?"

Adelaide blinked, her eyes fixed on the open door to the living room behind us.

"Of course I still see him. Why? Can't you?"

The temperature in the apartment dropped like a stone, and the kitten yowled like it had been stepped on.

"I feel sick." Blood leaked in globules from Sarah's mouth.

"Sarah!"

She popped like a soap bubble, gone, as an arm reached out of the shadows and yanked me back into the other room.

FUNNY PAGES

For a dizzying instant, I thought Mr. Mueller must have returned, or had been home all along, watching me talk to myself in his bedroom. But as I was dragged to the kitchen and scrambled to grab hold of the counters or chairs as I passed, every light in the sordid apartment was flickering on and off. The stovetop caught fire and the fire alarm wailed as I kicked my legs, knocking a coffeepot from a table.

My captor dragged me, gagging, to the living room, where the television switched on and stuttered through channels at a breakneck pace. I couldn't see my attacker's face, but I knew the fuzzy, warm sensation of his arm around my throat. This wasn't the heat of a living person, but the soft, needling pressure of a dead one, but one with more strength and presence than I'd ever felt from Sarah or Patricia.

Oh god, Sarah, what is happening?

The man spun me, pinning me to the wall. But it was generous to call this man—this *thing*?—a ghost.

He looked nothing like Sarah or Patricia or Addy. He looked nothing like anyone. This thing had masculine shoulders and every time it moved, a wrenching, ear-popping screech filled the air, like tires on asphalt, like metal on metal, like dinner plates shattering against the floor. He had a man's arms and a man's torso and height and wore a man's clothes—some kind of undershirt and dress pants combination. But where his face should have been, there was nothing but a ball of goopy black tobacco tar that slipped down onto his shoulders in a constant, churning stream.

The dead man pulled a pack of cigarettes from a pocket. He shoved one between my teeth, and then, when I spat it out, he jammed another one in. It was then that I noticed that he had more than two arms. Could he have as many as he wanted? While one pasty white hand forced cigarettes on me and another held my jaw, another pinned my throat and a fourth reached into his other jeans pocket.

He retrieved a length of rope.

The pressure on my throat increased. I saw pinpricks of snow in the room. The light bulbs burst throughout the apartment and the sofa caught fire as the lamp exploded beside it.

The thing grew taller and taller, slowly inching me up the wall until my head brushed the ceiling and my feet dangled free. Somewhere that kitten was still mewling.

Where the man's features should have been there was only a void. And it was growing, this cone that projected from his head to ensconce mine. As the dead black substance extended over my face, trying to hold me in its nothingness, the tendrils felt a lot like unwanted fingers in my hair.

The familiarity of that made me *so* fucking angry.

I reached for my stupid fanny pack, fumbled for the first

object I could find, and whipped my arm upward. I'd hoped for the salt, but instead I threw the Bible at him. The book passed through his body and out the other side, proving as useless to him as it had always been to me. The book thunked against the floor behind him.

The cone recoiled for a moment, and then a wailing, piggish squeal emerged from its throat. It sounded like sneering, if sneering had a sound. It sounded like jubilant condescension.

My throat was a wad of paper in his fist. I wasn't in a trance, but choking to death. I thought of Sarah and Patricia and Addy, who'd faced similar fates, and the unrighteous bullshit of the reality that people could end each other simply by squeezing their fists.

There came an almighty crash as someone—Sarah? No, not Sarah, Addy—burst through the bedroom door, dragging the invisible bed with her, arms pulled taut as she fought the invisible weight.

"What?" she demanded of the monster, eyes flaming. "I'm not enough for you? Leave the kid."

The dead man whipped his eyeless face toward her.

I found the cylinder of salt and smashed it against the ceiling. Glass and salt filled my fist and fell down like bloody snow over the dead man's body. Where the salt struck his flesh, it sizzled and hissed, and he recoiled. His grip loosened and I fell from the ceiling to the floor with an unhealthy crunch.

The thing, furious as the television caught fire and the smell of cigarettes filled the room, leaned down as I gasped for air, wrapping the rope around my neck, whistling some song from a musical.

I curled my salted, stinging, bloody hand into a fist and swung it into the black pit of his face.

This time he fell silent, as if a scream couldn't contain his pain, and suddenly, without warning, he vanished.

I didn't buy it for a second, but I didn't have to. Addy stood wild-eyed in the firelight.

"Go on," she said calmly. "Now. While you can."

I gasped, eyes watering, coughing on the smoky air. "You too," I rasped.

"No, no. He'll be back for me," she said again, shaking her head. Addy was already retreating through the door, already letting her arms go slack.

"You can't stay here."

"That's how it is," she said; the horror, the finality seeped from her voice. "There's nowhere he won't follow me."

"Go on, and take that kitten with you," she said. "And don't come back here."

Addy was pulled into the darkness, and the bedroom door slammed behind her, as if the strongest arm had closed it.

MIRACLE-GRO

I don't know how I found it in the smoke, but seven scratches later, I made my way to the door, the squeaking kitten zipped up in my hoodie. As much as it had fought when I dragged it out from under the filthy coffee table, the little creature settled once it felt the warmth of my body. Its little heart beat against my bruised ribs. Together we stumbled through the scorching living room and kitchen—those newspapers had been kindling for the flames.

In the room behind me, I thought I heard Addy cry out.

How many times did Dad hit Mom before we finally left? How many times did he hurt us before it was enough? How close were we to death, to resignation?

Why was I able to leave her there?

I burst out into the frosted air and was met with the glare of amber headlights. I threw my hand up, squinting in the light.

"Sarah?"

But it wasn't her. I knew this silhouette and gait.

Seiji Grayson. His expression wasn't unreadable anymore, but horrified as the motel caught fire behind me.

"Seiji?"

"Hi. I called 911."

"Seiji?"

He pointed. "Your motel is on fire."

I fell to my knees in the snow.

Seiji helped me to my feet, but I cried out when I put weight on the foot that had taken the brunt of my fall, so he hefted me up over his shoulder. I was too relieved to feel resentful or anything else as he led me to his truck and lifted me onto the open truck bed. The flames rose higher. Moments later, he joined me on the truck bed. My legs dangled, but his hardly did—he was so damn tall.

"Why are you here?"

"Your backpack." His face was calm again, but his eyes reflected the firelight. "You left it in my truck."

I thought we might be dreaming.

"Oh, yeah, thanks."

"This all looks bad. Are you okay?"

"I'm fine."

"Your apartment is on fire," he reiterated, as if reading a report.

"That's not my unit, not specifically."

He sat up. "Is there someone in there still?"

I bit my lip and shook my head, Addy's expression seared behind my eyelids.

"Your neck is bruised to hell."

"Oh yeah. See, no one *living's* in there. I was fighting with the ghost of a douchebag murderous fuck."

Maybe the oxygen deprivation was making me talk, or maybe

180

I didn't care to keep secrets anymore. As the flames licked the roof of the motel, I felt some kind of dark pressure rising in the air. I felt it, and wondered what it meant.

Somewhere in the burning building, had the murderous ghost evaporated? Or was it just wishful thinking that anything we'd done in there had made the slightest difference? That we'd done anything but enrage a monster?

What kind of person was I to leave Addy there?

You'd have left Patricia, too.

"Oh god," I said numbly. "How can I ever face Sarah?"

"Who's Sarah?"

"My best friend. The ghost who lives in your old Game Boy sometimes. She died in the seventies and now she's stuck with me."

"Oh."

The motel roof caught fire in earnest. People from the other apartments ran out into the parking lot, and neither of us said another word until the fire truck and ambulance appeared. Soon after Mr. Mueller leaped from his truck shouting, "Plumbing issue, my ass! My *ass*!"

Seiji and I watched him rant and rail, as if he were in a film we weren't part of.

We existed in this bleary reality, me and silent Seiji and the kitten in his lap. I thought I might never speak again once the swelling rose in my neck. The kitten, on the other hand, seemed like it would never stop protesting the horrors it had seen.

"Calm down, little guy," I said, as it screeched in Seiji's reassuring hands.

"Little girl," Seiji amended. "Calicos are almost always girls. It's a genetic mutation."

"How do you know that?"

Seiji shrugged. "I really love cats."

"Really?" I paused. "You love cats and gardening."

"I love cats and gardening," he agreed, "and *you* fight ghosts."

"Well, I don't usually fight them. Usually I try to help them."

"But not today."

I thought of Addy's resignation, the door slamming behind her. I trembled. "Not today."

Seiji said, "Anything else you want to tell me?"

There was something about the snow and my bruises, something about the surreal events of the evening. "Why not. Here's something: I'm a boy."

"Oh?"

"Yeah. I'm definitely a boy, but no one sees it and that's super fucking annoying."

"Oh." Had anyone ever said oh so many times, and had it ever been such a ridiculous and perfect response? "So you're transgender. That's tough."

I looked at him. I never thought anyone would know the word or say it so matter-of-factly, as if it were legitimate. We lived in an ass-crack northern Michigan town, where people still played "Smear the Queer" at recess and thought "shim" was a clever thing to call girls who dressed like boys.

Seiji Grayson watched the flames grow. Orange reflected off his black eyes.

"Yeah, it *is* tough." I had never imagined I could say so.

"No wonder you're so angry. Trans, seeing ghosts, and besties with a dead girl."

When he put it like that, I longed to laugh, despite all the ways it would hurt. I settled for a dozy grin. "Well, what's *your* excuse?"

"My mother died, my father left, I'm gay and Asian and in Podunk."

"That . . . that's tough, too."

"Hey," he added suddenly, "I'm pretty sure a ghost's haunting our flower shop. Think you could help her?"

"Um. Is that why you said you talk to dead people, too?"

"No. It's more general. Like, asking her for advice. She never answers. I can't actually see her. But can you help her?"

"I could try?"

We didn't speak again. Smoke rose to the sky. I couldn't stop seeing Addy's face, etched in orange and charcoal, and the scribble of the tarry bastard, too.

I ended up in the ambulance because of my bruises and wheezing and sprained ankle, and because of the glass in my hand. Seiji watched with one hand in his pocket, the other wrapped around the calico kitten.

Maybe it was the adrenaline, or maybe it was the intoxicating power of honesty. Or maybe we had always been aiming for fucked-up friendship, Seiji Grayson and me.

I waved at him before the ambulance doors shut.

OXYCODONE

Mom showed up to the hospital in her work outfit: black pants and a black apron and a low-cut shirt revealing a hint of what she called her "tip makers." Her makeup was a mess and she'd clearly been crying. The smell of cigarettes accompanied her as she burst into my hospital room.

"Is she all right?" she demanded.

"It's a badly sprained ankle, so she'll be on crutches for a while," the nurse said, "although we need to have a word with you about her other injuries."

Mom blinked, then nodded. How many times had nurses asked my mother to step out to the hallway to explain away her bruises and black eyes to doctors and social workers? And how many times had Mom lied, called Dad a saint and a victim, before she couldn't lie anymore?

I dozed for a while—whatever drugs they were giving me made me *very chill*—and when Mom returned, she seemed less frantic. Her expression expunged the calm I felt, leaving something cold and sad and *angry* in its wake.

"What the hell's been going on, Dani? I know we haven't

been talking much lately, but I'm still your mother. I love you, you know?"

I couldn't nod, because that hurt a hell of a lot.

"The doctors tell me you won't say where those bruises on your neck came from. They say you told them you fell on the ice when you ran outside to see the fire. Daniela Rae, I'm not buying it."

My throat had swollen in the minutes since I'd arrived, and though I knew I wasn't in any specific danger, I was grateful for an excuse not to speak.

"Was it that boy at school?" I knew Mom meant Charley, and the idea, how near and far from the truth that was, made me nauseated. "I told you, you have to be careful—"

"No, Mom, it wasn't a boy at school," I rasped. "I don't want to talk about it."

"So you're dating someone *not* at school?" She leaned forward. "I warned you—"

"No—no! And you didn't have to warn me. I remember life with Dad."

Mom fell silent. We rarely spoke of Dad or what had happened, that final straw that broke us all, but with the bruises fresh on my neck and the memories sharper than they had been in years, pretending felt downright stupid.

"Dani . . ."

"You never warned me about Dad, did you? You just let him do what he wanted." My ears rang like sirens. "You let him do it."

Her posture stiffened. "I didn't *know* he was doing that."

"You knew, or you suspected. You knew, and you ignored it. You ignored *me*."

"If you're telling me I'm a terrible mother," she said, shaking all over, "I *know* that. Believe me, I do. You think other people haven't told me as much? You think I haven't told myself as much every damn day? You hate me? Well, I hate me, too."

"Then *why* do you take his calls?"

She shook her head. "Christ, I don't know. At the shelter I learned about patterns of abuse. I know he won't change—I *do*, Daniela. And I'd kill him, I really would, if he touched you again."

I stared at the hospital blanket, my pale knuckles.

"But there's still part of me that thinks he loves us. That thinks maybe, just maybe things would work out, if I tried harder." She lifted her head. Her eyes were glassy with tears. "But he's not coming back. I can promise you that, Dani."

I didn't want to hear this. I wanted to hear her say that she was wrong. I wanted her to admit, finally, that she'd known what was happening to me in that trailer. But I didn't think she could. I didn't think she ever would.

God, I *wanted* to hate her. I wanted to.

"Right." She stood, adjusted her hair. "I better head back home. Our place is intact, but there's gonna be a lot to deal with in the morning. The fire tore through that whole building. No one's hurt, but George is having a fit." George was the owner of the building. If he didn't have fire insurance, that was his own stupid fault. "We'll be fine, but obviously the tenant in 7 has to move out to some motel for a while, and 9 and 5 will, too. Don't suppose you'll tell me what you were doing in there?"

I shook my head, and she sighed.

"Well, so long as you didn't set the damn fire. You didn't, right?"

186

I couldn't even blame her for wondering. It wasn't like we knew each other.

"No. I didn't."

She squeezed my hand before she left. Her grip felt cold, or maybe mine did.

BOUNCE

My eyes shot open in the half dark of the hospital room.

Sarah, caught in the green glow of the monitors, lay beside me, looking closely at my face. "You never told me that your father hurt you like *that*."

"Sarah!" I could have cried at the sight of her. She looked like herself, no blood on her chin. "How'd you get here?"

"I hitched a ride inside your mom's phone. Why, did I scare you?"

My eyes welled. "I'm so glad to see you. In the motel when you disappeared, I thought—"

"I know, I don't know what happened. It was like the me was sucked out of me. I'm so sorry I left you alone with him. But tell me, because I have to know—is Addy okay?"

Sarah lay alongside me like she had a thousand times, face close to mine. Sometimes looking at Sarah felt like looking at my reflection, or the reflection I might have had if things had gone another way, a thousand other ways. But I couldn't face my reflection or the truth of what I was.

"Dani? Did she get out?"

"Yeah, yeah she did," I lied. "She got out."

Sarah's posture changed. Joy shone in her eyes. "Oh wow, really. *Really?* That's amazing. That's so—but Trish said she didn't come to the shelter. So where did she go?"

I fumbled for words. "Um. Away, I think."

"What, to heaven?" Sarah snorted. "No way."

"No, I think . . . she walked off into the woods." God, I couldn't believe myself. I shut my eyes and prayed Sarah couldn't see me for the worm I was. "She didn't want to live with us, I guess. Had her own plans."

"Oh." Sarah sounded hurt, but as though she was trying not to be. "I mean, that's her choice."

"Yeah."

Her choice, locking herself in with her killer. But my choice, letting her do it.

"And? What about you? You okay, Dani?"

"I'm okay," I told her.

"'Course you aren't." Her marble eyes caught the emerald light of the monitors. More than ever, she looked like I might be able to touch her. "But I'm jealous. You were out there kickin' some murderer ass, playing the hero, and I . . . I couldn't keep it together."

"Where did you go, Sarah?"

"I don't know. I just felt so sick, and then I . . . *wasn't*, for a while." She spoke calmly, but I could sense her frustration. The exorcism had been her dream, not mine, and I could not tell her what a nightmare it had been. "I tried to go back to apartment 7, after the fire, but I felt too sick again. I felt myself dissolving all over again. I don't understand it. If he's gone, and Addy's gone, why can't I go in there?"

I closed my eyes. "Maybe because it was haunted for so long."

189

"Maybe. Even after the fire was put out, even after I went back . . . that buzzing's carrying on, like a swarm of insects. Patricia won't go in there, either, obviously. But I feel like such a waste of space."

"It's not your fault."

"Trish said that, too. But I feel . . . Dani, I was actually *helpless*." Sarah shook her head. "I couldn't help you, or her, or myself."

Tears started pouring down Sarah's cheeks.

"*So why*? Why wouldn't she come live with us? Did we do something wrong?"

"She had other places to be." I longed to wipe away Sarah's tears.

"Or maybe she didn't like us."

"No, Sarah." That part I could tell her. That part was not rotten. "Addy—she saved me, you know."

Despite my sore throat, I told her about the events of the evening. I explained the murderer's melting face and multiple hands and the normalcy of the rest of him, how he might have been anyone's uncle before he vanished. I deleted Seiji and his help, and I deleted the awful truth:

Addy and her killer were still in the wreckage of that apartment, and I'd left them there.

"So salt and fire did it, then? I can't believe it. Seems so simple. But next time we'll be more prepared. Double the salt, and a bunch of matches, too."

Next time. I shuddered. "Sarah, I'm not sure we should keep this up."

She ignored that. "How did you get out on that messed-up ankle?"

190

"I don't know. Adrenaline, I guess."

"Sure. I read once that mothers lift cars off their kids sometimes." She hesitated. "Did you . . . um . . . that kitten?"

In answer, I pulled down the collar of my nightgown, revealing a few scratches on my collarbone. "She's fine. She got out, too."

"Okay. Good."

I clung to the cat rescue, my only truth. "Aha. You like her."

"No."

"You do." I inched closer. "You're becoming a crazy cat lady in your old age."

"Hush."

And wow, the meds must have been kicking in again, because I felt a little loopy. I was almost dozing against Sarah's shoulder when she spoke, very quietly. "Next time, I'll be there with you. Next time, I—I won't leave you there alone."

I nestled my head under her faint, warm chin. "Okay, Sarah."

She shook her head. "I wouldn't exist without you, you know."

"Rightbackatcha."

"I'm serious." There was nothing to buffer the hollows in her expression, and a massive grief weighed her words, which was something my garbled mind couldn't parse. "I have to look after you, for my own sake. What do people say in movies? 'Don't go dyin' on me.'"

I laughed, teary with the pain in my ribs.

"Whoa there."

Breathing could stop at any moment, at the hands of almost anyone or no one.

Sarah looked at me with a pained expression I didn't quite understand. Then suddenly, the world flipped over, and everything I thought I knew went sideways.

Sarah pressed her lips against mine.

It was like being kissed by a feather. I was so surprised I didn't pull away, and then she was kissing me with her spectral fingers pulling me against her. She wasn't breathing, but I was. I was downright gasping. Her touch enveloped the pain that spanned my entire body, wiping out everything but her presence. Her sudden realness, terrifying and undeniable.

And then it ended. Sarah pulled away and dissipated slightly, blurry as a fogged window. I felt my strength leave almost every particle of my body, as if she'd sucked my soul from my mouth.

I stared. "Sarah. What . . . I mean, Sarah, *what*—"

"Shit," she said. "Shit. No. This is *such* a bad idea."

"Sarah, I—"

She vanished, leaving me alone with the bleeping machines and all my twisted thoughts.

STELLA

SPRITE

I spent a night in the hospital before Mom bundled me up, wheeled me to the truck, and promised me cocoa and bed rest on the couch, movies, and whatever snacks I wanted. My ankle and my bruises laid me up for the next week, so I missed the remainder of school before Thanksgiving.

To my dismay and confusion, Mom seemed reinvigorated with motherly instinct after my accident, or maybe she was responding to my accusations. I didn't know how to feel about her sudden devotion to me. She took the week off work to keep an eye on me, and fed me Sprite as if I had the flu again. I still hadn't given her (or the social workers or doctors or anyone else) any explanation for my injuries. I knew something of what Mom must have felt, seeing lies work when they really shouldn't have.

Mom's unending presence at my side meant that I hadn't seen Sarah since she kissed me in the hospital. I ran a dozen excuses for her behavior through my mind. Maybe Sarah was scared, or maybe she was trying to make me feel better, or maybe it was a misunderstanding.

But the truth? The truth was she had kissed me, *not* like a sister, but as though she loved me, and I had no idea what to do with that knowledge. I knew we needed each other, but I had never needed Sarah like *that*, and I had no idea what I could possibly say when I saw her again.

I tried not to think *if* I saw her again, tried not to think of the blood that had poured from her mouth before she vanished in that motel room, the fear in her face when she said, "I wouldn't exist without you."

I was grateful for my windowless room, grateful I couldn't see the blackened shell of apartment 7 even though I could sometimes smell the ash from it, taste it in the tap water.

———

The first ghost to visit me in the days after I got home was Patricia, making a rare appearance outside the lobby. Mom was dozing on the couch while an infomercial advertised cleaning products. Suddenly Patricia was there between us.

It was the second time I'd ever seen her leave the lobby.

"Patricia!" I threw my arms around her. She shrank slightly, but seemed grateful for the hug. "Thanks for coming to see me."

"I had to see how you were doing, after everything."

"Everything."

"You did a brave thing, helping Adelaide."

"She goes by Addy," I said, looking away.

"Addy, next door all along."

Patricia had a preternatural teacher-based ability to read the lies in my voice, so I simply nodded. "Did Sarah tell you about it? About Adelaide leaving?"

"I'm a little fuzzy on the details. Did she really just walk out into the woods?"

"I was pretty confused. But yeah, I think she did." Maybe if I retold the lie enough times, I'd believe it. Maybe I'd stop seeing, on endless looping repeat, Addy's expression as she closed the door, as she told me to leave her alone.

Patricia pursed her lips. "The woods are no place to be. I wish she'd stayed with us, at least a little while."

Patricia pointedly did not ask about the exorcism, and I pointedly didn't say a word about it. Somewhere out there, her own killer might be lingering on the path.

"But you know Sarah's been cagey about all of it; she's been spending a lot of time in that basement. Did you two have a spat?"

I had never wanted to change a subject so badly.

I spoke over Mom's snoring. "She may have . . . um. She kissed me."

"She *what*?"

"She, um . . . kissed me?"

"I see. And how do you feel about that?"

"I don't know." My face flushed. "It was sort of a shock. Sarah's like my sister. Obviously I *love* her, but not . . . and she gets that, I think she does, because she says she wouldn't exist without me. I mean, she's like another part of me."

"No one is *part* of anyone else," Patricia said sharply. "But if Sarah feels that way, or if she feels you belong to her, or . . . oh, what an absolute mess."

"I don't care if she's gay!" I couldn't seem to make a single thought coherent, and I couldn't seem to stop talking, either. "I mean, I don't know what things were like in the seventies, but obviously I don't care if she's a lesbian, I just don't love her like *that*, and—"

"*That's* not the messy part, Dani."

"What? Or do you think because I'm trans I should like girls, because I'm not sure I *do* like girls, I'm not sure I *like* people romantically, and—"

"*No*, Dani. It's not that, either! Believe it or not, not everything that happens is about whether or not you're queer. It's—sometimes you forget, don't you," Patricia whispered, with this strange, sympathetic smile. "You *forget* what we are."

Blood warmed my face. "I *don't* forget."

"You *do* forget. And honestly? That's nice. Around you, Sarah and I, we're just people, Dani, and not necessarily even *dead*. The fact is, as complicated as your identity is—can you imagine how difficult things would be if you also had to face the reality of your own demise on top of the rest of it?"

I shook my head. "Of course I can't. How could I ever?"

"I'm glad you can't." Patricia stared at her fingers. "Sometimes I don't feel real. I feel like less than the wind, and I wonder whether I'm myself or just some *echo* of Patricia-who-was. I wouldn't wish that sort of doubt upon anyone, and I suspect—no, I *know*—Sarah doesn't want to share that sensation with you. But still, she kissed you. She did something a living girl would do. She forgot herself."

I thought of Sarah's confession, her admission of her fragile existence. Maybe she hadn't meant it romantically, but literally. Maybe she only meant that without me, she'd still be haunting the underside of a bed.

Like Addy, haunting the bedroom.

I felt sick in every way.

"Just keep that in mind, Dani. I'll talk to Sarah. I'm not sure exorcisms are the way to go about solving anyone's problems. Look at what this did to you both."

"Has Sarah . . . I mean, has anything happened with the hotel room?"

Patricia shook her head. "I haven't . . . you know I haven't gone there, and Sarah hasn't either. There's still caution tape all around it; I don't think the tenants have even been let back in. Maybe they'll condemn this old place, and we'll have to move."

"Don't worry," I told her, sensing what she wasn't saying. "Nobody bothers condemning anything in towns like this."

"If only we'd been able to give Adelaide a coat, or something. Or . . . anything. I'd have liked to meet her."

"Patricia . . . can I ask you something? Something personal?"

Her nod warmed me. "Always."

"When we found you, in the woods." I thought of Adelaide's expression, her certainty as she shut me out. "Why didn't you . . . why had you stayed? Why couldn't you have left the trail on your own ages ago?"

"It's hard to undo what's already been done, and hard to break even the worst of habits. I think you know that. Sometimes there's comfort in the horrific."

I thought of Dad, of Mom, of words that could not be overwritten.

"Do you think you'd have stayed there forever, if we hadn't come?"

"Forever?" Patricia lifted her hands, as if she could hold mine. "I laid on that path for a decade, you know. I never considered there were any other options. Maybe exorcisms *can't* work, because they only impact the monsters and not the victims. Being dead is a lot like being alive. There are no simple solutions. Yes, I'm haunted, and Addy will always be haunted. Like, I suspect, you will be, too."

I closed my eyes. "So *rescuing* ghosts might be pointless."

"Dani. Listen." When I open my eyes, Patricia's looking at me with so much warmth and kindness. "I thought my life, my unlife, my *everything*, was done. But do you know what?"

"What?"

"I read an amazing book the other day. I've got a home, and a new family, and a roof that keeps me dry. Haunted or not, I'm here. That's not pointless." She smiled gently. "It's not pointless in the least."

I nodded, wordless, and she kissed the air above my forehead, and I thought of Sarah and all the things she would not say, the secret spirits that plagued her.

I couldn't know what it felt like to be an echo. No matter what, I still had a future, while my friends were already things of the past. While Mom dozed beside me, talking in her sleep, I felt like Patricia's point was a little unfair, even hypocritical.

The future could seem so impossibly pointless, and lonely, too.

But it could also, maybe, be the opposite, populated by as many good ghosts as bad ones.

BUTTERBALL

On Thanksgiving morning there was a knock at the door. Mom got up from the couch and answered in her robe. A woman's voice cut through the morning air.

"Happy Thanksgiving!"

Mom shied away from the sheer enthusiasm. "You here to complain about the fire damage? Because the insurance company is on it, and—hold on. Are you even a tenant?"

"No, ma'am!"

I craned forward on the couch cushions and recognized the visitor's bright face. It was Sophie, the woman I'd met at reception at the Green House. She wore a lurid penguin-patterned holiday sweater and reindeer antlers. Sophie beamed when she spotted me.

"I'm Sophie Alldridge. I work at the Green House, the local women's shelter."

"I'm familiar." Mom's posture remained stiff. "Is this about what happened to Daniela?"

Sophie shook her head. "Not exactly. Someone told us about the fire and her accident. We wanted to invite you and any interested tenants to our annual turkey dinner at the Knights of Columbus hall. We'll have all-you-can eat stuffing and mac-cheese, no charge."

Mom hesitated, glancing at me. "I dunno . . ."

"Will Seiji be there?" I asked.

"Yeah, he'll be working the line, serving up pumpkin pie." Sophie winked knowingly again. She had it wrong, but not *entirely* wrong. I did want to see him, and I'd been couch-bound and stinking for days.

"We'll think about it," Mom said.

"Neat! If you decide you're interested, come on by at 1:00 p.m., and bring these tickets." She pushed two slips of red paper into Mom's hand. "I'll keep door-knocking, if you don't mind."

"Okay—"

"Wait!" Sophie turned, and Mom looked downright apprehensive. "I forgot to mention—there'll be karaoke!"

"Sounds great!" I said loudly. "We'll be there for sure!"

Mom whipped her head back at me, then wished Sophie goodbye before closing the door and sitting on the arm of the couch. "Say-gee? Is that a boy's name?"

"*Mom*. Believe me—Seiji has nothing to do with my damn bruises, okay?"

Mom played with the loose threads on the sofa. "I guess we can go. I've only got a mediocre lasagna in the fridge."

"Cool. I'll have to wash up first."

"But!" Mom added. "We'll only go if you tell me who hurt you."

She was as tenacious as I'd ever heard her. I'd finally have to say something.

"Don't tell the cops, okay?"

Mom pinched her lips but nodded.

For a heartbeat I considered telling her the truth. Who knew? Maybe she'd take the news as easily as Seiji had. Or maybe when she was my age, Mom also saw ghosts. Maybe it wouldn't sound like madness to her, maybe it would knot us together. But I also knew reality was hard enough for Mom even without paranormal nonsense thrown in.

"It was a stranger." I looked down at my lap. "Some guy in the alley between Ace Hardware and the 7-Eleven. I didn't even see his face. He grabbed me from behind and shoved me against the wall."

"And you have no idea who he was? Did you see what he was wearing?"

My mind flashed back to the horror I'd felt, and bile rose in my throat as I answered truthfully: "Black leather shoes and suit pants."

Mom placed a hand on my shoulder. "Let's get ready for the party."

"RUDOLPH THE RED-NOSED REINDEER"™

The K of C hall was crowded. The crutches weren't ideal on ice, so Mom insisted I use the wheelchair the hospital had loaned us instead. When we entered the brownish foyer the smell of ham and sugar and the distorted echo of music couldn't banish the general forlornness of the aging bingo hall. Peeling linoleum covered the floors and the walls were probably built before Sarah was born.

Staff had draped garlands across the tables and along the ceiling, like it was Christmas, not Thanksgiving. It was weirdly nice, though, watching families and loners all gathered around long foldout tables, bundled up in festive clothes and trying to keep their children seated. A little girl jumped up and down to Christmas music on the makeshift dance floor, a candy cane stuck in her hair.

I felt self-conscious in that wheelchair, but Mom wouldn't let me up. Maybe I'd see some classmates here, but even if I did, that'd make them either a volunteer or as poor as we were, so what did it matter? I had a scarf around my neck, but there was no hiding my busted foot.

Midway down the buffet line, I spied Seiji; he'd pulled his hair back from his face into a short ponytail that exposed his high cheekbones and large eyes. To my amazement, he smiled at people as he scooped pie onto their plates, and for once he didn't look fearsome, though part of that may have been the candy-cane-patterned apron and a bow tie. By the time we got to him, he'd gone through two pies, and was pulling another from a box behind him.

"Hey," I said.

He turned, so red in the cheeks and forehead that, for a moment, I thought he was about to yell. Instead he asked, "Want some pie?"

"Definitely," Mom said. "Two slices each. Those are basically slivers."

I grimaced. "One slice each is fine, Seiji."

"Seiji?" Mom sized him up, frowning at the tattoos on his knuckles and the piercings in his eyebrow. "Huh."

Seiji dropped the spatula twice before serving us.

By the time we made it to a table, I was wishing we hadn't come.

"Honestly, he doesn't look like your type."

"He's *not*, Mom."

"Huh." She poked at her stuffing and glanced up again. "Aw, hell. There's Mueller. I gotta go talk to him about the insurance and fire damage. Don't go anywhere."

I sighed in relief as she departed, but almost choked when Seiji took her spot.

"Your mother doesn't like me."

"She doesn't trust boys."

He raised his eyebrows, and I knew what he wasn't saying.

"Yeah, no. She doesn't know about my situation."

"Ghosts or gender?"

"Both. So maybe don't mention either?"

Seiji drew back. "I am not known for being talkative."

I snorted over my canned beets. "No kidding. You're pretty closed off. I think this is the first time I've ever seen your whole face without your hair in the way."

He started pulling his hair over his forehead, skin reddening. "Soph made me tie my hair back. Health code."

"You've got a good face." I envied its angles and definition, the lack of soft flesh. "Maybe if you showed it occasionally, or smiled like you were a second ago, people wouldn't say you were in the yakuza."

"They still would." Blunt as ever. "I'm Japanese and they're racist. Also, I don't like my face."

"Why not?" I pointed at my most infamous feature. "*You* haven't got a lazy eye."

He frowned. "Do you think your eye helps you see dead people?"

"I have no clue. Why do you hate your handsome face?"

"My face gets red really easily. It's a genetic thing."

"I hadn't noticed." I snickered. "I just thought you were drunk."

"Hey."

"Or maybe really, *really* cold."

"*Hey.*"

"Seiji the red-faced pie man, had a very scary face," I sang.

"*Hey.*"

206

"And if you ever saw it, he would pull down his bangs!"

"You're a bad singer," he declared, glancing over his shoulder, his cheeks as red as roses.

Now that I was getting to know him, he sounded mean when he was embarrassed. I wondered if that was coded in him like my back talk was.

"Hey, how's the kitten doing?"

"I named her Chestnut." I wondered if he realized how cute that was. "How's . . . how are your ghosts?"

"They aren't pets, so I don't know how to answer that." I looked away. "But I'd say not so great."

I caught him eyeing my scarf. "Hey. About you helping me, with mine. My ghost."

"Oh." To my shame, it had slipped my mind. "I mean. I can't promise anything."

He nodded. "I'll give you a ride to the shop after school on Monday. But you'll have to wait for me a little while."

"Right. Because you've got detention after school."

Seiji blinked twice. "I haven't had detention since middle school."

"But everyone says—"

"Everyone says I'm in the yakuza. Everyone says you're a lesbian."

"Point taken."

"I have to go back to work." Seiji stood up, but I grabbed his hand.

"Did you tell the Green House people to invite me and my mom?"

He shrugged, which I thought meant yes. His shrugs could mean all sorts of things.

"So why *do* you stay after school?"

"To look after the iguanas in the bio lab."

He said this like it was the most obvious answer, and I was still chuckling when Mom came back to the table, looking harried.

"Mr. Mueller says *you* set his place on fire, but I told him that was nuts and to shut up about it. What's so funny?"

"I wanna try karaoke. Can you put in a request for 'Rudolph the Red-Nosed Reindeer'?"

Behind her, Sophie was scolding Seiji about his unruly hair and he begrudgingly pulled it off his forehead again.

"Are you serious? Karaoke?"

"Yeah, Mom."

"Okay."

Mom wheeled me to the dance floor. When my song started, I watched Seiji turn pale as they lowered the microphone. When he heard me singing the traditional lyrics, he flipped me the bird. The little girl on the dance floor was head-banging like there was no tomorrow while her mother tried to peel the candy cane from her hair.

I didn't feel the least bit haunted.

THE HUSTLE

By the time we left the hall, Mom was flushed from eggnog and dancing. I was woozy from the meds and the company, and frankly, all the singing. It turned out I had a secret desire to belt a dozen cheesy Christmas songs, and Mariah Carey wiped me out pretty quickly. As we left the little head-banger was snoring in her parents' arms. Sophie gave us colossal hugs and helped us to the car.

As Mom wheeled me into the apartment, she said, "I haven't danced in years."

"I'm not sure doing the hustle counts as dancing anymore."

"Sorry I don't know the cha-cha slide or whatever."

"Don't be sorry; it sucks."

Her cackle set off her smoker's lungs. Once the coughing cleared, she said, "That boy seems all right."

"I think he might be, Mom. But I told you, it's not like that."

"Because you don't like boys." She spoke without inflection, careful as she'd rarely been. The lack of judgment in her tone left me reeling. That was only part of the story—but it was a start.

"Fair to say yeah, I don't like boys," I agreed.

"Okay," she said, exhaling. "Okay."

"*Is* it okay?" I asked, heart in my throat.

"Sure, honey."

I looked at her. Her expression was gentle, almost *motherly*. "I wish I didn't like them, either."

I laughed, my body a thousand times lighter as she mussed my hair.

"I'm gonna head to bed," she said. "Back to work tomorrow, and you know Black Friday is hell."

My eyes were damp as I limped to my bedroom.

Sarah was waiting for me. Not on my bed, but sitting in my desk chair, staring at the ground. I wondered if she'd heard Mom and me talking. I wondered whether it mattered.

"Sarah. Hey." I swallowed at the sight of her. "I've missed you."

"I've been avoiding you," she said bluntly.

"I figured."

She glanced at me. Her eyes seemed a little hollow, and her skull was showing more than usual through her translucent skin. "What else was I supposed to do?"

"It's casual." I plopped down on the bed, setting my crutches beside me. "It's not like I went looking for you, either. I . . . I get it."

"You *don't* get it. You're still alive, Dani."

I sighed. "*Every* time you folks pull the 'we're super dead' card, how am I supposed to win an argument? Just—you don't have to worry about it. Patricia talked to me."

"She talked to me, too." Sarah watched me. "I should never have done that."

"Done what, Sarah?"

For once, Sarah couldn't seem to speak her mind.

"*What*, Sarah?"

She shrank two sizes. "Kissed you."

The tension in the air was another person in the room, like we were putting on a performance.

"Sarah. It's okay. There was a lot happening."

"Tell me something, because I can't seem to remember." The blackness of her eye hollows spread like fetid moss. "Did you kiss me back?"

"No, Sarah. I love you. But not like that."

"No," she says, shaking her head. "You kissed me back. I know you did."

"I didn't."

"Well, maybe you did! Maybe it was an accident!" she cried, and the lights flickered. "Didn't you ever kiss your father back, by accident?"

That was a blow I'd never expected, and it left me reeling.

Sarah backpedaled, but the words had been said, a taint like poison in the air. "I know it's not the same. I know you didn't—I mean. I don't know why I said that."

"Stop." I felt emptied, horrified at the implications. But more horrifying to me was the confusion on her face, a sense of loss I'd never seen in her. Maybe I was finally more mature than Sarah was. Maybe I had been for a while, but hadn't noticed.

"Sarah, you are *nothing* like him. You weren't trying to hurt me."

"Can you be sure?" She trembled. "You've seen how malicious ghosts can be."

"Sarah. Stop that. We're good. Okay?"

"It's casual," she said, and it had never sounded so false.

"It's not. You're upset. *I'm* upset." I hesitated. "Maybe there are secrets we both should have been sharing. We could talk about them? Like we used to?"

For an instant, I think I'm about to hear her whole story, her life and her death and her feelings and thoughts, and maybe she'll hear mine, and we'll be closer than ever—but then her eyes shutter.

"I hardly think this compares to a folder full of magazine clippings of boy bands. Besides, you couldn't even talk about that. So what do you mean, 'used to'?" She laughed bitterly, fading to a fog, a girl-shaped distortion that twisted my bedspread and wallpaper together. "No. The moment we start telling each other the truth, there's no reason for us to be together."

"What is that supposed to mean?"

Her tone was more than disparaging. "Oh come on, Dani. What would we have in common, if our fathers hadn't hurt us?"

Heat filled my eyes. "You're my best friend."

"I'm just another dead girl, an itch that won't go away."

This all felt so wrong. I struggled for normalcy, to spark our usual banter, but came up dry. "Sarah . . . please . . ."

"On my map. There are other ghosts. Other murderers to exorcise, other dead girls out there waiting for help."

"But . . . we haven't . . ." I bit my tongue, bit down the vision of Addy. "I don't think I'm ready to face that."

"Really? Didn't you just *heroically* save a tortured ghost?"

"I . . ."

212

"You *did* save her, right?" Her gaze was intent. "Because that's what you told us."

"Yes, I did!" I blurted. "Yes. But . . . now I'm worse for wear."

"So?" She shrugged, feigning indifference. "Dani, while you're hung up on your twisted foot, there's always going to be more of us. Girls like me are just ten-a-fucking-penny."

TEEN SPIRIT

I woke to violent screaming, followed by a high-pitched wail that resonated through the walls and set my veins shivering.

"Sarah?"

But it wasn't her voice. I stumbled out of bed, forgetting my busted ankle, and cried out as I fell against my dresser, knocking deodorant and lotions to the floor.

Somewhere in the near distance the piercing shriek continued, muffled now, as though someone had clapped a hand over the screamer's mouth.

The air pressure in my room suddenly increased, as though I were underwater, and the act of breathing suddenly felt like a burden. My wrists stung like they'd been burned, and I felt my arms being pulled apart, spread like wings, like I was being tied down. Something invisible weighed on me, some experience that wasn't mine.

"Addy?"

The air fell still, like a balloon had been punctured, and my arms fells slack.

I turned around.

Addy was on my bed, tears streaming, wrists bound.

She stared at me, eyes wide, shook her head, and then was gone.

Her parting sob echoed in my head until the morning.

SHARPIE FINE POINT
(REPRISE)

When I returned to school, the holiday weekend, the news of
the apartment fire, and the sight of my crutches eclipsed the
news of my binding debacle. If Corina had spread rumors, they'd
been buried in the other drama.

Coach Ma found me in the hallway at breakfast. "Look, I'd
already let you quit the team. You didn't need to go out and
twist your ankle to convince me, Dani."

"Sorry, Coach." I smiled tightly.

"Don't apologize for things that happen to you. Got that?"

"Right."

"And if you want to tag along and play water boy at regionals, I could use an assistant coach. Think about it." She clapped
me on the shoulder, almost knocking my crutches out from
under my arms.

"Hey, Dani!" Charley said with his cheerful smile. Had it
always been that false and horrible? "Heard about the fire! Glad
you're okay!"

"Are you glad?" I asked. "Or are you saying that because
there are people watching you right now, and you like to look

like a good person when really you're the absolute fucking worst, Charley?"

One of the kids behind him said, "*Damn!*" and another one whistled.

I stared at Charley until his grin slipped off his face and he walked away.

When I started down the hallway, Seiji was there, towering over me with all that black hair in his eyes. "If I offer to carry your books for you, are you going to yell at me?"

"I *probably* won't yell." I tapped my turtleneck. "Hate to strain my throat."

"Too risky." Seiji pivoted away with his hands in his pocket, and got halfway down the hall before I laughed and called him back.

"Fine, fine! I *definitely* won't yell."

"Very kind of you," Seiji grumbled, taking my bag from me.

I bit my tongue before I could rightbackatcha him.

————

School passed without any disasters of note. I sat with a few classmates at lunch, and despite Corina's and Charley's whispers, they asked to sign my cast and talked about their Thanksgiving vacations. I'd thought our friendships were shallow, but being distant meant they didn't hold grudges, or care much about whatever whispers trailed me. I hadn't seen that as an advantage before.

But when Seiji approached our table and wedged himself between me and Liz Fay, the entire table went quiet. Seiji didn't seem to notice.

"Are you still coming over tonight?" he asked.

"Oh my *god*," said Maryanne, laughing. Liz elbowed her and started a new conversation in a futile attempt to distract from the presence of the giant at our table.

"Sure. Where should I wait for you?"

"Come help me with the iguanas," he said, and then stood up to leave. I grabbed his sleeve, almost snorting.

"Is that code? What iguanas?"

"I told you. At the bio lab. Mr. Carson's classroom. They need their lettuce."

Maryanne laughed again. This time Liz just put her head in her hands.

GREEN GIANT

It turned out Seiji's after-school activity was actually more like what I imagined Care of Magical Creatures class to be, except that these creatures were less magical and more unlovable.

I watched Seiji throw heaps of greens at wide-eyed iguanas named Jerry and Banana, then watched him dodge sharp yellow teeth in a bid to refill the water bottle of a red-eyed rat named Santa, then watched him promise a delicious mouse to an enormous one-nostriled snake named the Long Man.

"Who named these animals?" I asked, but I already knew. "Okay, never mind. Tell me why you named the rat 'Santa.'"

Seiji remained deadpan. "It's an anagram of Satan."

"Of course it is. Have you done this all year? Looked after the beasts?"

"I've done it since junior high." Seiji pulled on a pair of thick gloves and plucked an angry gray mouse from a small, isolated cage labeled Billy the Squeak.

"You've been hiking over to the high school laboratories since *junior high?*"

Seiji lifted the lid of the Long Man's terrarium. "I like animals."

"Okay . . ."

"I like animals." He set the mouse into the cage and closed the lid again. "And my mother died and my dad left around the same time. People at school didn't like me. All of those things were happening at once, so I started coming here."

My chest constricted. Before Seiji's suspension, a *lot* of people had liked him. That gaggle of laughing boys. Maybe they were assholes, but they were his friends.

"Seiji. I've never apologized—for the time I faked that black eye."

"And you still haven't," he observed, watching the Long Man unfurl and inch toward a scurrying Billy the Squeak.

"I know. But—look, I was so *angry* about the 'whore' thing. I had just moved here, and I was poor and I didn't know anyone, and that was my introduction to Rochdale. How could you call an eleven-year-old a whore?"

"I told you, I never did." Seiji looked at me over his shoulder. "My mother met my father while she was working as an escort. A lot of people are sex workers; it's just a job. I never wrote that word on your desk."

Behind him, the sluggish red-tailed boa began to unwind itself.

I felt so ashamed, smaller than the mice in the plastic cage beside me. Of course I knew what he said was true, and of course I knew Addy was more than her job, too. There was nothing I could say, apart from what I'd been withholding.

"I'm sorry, Seiji. I didn't realize."

"And I didn't realize you had dead friends."

"I guess we've really misunderstood each other."

Behind him the Long Man snapped and wound its body around the screeching mouse. Seiji closed his eyes, looking truly pained.

"I don't like to watch," he murmured, "but snakes have to eat, too."

NESPRESSO

The sun was setting by the time Seiji pulled his truck into a small parking lot behind the Main Street businesses. We climbed out and our boots hit the snow-covered pavement with a crunch. The sky glowed a fiery red.

"It's going to be dark soon," he observed, leading the way to a windowless door.

"That's good. Ghosts don't come out in daylight."

"I thought that was a vampire thing."

I laughed. "Yeah, I used to think that, too. But I don't think vampires exist."

Seiji frowned, jangling his keys. "Are you certain?"

"I'm not. But *I've* never met one."

"I've never met Keanu Reeves, but I know he exists."

"Huh." Did Seiji realize he was vaguely hilarious? His expression never seemed to say so.

He propped open the door, and we stepped inside what looked like a storage room. The smell of flowers hit me like a tangible force, a wall of unseen petals crushing my nostrils.

"I'll go tell Aunt Lavonne we're here."

"Should I come, too? To introduce myself?"

Seiji considered this. "She's weird."

"Who isn't? That's not an answer."

"Oh. Are you Christian?"

"No," I said, thinking of that useless Bible. "I mean, I've never thought about it either way. Are you?"

"I don't know. But if she asks you about the lord, just smile and ask about her flower arrangements instead." He paused, then doubled back. "Also. Don't tell her I'm gay."

Abruptly anxious, I followed Seiji past stacks of boxes and rolls of cellophane and shelves of ribbon. An industrial silver-colored table occupied the length of one wall, lined with vases and flowerpots and yet more ribbon, bottles of glitter, brushes, and paint.

Seiji pushed open a swinging door and we stepped into a space between the storefront and the storage room. I gaped, sorry I hadn't been there before. The room was warm and damp. Where I assumed there'd be a roof, there was a ceiling composed of several glass skylights. The walls of that long, narrow space were lined with blooming planters and pots on tables, blossoms in colors precious, rare, and unknown to autumn.

I didn't really know flower names, but I knew they were beautiful. I recognized orchids and lilies, and some other flowers I was certain shouldn't be blooming in November, but then again, what did I know about pansies?

"Is this an actual greenhouse?"

"We don't call it the greenhouse, because the women's shelter is called the Green House."

"So what do you call it? The Satan House, an anagram of Santa?"

"We call it Stella's Garden, after my mother," he said.

"Oh. Right."

"Most florists don't grow flowers; they get their stock delivered. We don't use most of these flowers, but my mother used to."

"I'm sorry."

"Thanks," he replied. "This way."

There really was no telling when Seiji was being serious or not. He dropped deep thoughts into every conversation as if he were adding minor chords to pop songs. But then, he didn't seem offended, no matter how I reacted. Maybe that was why honesty was starting to feel less like an awful mistake.

We didn't speak as we crossed Stella's Garden. I watched the condensation trickle down the roof, the red sunset prismatic through the glass.

We passed through plastic flaps and another door and entered the actual store.

The scent of flowers was met with the smell of warm coffee, and I was surprised to spot, amid displays of poinsettias and Christmas wreaths and roses, a few small tables occupied by patrons wearing headphones or reading books, sipping coffee in floral-patterned cups. The entire room, from the rustic wooden floors to fairy lights along the walls to the overflowing bookshelves topped by decorative arrangements seemed incongruous and strangely metropolitan. I'd had no idea such a pleasant place existed within a hundred miles of Rochdale. If Patricia weren't so afraid to leave the motel, I'd bring her here.

"It's a coffee shop, too?"

"Flowers don't sell around here, except when there are funerals or high school dances," he said.

I followed Seiji to the counter, where a bony white woman wearing a checkered apron was wiping down an espresso machine.

"Aunt Lavonne."

The woman let out a small squeak and put her hand on her chest. As she turned around, her eyes were spooked and strangely familiar. She reminded me of my mother, although I couldn't say how. My mother was not thin, and she had never looked as coiffed as this lady, whose hair was neatly drawn into a ponytail, lipstick perfectly placed.

"Seiji! I've told you not to sneak up on me."

"I'm not sneaking. I'm quiet."

"Yes, I know." Her eyes fell on me. "Do you need a coffee, dear?"

"This is my friend," Seiji declared. "We are going to hang out."

"Oh, really?" Aunt Lavonne's eyes widened, but she cleared her throat and tried to hide her surprise. "Of course! I'll make some lattes for you in a minute. There aren't a lot of orders today. What's your name, sweetie?"

"Dani," I said. "Hi. I like your business."

"Well, thank you, but it's not really mine. I mean, I do what I can, but this was my little sister's business first."

"But she's not here anymore," Seiji said. "It's yours now, Aunt Lavonne."

She seemed as discomforted by Seiji's blunt manner as most people were, and my chest ached for him, misunderstood in his own home. Aunt Lavonne plastered on a smile. "You two get settled, then."

"We'll be in the back room," Seiji told her. "At the ikebana table."

"Okay." She frowned, but didn't ask why her nephew wanted to hang out in a dark storage room with a stranger. I got the impression she didn't question him at all, almost as though she were afraid to—another familiar tragedy. "What should I bring you, sweetie?"

"Um, I don't need anything."

"We'll take two caramel cappuccinos," Seiji said. "Thanks."

As we walked through the garden oasis and reentered the back room, he said, "If you don't accept a drink, she'll be offended."

"She seems a little on edge."

"She is," he agreed, but offered no further explanation.

Seiji flicked on a dim fluorescent bulb and we sat on stools behind the silver table.

"What did you call this thing?"

"The ikebana table. My mother used to practice Japanese flower arranging."

"But . . . she wasn't Japanese?"

"No, my dad was Japanese. Mom and Aunt Lavonne are from Ohio. She just liked the style. She thought most arrangements were too cluttered. She said that busy arrangements were a smelly headache for the eyes. Ikebana is a lot more minimalist."

I smirked. "Like you."

Seiji's face turned rosy right away.

Aunt Lavonne appeared, carrying two cups. "Let me know if it's too sweet for you. Seiji has a mean sweet tooth."

"Thanks." She waited in the doorway until I took a sip. "It's delicious," I added, and then her posture relaxed and she left us alone.

Again, something about her reminded me of Mom. Maybe it was the buzzing anxiety in her aura, or her uncertainty, or—

"Hey, your aunt. Did she ever spend time at the Green—"

"Did you sense my mother's spirit in her garden?"

"What?" That was the first time Seiji had ever interrupted me. He must have been dying to ask, and I almost spilled my drink. "Your *mother's* spirit? Your mother—she's the ghost that's haunting you?"

"Yeah. Didn't I say?"

"No. No, you didn't." I set down the mug.

As if it made no difference whose ghost it was. "So? Did you sense her?"

"Um, no. I mean, it's not a sense, exactly. If she's here, I'll see her, like I see you. After dark, if she wants to be seen."

Seiji's shoulders slumped. "Do the dead have a lot to say?"

"Oh, hell yes."

Seiji considered this. "I wonder what Mom'll say."

"Seiji. What makes you so sure your mother's ghost is here?"

"Well, plant pots in her garden fall over. Especially when we set them on the table closest to the back door."

"Oh." I tried not to sound discouraging. "Is there anything else?"

"I sometimes feel a very cold wind in there, too."

"Okay." I couldn't bring myself to point out that the skylights were probably letting drafts inside.

"Also sometimes the flowers on this table arrange themselves," he added.

I spit out my cappuccino. "What do you mean?"

"I'll come downstairs and there will be an entire ikebana arrangement sitting on the table, perfectly balanced and styled like Mom used to style them."

I stared at him. "Why didn't you *lead* with that?"

Seiji shrugged.

"Okay, okay." There was one more question I had to ask, though I didn't want to. "Seiji, how did your mother die?"

Seiji didn't blink. "She had Lou Gehrig's disease. It affects the nervous system. She died a few years after she was diagnosed. Her muscles got really weak, and eventually she couldn't get up, and then she kept choking and . . . later she died."

"Oh." This didn't line up with what I knew about ghosts—she'd had a sad death, but not a violent one. "Did she die here, in her garden?"

"No, she died at the hospital. I was ten."

This really didn't fit. If there was a ghost in the flower shop, it might not be his mother, but I didn't say so.

"Do you want me to invite her to live at my place, with the other ghosts?"

Seiji looked at his hands. "I don't know if she's happy here."

"But maybe she *likes* haunting this place," I said. "Maybe she likes arranging the flowers, watching you grow up, and seeing her sister."

Seiji shook his head. "She and Dad started this business together, but he abandoned it when she died. He said all he needed was Mom and the shop and a fresh start in America; he wouldn't talk about family in Japan, but I think they may have disowned him. But a few days after she died, he left for good, and he didn't say goodbye. I've lived with Aunt Lavonne ever since. Being here after all that probably makes Mom very sad."

"Seiji, maybe she likes being around *you*," I reiterated gently.

"She probably doesn't. She didn't like gay people. And I look a lot like Dad."

I couldn't tell him how sad that sounded.

"How about I ask her what she wants, then?"

Seiji nodded. "Okay."

"And if she moves into the shelter, you should come visit."

Sarah wouldn't like that, but I didn't really care. I was tired of putting Sarah first when she kept putting me behind.

Seiji looked at his phone. "It's probably dark now. Should we go in?"

POP SECRET

When Seiji and I stepped into the room, the red sky had gone black. Moonlight provided enough illumination to see by, and left many of the misty leaves glossy and white. The air remained warm and damp, but as Seiji had mentioned, there *was* a breeze poking through the humidity, like a needle of ice.

Seiji gestured at the small table on his right.

"This is where things always fall over. I'll show you." He pulled an empty ceramic pot onto the table and took a step back.

We waited a few minutes, and nothing happened.

"Won't your aunt come back here and wonder what we're doing?"

"The shop gets busier in the evenings, when people get off work. She'll be busy up front for a few hours."

I hoped it wouldn't take that long. But if it did, I wouldn't complain. Seiji had trusted me with this vital task. I had never thought anyone would believe me, let alone trust me.

Our legs got tired, so Seiji retrieved the stools from the back room and we perched on those in the doorway. By the time I heard the plastic door flaps on the opposite side of the room move, I was yawning.

"Oh, hey," I said, assuming his aunt was making an appearance after all.

"What is it? Do you see her?" Seiji asked.

Which meant he couldn't see the newcomer.

I noticed the wrongness of the approaching silhouette. It was taller than Aunt Lavonne, and broader in the shoulders. Could this really be Seiji's mother?

When the figure stepped forward, I recognized the buzzing pallor of its skin at once. But it couldn't be Seiji's mother, because it appeared to be a man.

He wasn't alive, but he wasn't a murderous monster, either. He had more in common with Sarah and Patricia and Addy.

"Is she here?" Seiji whispered. I put a finger on his lips, wondering how the hell to break the news.

But as Seiji fell silent, the man stepped into the light.

I shut my mouth to kill a gasp.

The ghost met my eyes and dipped his chin, but he didn't stop walking toward us. In his arms he held a length of rope. His face was haggard and sad as he threw it upward, catching it on the rafters and pulling it back down into place. He tied the rope into a noose and climbed onto the table, sock feet passing through the planters.

"What is it?" I'd never heard Seiji sound so emotional. "Is it really her?"

I watched the ghost reenact his death. As he fell from the rafters, a flailing foot struck the plant pot and knocked it from the table.

"See that?" Seiji cried as the pot shattered. "See!"

I couldn't tell him. I couldn't tell Seiji that he was right after all, not about his mother's ghost, but about something else he'd said: Seiji *did* look a lot like his father.

"No." I squeezed my eyes shut. "I don't see anything."

HOOVER

If Seiji was disappointed, he disguised it well. He told me we could try again in a week or so; maybe we'd get lucky. He told me to come over anytime, told me he was grateful. I said sure and that I was tired and had homework. We said goodbye to Aunt Lavonne (what did *she* know about Seiji's father?) and Seiji drove me home.

I'd seen his father falling, suffocating to death, and fading to nothing.

I'd watched his father commit suicide. But Seiji didn't know his father was dead, so how could I tell him that? I couldn't look at him. All the other secrets I was keeping seemed like nothing, maggots to snakes in comparison.

Seiji helped me carry my books to my front step and thanked me again.

I waited for him to pull away, then made straight for the lobby, cursing my awkward crutches. I burst through the side door and threw them to the ground.

"Sarah? Sarah!"

"What is it?" Patricia asked, turning away from the wall she'd been reading.

"I need to talk to Sarah. Where is she?"

"I'm here." Sarah appeared cross-legged on the counter, as if nothing had gone crooked between us. "What is it?"

"Sarah," I said, too upset to care about her folded arms. "Can you look something up for me? Please? It's important."

She straightened, searching my face. She raised her hands as if to hold me, but then lowered them. "Sure, Dani." She slipped off the counter. "Whatever you need."

———

An hour later, Sarah returned from the library. Her expression was grim.

"Patricia? Do you mind? I need to talk to Dani alone."

Patricia looked to me first.

"It's fine," I said.

Moments later, Sarah and I were alone.

"I did what you asked. I looked up deaths under the name Grayson. And here's what I found out. First, a woman named Stella Grayson died in Rochdale County about five years ago. I found her obituary, no problem. Seems like she owned the flower shop. I didn't find any other Rochdale obits with the name Grayson, not recent ones anyhow."

"Really?" I allowed myself a moment of relief.

"I found something else, though. According to police reports, a man named Yukine Nakamura-Grayson died in Rochdale county about five years ago, too, but it wasn't reported in the papers, because the family demanded privacy. He wasn't buried in Rochdale, but cremated a few towns over. I don't know what happened to his ashes, but there you have it. Two dead Graysons."

"Shit," I said quietly. "*Shit.*"

"So who the hell are the Graysons?"

I hesitated. "They're a friend's parents."

"A friend? What, from *school?*" She tasted the word again, eyes narrowing. "Grayson. *Grayson.* Wait. Isn't that the name of the boy who used to harass you?"

"I harassed myself," I argued, and that was more than enough answer for her.

"Are you *kidding* me? You're hanging out with that asshole?"

"He's not an asshole." I tried to draw myself up. "And you know what, Sarah? It's not really your business."

"*Excuse* me?"

"You can't have it both ways. You can't shut me out and then shut me down."

I thought she might scream. Her eyes were incredibly black, and the walls felt very close, almost suffocating. Her pigtails rose from her shoulders. But as pages began to rustle on the walls, she came back to herself and sank into the couch.

"I don't care who you hang out with." Her gaze was heavy. "I just wish we could be close like we used to be."

I wanted to argue with that, to tell her that was as unfeasible as any fate other than death. If anyone knew time would not stop, it was Sarah.

"Me too," I said finally. "Let's work on it."

After a moment, she nodded. "There was something else. At the library. Ever since we learned about . . . about Patricia's family's situation, I've been keeping tabs on the family's fundraising page. I signed up for their email newsletter."

There was only one reason Sarah would share these facts with me.

"What is it?" Patricia demanded. She appeared larger than life between us, looming and pale. "Tell me."

"Patricia. I asked you to leave."

"You don't own me," Patricia declared, jabbing a finger into Sarah's chest, livid like I'd never seen her. "No more than you own Dani. And you don't own information, either, like some hoarding dragon. So tell me."

"You asked us *not* to tell you," Sarah said, deeply affronted.

"Things have changed." Patricia said. "Is she . . . has she . . . is she gone?"

"No . . . but she's in a coma. The family has thanked everyone for their support, and they've announced that they'll be taking Patricia Junior off life support this weekend, after her relatives have said goodbye."

The lobby went black. A rumbling began underfoot, and I heard Sarah yelp in the darkness as paper tore off the walls.

When the storm had passed and light returned to the lobby, Patricia knelt sobbing on the floor amid a thousand torn pages, Sarah's arms around her shoulders.

"Shh," Sarah said. "I've got you."

"Patricia." I hobbled forward. "The offer still stands. Do you want to go see your granddaughter?"

Patricia raised her head. "How will we get there?"

"I know a decent guy with a truck."

DUVET

She never appeared when Sarah was with me. She never appeared unless I was alone.

This time, Addy floated near my ceiling, arms out and bound, suspended like a trapeze artist while I lay supine in the bed below. Her gag was fixed but her stare was more so.

For a long instant we looked at each other.

"I'm sorry," I whispered.

She shook her head. Her eyes were scared.

I wanted to be brave enough to help her. I wanted to get out of bed and stand on tiptoe and reach up to the ceiling and pull her down.

Her tears fell from her cheeks but never touched mine.

Slowly, I pulled my duvet over my head and waited for her to disappear.

FRAPPUCCINO

The next day, I pulled Seiji aside as he lumbered past my locker.

"Is it about my mother's ghost?" Cutting straight to it, as usual.

"It's not that," I said, with a pang of guilt.

He listened to my request with a furrowed brow.

"So you need a ride to the children's hospital in Faylind."

"Not just me. Some of the ghosts, too." It felt so strange to say it aloud.

Seiji didn't hesitate. "Should we leave now?"

This boy was no asshole, no matter what Sarah said.

In the end, we decided to make the journey to Faylind later in the evening, to give Seiji time to talk his aunt into letting him borrow the truck. I also suspected Patricia would need a little more time to steel herself.

After school, Seiji attended to the iguanas and company, so I accepted a ride home from Corina of all people. I was pretty gimpy, and I suspected I couldn't avoid her forever.

We'd just pulled out of the parking lot when she blurted, "Are you and Seiji Grayson a thing now?"

I sighed. "What do you think, Corina."

"I don't know what to think. That's why I'm asking."

"Remember those crappy rumors you were so happy to tell me about, that day I fainted? About me being a lesbo? They're not true exactly, but they're not too far off. Go ahead and spread the gossip, if you want. I don't care."

"I wouldn't gossip about *that*!" she shrieked, almost spilling her bottled coffee. I glanced at her. She was angry. "I didn't tell anyone about your bandages, and I won't tell anyone if you're a lesbian or anything else, either. Not if it's the truth and you don't want me to."

I was probably staring, so she continued, "My aunt's trans. She used to be my uncle Joe, but now she's Aunt Jo, and I love her. I'm not as shitty as you think I am."

I swallowed hard until my desire to cry had passed. We were almost to the motel when I asked, "Would you mind if I send your aunt a Christmas card?"

"She's Jewish," Corina said, "but I'll give you her email."

It wasn't only Seiji I hadn't seen clearly. Maybe I'd been too submerged in my own depths to see anyone else.

THE THIEF

As I entered the lobby, Sarah was lying on her stomach on the floor, staring at a closed book. I thought about telling her about the night screams, about Addy's apparitions, about my cowardice.

I thought about it, but I didn't.

"I think you have to *open* the book to read it."

She didn't laugh, but didn't roll her eyes, either. "I'm trying to make it levitate."

I bit my tongue. She rose to her knees and looked at me. "You told me Addy's murderer lifted you all the way up to the ceiling."

Addy, on the ceiling. I shuddered.

"Dani? That's what you said, right?"

"Yeah, he did, but I don't know how he did that. He wasn't like you, Sarah."

"But you *can* feel us, a little. I know you can feel me."

My cheeks flushed. "Yeah, but only like . . . you feel soft like felt."

"But that murderer left *real* bruises on your neck."

"Yeah, but I dunno, Sarah. It was like he was . . . powered by evil," I finished lamely. "I don't think all ghosts can do what he can."

"Do you know how many times folks told a girl she couldn't do something?"

I cringed. "I didn't mean—"

"If I couldn't do all the things folks said I couldn't, I'd be a potato in a sack." She stared at the book again; there was a boy on the cover.

"You seen Patricia?"

Without taking her gaze off the book, Sarah jerked her thumb toward the counter. "Check the boxes."

I peered into every little mail cubby until I spied a small lump huddled on one of the tiny cardboard beds.

I prodded the bed with my finger. Patricia lowered her hands from her minuscule face and sighed.

"I'm acting like a child."

"I don't think you are."

"You'd think ghosts wouldn't be afraid of death, but I still am. Not of my own, but of all the other deaths in the world." She wrapped her arms around her knees, looking more frail than I'd seen her in ages. "I'm still so afraid for the living."

"Me too," I confessed, thinking of Seiji, of the things I could not begin to tell him. "But we'll be there with you."

Sarah didn't say anything, but put her back to us. I frowned.

Patricia's face was so little and so lost. "What will I say to my son?"

"I don't think he'll be able to hear you . . ."

"I still need to say something." Patricia climbed out of the little bed. "To my son, and to my daughter-in-law. To my grand-daughter, who might not even know how to speak. All my advice, all my education and experiences, they amounted to nothing. Look where they led me. I'm hiding in a mailbox."

"Nothing you did led you here," Sarah called. She was still kneeling on the floor, staring at the book. "Don't be stupid, Trish."

Patricia materialized beside me at her usual height, clutching her upper arms in her hands. "You say that. If I hadn't gone jogging . . ."

Sarah raised her voice. "If you hadn't gone jogging! If you hadn't walked alone at night! If you hadn't made your own choices or lived your life! If you hadn't been a woman! All those things—they aren't a reason!" She threw up her hands and the book lifted from the ground and collapsed again, landing splayed open on its spine.

At the same time, I staggered, as if the wind had been pulled from my chest. I leaned against the counter, dizzy, staring at the sudden color in Sarah's cheeks.

"Did you . . . the book—"

"Holy shit," Patricia cussed, then covered her mouth.

"There you go," Sarah breathed, eyes wide. Her face was victorious. I loved her, but I could not help but see her as ghoulish.

"Moving things is not about being evil. It's about getting *furious*."

We all stared at the fallen book, weighing the implications.

"Tonight." Patricia squirmed, looking at the walls and not at either of us. "Are you coming with us, Sarah?"

Slowly Sarah straightened, and then she shook her head.

"There're three things you should say to your granddaughter. First, tell her she matters. You should also tell her you love her, obviously." Sarah looked at me, and dread filled my stomach. "And finally, tell your dying baby granddaughter not to trust anyone, especially the people she loves."

"*Sarah*," I chided, as Patricia crumpled.

I strode out from behind the counter, forgetting my ankle in my anger. It was one thing for Sarah and me to argue, but another for her to attack Patricia on a day like this.

Sarah was fading from view, but I reached for her hand.

To my utter amazement, she felt almost real, as if that surge of anger had brought her closer to living, or me closer to dying. When I reached for her hand, there was something to grab, like the lightest silk handkerchief.

"*No*, Sarah! That's unfair. You don't get to be cruel and then vanish! Apologize!"

"Putting your hands on me now?" She tore her hand free, and I cried out—it felt like sandpaper scraping my palm. "*I'm* unfair? I'm trying to help these women. Maybe that means being angry—maybe it means killing their killers. But don't call *me* unfair, when you're *using* all of us, Daniela!"

"Using *you*?" I sputtered, overwhelmed by her fury.

"*Daniela Miller* spends all her time with ghosts because living people don't care about her! Have you considered *we* don't care, either?"

"Stop this, you two," Patricia began, but Sarah wasn't finished.

Her skin glowed fluorescent white. Pages rustled, furniture shook and broke.

"Poor Daniela Miller, teased at school! Poor thing, crying about bullies on the shoulders of women who've been *molested* and *murdered*. But *no*, it's unfair for *us* to be angry, because we should only care about Daniela and her stupid, constant, *living* angst."

"Stop it," I gasped. "Stop calling me *Daniela*."

"Yes, because *that's* what's important right now. Me, calling you your actual name. Why are you so afraid to be yourself, *Daniela*? Are you afraid of being a girl? Do you think girls matter so little, that you can't bear to be one?"

"It's not like that!" I couldn't begin to say what it was like.

"Maybe it's not." She began to fade, but her rage remained. "Maybe it's not about being alive or dead. It's about being selfish. If it weren't for me, Patricia would still be in pain and alone. If it weren't for me, would you even be thinking about trying to save another dead girl? Tell the truth. Would you be thinking about *anyone* but yourself?"

I shook my head, eyes welling, throat swelling.

The screaming in the walls, the voice that haunted me.

"Right. So don't you *dare* act like a saint now." She turned on me. "And for fuck's sake, I'll vanish whenever I damn well please."

She did.

I couldn't say . . . I couldn't say anything, and neither could Patricia, who waited for the walls and furniture to settle, staring only at the carpet.

CLOSE ENCOUNTERS OF THE THIRD KIND

In the face of Sarah's explosion and Patricia's fear, my nerves about revealing the lobby to Seiji had all but evaporated. I opened the hidden door and let him into the cluttered space. He couldn't see Patricia, but he made an effort to seem friendly, an effort that might have made me laugh on any other day.

"HELLO, GHOSTS," Seiji announced in a booming voice. "MY NAME IS SEIJI GRAYSON, AND I COME IN PEACE."

Patricia smiled wanly. "You can't say he isn't trying."

"Seiji, you don't have to yell. She's right next to you."

Seiji looked left and right but to his credit didn't flinch.

"Tell him I'm grateful for his help."

I relayed the message, and Seiji addressed the air in a whisper. "You're welcome. I'm sorry about your granddaughter."

". . . thank you."

Because it was after dark, and because she was not alone, for the first time since she'd come to us, Patricia walked freely out into the night. She paused on the precipice, but not for very long, and then let the moonlight graze her.

Seiji kept looking over his shoulder as if he might catch a

glimpse of them. I didn't tell him Patricia was beside him. He held the door to his truck open for a minute before I told him that they'd already phased through the side.

"Don't mind the soil," he said awkwardly, and we hit the road.

As soon we left Main Street behind, snow began falling in gentle puffs of white.

"You're upset?" Seiji asked, as we approached the I-75 north on-ramp.

"I'm not."

Seiji glanced at the rearview mirror. "Dani's upset, isn't he?"

"Definitely," Patricia replied.

"The ghost agrees with me, I bet," he said. "Is it because of where we're going?"

"Seiji . . . do you think I'm selfish?"

"Yes," he replied.

"Okay. Wow."

"But I'm selfish, too. Everyone is selfish. Some people just hide it better."

"That's a pessimistic perspective."

"Not really." Seiji signaled left and entered the fast lane. "It's reality. Humanity survives by being selfish. It isn't necessarily bad. I used to be angry about my mother being selfish, not telling us she was sick. And then about my father being selfish, leaving us behind."

I closed my eyes.

"But I realize they were trying to survive. And also, in a way, being selfish made them want to be greedy about their problems to protect me. In a way, *that* was kind of selfless."

246

"That's either nonsense," I said, "or very deep wisdom."

"Nothing is simple."

"I used to think you were," I observed. "I thought most people were."

The snow continued to flurry around us, clumps like ghosts hitting the windshield as we sped toward the hospital.

HIGHLIGHTS FOR CHILDREN

The snow fell thicker as we traversed the Faylind Children's Hospital parking lot. Patricia hadn't spoken again during the trip. I reached back as if I could hold her hand while Seiji pulled up in front of the main entrance. Through the glass doors, I spotted a Christmas tree decorated in green and red and gold. It was December. I felt my chest hollow out.

Little Patricia had almost made it to her third Christmas.

"I'll drop you off and go find parking."

"We'll meet you in the lobby."

Seiji touched my arm. "Should I be here? I can wait outside."

"No, please come in with us." I pulled a stack of Get Well cards from my backpack. "I have a plan to get us in, and it'll be more convincing if you're there, too."

Seiji turned around in his seat. "Is that okay with you, Ms. Patricia?

To my immense relief, Patricia nodded. "Yes, it is, young man."

"She says it's fine."

Waiting in the lobby with an invisible woman beside me, I

must have looked pretty lost. I tried not to speak to her, to appear like a normal kid on crutches.

A nurse seemed surprised when I said I was there as a visitor.

Patricia stood very still, fading in and out of focus beside the Christmas tree.

When Seiji rejoined us, shaking snowflakes from his hair, we approached the garland-draped reception desk.

"How can I help you?" The receptionist wore festive cotton scrubs.

"We're here to see Patricia Lyttle."

"It's past visiting hours, and the family has asked for privacy."

I glanced at Patricia, but her eyes were closed and her face was drawn.

"Please, won't you call Mr. Lyttle? We're students from his class." I reached into my bag and pulled out the stack of dollar-store cards that I'd filled with illustrations and well wishes. "We brought prayers from our classroom."

"You kids just keep coming. He must be some teacher." I could see her relenting. "Let me call and check with him. Can I have your names?"

Somehow I hadn't prepared for this, hadn't thought she'd verify our answers.

Patricia spoke up. "Say that you're Sammy Wallace and Dan Roanoke."

I repeated Patricia's words. Seiji's impassive face was good in a pinch, because he didn't look the least bit surprised by his new name.

"He says you're welcome to go up. It's room 624, in the hospice ward. Go to the end of the first hallway and turn right. There's a reception area where he'll meet you."

In the elevator, I could hear Patricia breathing. She didn't need to, but maybe the inhaling and exhaling was steadying her. I stopped glancing at her, because it seemed to make her breathing louder, and staring never helped anyone.

As we left the elevator and walked down the teal hallway, Patricia's breathing became more staggered.

My doubts resurfaced when we reached the second lobby. All the chairs were occupied by children and adults. All strangers but not entirely—I didn't recognize their faces exactly, but some of them had Patricia's features, and I *did* recognize their defeated expressions.

Patricia freed her hand and stepped forward. She walked quietly among them, peering at their faces with one hand over her mouth. She brushed her fingers in their hair and touched their shoulders softly as she passed.

The people didn't notice her, but they did notice Seiji and me. Patricia's family treated us to expressions of anger, confusion, or a numb nothingness.

It suddenly felt very wrong to be there, like we were staring at a car accident.

I took a small step back and felt my spine hit Seiji's chest. He put his big, warm hands on my shoulders.

"This trip is not selfish," he said.

I nodded and stepped forward, holding aloft the forged cards. "Excuse me. Are you the Lyttle family? I've brought cards for you and baby Patricia."

"I hope they aren't get-well cards," snapped an older woman. "That'd be tactless."

"Um, no. They're just . . . cards."

"You aren't my students," said a weary voice behind us, "and you *definitely* aren't my childhood friends Dan and Sammy. Who are you, and what do you want?"

We turned and there he stood: Patricia's son, Gary Lyttle. It looked as though he'd aged a decade since that video interview I'd seen in the library.

Patricia walked toward him, shoulders rising and falling, her breathing louder than ever, so that it seemed to echo like another respirator or monitor. I made the grave mistake of looking at her face: love and pain in equal measure. I can't imagine how she felt when her son looked right through her.

"As if she were a ghost," I mumbled to myself. I'd accepted the surreal for so long that seeing my friends discounted in person, treated as shadows, not the fascinating people they were, felt like a slap.

Seiji said, "You don't know us, but we need to talk to you."

"I'm not in the mood. Please, leave my family in peace."

I couldn't think of where to go from there. Just behind her son, I saw Patricia's trembling shoulders, her hair and clothes in disarray again.

"Your mother sent us here," Seiji said, as the blood left my face.

I'd known he was blunt but I wasn't expecting that.

Gary's face shut down.

"My mother is dead," he said angrily. "Go, please. Now."

Seiji pointed at me. "This is Dani, and Dani sees ghosts. She brought your mother here to see you."

"You're despicable!" an eavesdropping old woman declared.

"Sorry, Gran," Gary said, and he beckoned us to follow him. When we were several yards from the lobby he spun on us.

"I don't know *why* you're here, but that's enough!"

"Your mother loves books," I blurted.

He blinked. "She was a teacher! Anyone could guess that. Now, please—"

"She loves science fiction and fantasy books, especially ones with maps in them. She also likes raspberry Slurpees, and she hums 'Singin' in the Rain' to herself when she's in a good mood. Her favorite color is turquoise, and she hates jazz!"

"Most people hate jazz," Seiji added, like it was helpful.

"I don't know how you know this," Gary murmured hoarsely, "and I don't care. Go find some other family to harass."

I cut in front of him again. "When you were seven years old, you hit another kid and called her a bitch. Trish was disappointed in you, because she raised you better."

He stared at me. "*Go.*"

Upset as she was, Patricia cleared her throat and readjusted her glasses. "Tell him he used to go everywhere with a Sesame Street plushie of the Count, but he called him Toothy."

I repeated these words. Gary looked shaken but still mostly furious.

"What, you're pretending she's *here*? Fine. Why not. Not like I have a daughter to grieve. If my dead mother is here, ask her this: What instrument did I play in elementary school?"

Patricia listened, then answered, and I recounted what she'd

252

said for Gary: "You didn't play any. You threw a tantrum when she tried to sign you up for piano. And when you were supposed to practice the recorder, you hid it behind your hamper until the night of the concert, and she had to wash the cobwebs off it."

He blinked. "Ask her what I liked to put on my pizza."

"Canned corn," I said, but stopped myself from calling him a weirdo.

"I don't believe in crap like this," he said, slumping. "But I don't have the energy to argue with you. So tell me, why would my dead mother come here?"

"To see you," I said. "And to say goodbye to your daughter."

He rubbed his eyes. "She's a bit late for that." He looked at us with bloodshot eyes. "My daughter died an hour ago."

I looked at Patricia. She drew herself up tall, her expression unreadable, more skull than face.

"Is she still here?" The tremors had left her, leaving cold determination in their wake. "Can I see her? Can I see my granddaughter?"

"I can't ask that," I whispered. "It's morbid."

Her eyes flashed and she looked furious with me for the first time ever. "The receptionist told us the room number. I can go check for myself."

I could not tell her not to. I could only watch her walk past them all, watch the way the walls bent around her, as if every one of her exhales might tug the building down around her.

"Sorry for your loss," I managed.

"Just go."

In the elevator without Patricia, I began to sob like an idiot.

Seiji said, "He was probably lying."

"What?"

"Why would the whole family be sitting in the lobby if she was already gone? They were waiting for something."

"Waiting for what?"

He closed his eyes, revisiting some memory. "They were waiting for the end."

Seiji's hand was cold and rough and real in mine.

HALLMARK

We sat downstairs in the ER waiting room, accompanied by a terrible Hallmark Christmas movie about some entrepreneur who remembered the charm of her hometown and fell face-first into a boring hetero romance. Seiji seemed absorbed in the film. He looked incredibly awkward, squeezed between the narrow arms of the functional furniture.

Sometime after seven, he got up, said the word "tea," and reappeared with two cardboard cups in his hands. As he passed one to me, he said, "The little girl's alive, but not for long. The whole family's here because they're pulling life support tonight. They're just waiting on a few more people to say goodbye."

"You got all that from the cafeteria?"

"People tell me things," Seiji said. "I'm not sure why."

"Because you seem honest."

"Or I seem like a brick wall." He sat on the coffee table across from me. "She won't be okay. Your friend."

I frowned at him. "You don't know that. She's been through a lot."

He shook his head. "She won't be okay."

"You're being mean."

"Time passes. Eventually not being okay becomes okay. But she won't be okay at first."

I thought of Sarah, asking if I was okay, but never saying it was okay not to be.

"I'm not sure it works that way for ghosts," I told him.

"Ghosts are people, right?"

On the screen, the lonely entrepreneur danced at a holiday ball and finally kissed the handsome small-town lumberjack. "Did you say goodbye to your parents, Seiji?"

"I said goodbye to my mother, but she was comatose. I don't think she could hear me. I didn't say goodbye to Dad, because he left without a word. He didn't even take his stuff with him. He never called or anything."

I bit my tongue and tried to shake the image of his father's dangling feet from my mind. "So how—I mean, what made you realize he was gone?"

"Oh. He left a note for Aunt Lavonne, telling her to take the truck and business."

If he'd really left a note behind, Aunt Lavonne hadn't shared the biggest part of it. There were many reasons why she might have lied to Seiji about his father's death, especially so soon after his mother's. I knew she was religious, and I knew she was facing the reality of having to raise a grieving kid alone. Maybe she feared the truth.

I knew I did. If I bit my tongue much harder, would it bleed?

"When I see Dad again, I might punch him," Seiji pondered. "Or I might hug him very tightly."

It was weird and shameful to admit, because my father was a monster, but I said, "I feel that way about my dad, too."

Seiji nodded, wide-eyed and serious. "We're twins, you and me."

MOBIL

Nine o'clock came and went. Patricia did not reappear. Then ten, and eleven.

Without warning, Patricia stood between us, distorting the TV screen.

I stood up and hugged the air around her. She accepted the gesture wordlessly. Her mind seemed far, far away, filled with forests again.

"Let's go home," Patricia said. "I'm tired."

To my right, a couple were whispering to each other, reacting to my outburst.

"What are you looking at?" Seiji asked them. "My friend is grieving."

The couple coughed and looked away.

"Seiji, you're so embarrassing," I muttered, which was unfair, because I really wanted to hug him, too.

Seiji led the way to the exit. Patricia walked silently beside me. I wished I could catch her if need be, and I wished Sarah was there to do it if I couldn't.

Patricia didn't stumble. She stood steady on her faint feet, but her calm perturbed me. She was usually so scattered and enthused. Her solemnity was heartrending.

The snow had not stopped falling. A solid seven inches coated the sidewalk and lawn, boding ill for our long drive home.

"Oh wow. It's a whiteout."

"I'll drive carefully," Seiji said.

———

Careful as he was, the snow had its own agenda. We traversed the frosted freeway at a snail's pace, and even that felt reckless. Because the silence was uncomfortable, I switched on the radio. Old Christmas classics were playing, and soon we were treated to a jolly pop revision of "Winter Wonderland," complete with runs and saxophone that nobody asked for.

"There's nothing *wonderful* about winter," Patricia said. "God, will I *ever* see the end of winter? Do you think anyone in my poor family will ever think of winter as a wonderland again?"

"Patricia—"

"No. Let me be furious. I died in the snow and rotted in a ditch for *months*, and then I found myself haunting those woods for years, and do you know, winter *never* stopped coming. And it *never* stopped being fucking awful. Every year, I watched the snow bury me, and I couldn't even suffocate to death, not a second time. And whenever the winter returned, so did my murderer."

Seiji couldn't hear her, but I wondered if he felt the temperature rising. A pickup truck passed us at breakneck speed; Seiji skidded slightly, clutching the wheel tighter. Outside, I couldn't see the road signs through the white.

"I might have to pull over," Seiji admitted. "Next gas station we see."

"Winter is heinous," Patricia muttered. "They thought my granddaughter wanted a white Christmas. But maybe she didn't. She was too young to say what she wanted."

"Patricia . . ." I began, but what could be said?

Seiji slowed the truck to a toddling crawl. "It might be *more* dangerous if we wait on the shoulder. I can't even see the exit ramps."

Sweat beaded on my brow and the windows grew foggy. In the rearview I saw only steam. Patricia was a livid haze.

"I'd kill him myself, all over again, if I could." Patricia's rage cut through me.

Seiji lost control of the slippery wheel for a split second, but that was enough to yank us toward the shoulder and an unseen pine-filled ditch beyond. Seiji cursed and threw an arm out in front of me, and for a second I thought that I, too, might be haunting a snowbank for the foreseeable future—

But the wheel jerked left, seemingly by itself. With a final squeal and some breathless zigzagging, we were back on track.

The temperature dropped. None of us spoke until we were home again.

———

"Should I come in with you?" Seiji asked.

The snow had stopped falling, but there was plenty of it filling the motel parking lot. Patricia had already phased through the side of the truck without a word.

"No, it's fine."

"Okay."

"Thanks for the ride, Seiji."

"You're always welcome."

I paused, hand on the door. "No, it's a bigger thank-you than that."

He waited, face placid, but I had finally begun to see ripples in his expression, the movement beneath the calm surface of the water. He was a pond I wouldn't mind falling into.

"Thanks, not just for the ride, but for believing me, about the ghosts. For helping me, even after how I treated you."

"You're helping me, too," Seiji reasoned. "With my mother's ghost."

"No, I'm not," I choked, unable to speak the truth of what was haunting him even after all this, perhaps *because* of all this. "I mean. I haven't yet."

"But you will."

I didn't want to lie to him, but I did. "Yeah. I'll try."

Seiji smiled, genuine and warm, and his trust all but cracked my ribs. "It's nice."

"What's nice?" What could possibly be nice?

"I haven't had a good friend in years," Seiji pondered, "or maybe ever."

What would a good friend say to him then? Would a friend tell him that his father was dead? Or would a friend want him to keep smiling like that?

"Yeah, well. There aren't a lot of queer kids in town."

"There are probably more than we know, but you're right. We have to look out for each other."

I smirked. "The queer squad."

"The queerkuza," he said, deadpan.

When he left, I felt colder than ever.

"AU CLAIR DE LA LUNE"

Patricia stood silently in the snow, outside the lobby, shoulders hunched, clothes askew.

"Let's go in. It's freezing."

"No," she said. "No, I think I'll spend the night outside."

"Come on, Patricia," I reasoned. "Don't. Come in. I'll let you read to me."

"Dani. You should get some rest."

My heart squeezed shut. "Patricia, you're scaring me."

"Am I?" She looked back at me with pity. "Only now?"

Patricia ignored my gasp, and no amount of reaching for her would hold her. She slipped between my fingers as her vacant outline walked into the white night. Patricia dragged her feet toward the trees, losing her shoes, losing her composure as she reached the woods.

At the treeline, she adjusted her ponytail, picked up her feet, and began running.

"Are you going to let her go off like that?" Sarah asked me, as if she'd been beside me the whole time.

"Are *you*?"

"I saved her the first time," Sarah said, jaw set. "And supposedly you already let Addy walk off into the woods. Can't let that happen again, right? It'll become a habit."

I stared at her, numb all over. She seemed like a stranger. Had she seen right through me in the one way I never could see through her?

"What are *you* going to do, Dani?"

Twisted as Sarah's attitude seemed right then, I knew she was right. I felt, down to my marrow, that if I let Patricia go, she'd be gone for good. She'd end up lying on another path somewhere, erasing herself from the world. And this time, if I let her go, I couldn't pretend it was fate or her choice. Not when I could have done something.

Not when I wanted her to stay.

I gritted my teeth and started running after her, my busted ankle crying bloody murder as I pushed past pine branches and stumbled over frosted snow that cut like razors. At first I saw the flash of her iridescent scrunchie in the dark between the trunks, but then there was nothing.

I didn't stop, even as my ankle gave out, even after I fell from the brush onto a snow-buried trail. My foot twisted against a tree root and my face scraped the ice.

"Patricia!" I cried, trying to pull myself up. "Patricia, please don't go!"

There was only moonlight on the trail, no sign of her silhouette. I let my face fall onto my arms and sobbed. If there was a murderer in the woods, he could have me.

Silent footsteps approached.

I opened my eyes and saw familiar Adidas trainers, spotted with blood.

"Dani," Patricia chided softly. "What do you think you're

doing, on a bum leg? God. Sometimes I wish I could suspend you."

I craned my neck to look up at her; the moon shone through her face. It didn't catch on her tears, but they glimmered all the same. Every centimeter of her was disheveled.

"It's okay to not be okay," I gasped, choking on my tears, "but please, Patricia. Please don't be not-okay alone."

She crouched in front of me and shook her head. "Oh, *Dani*. I admire you, but you are truly a hypocrite. Being not-okay alone—isn't that your modus operandi?"

"I know," I told her. "Please don't be like me."

She sank onto the snow, becoming smaller. "Do you know why I took so long tonight? After they shut off the machines, after I watched my granddaughter die? I waited until they moved the body to the morgue, until most of the family had left. Do you know why?"

There was nothing I could say; we listened to the creaking trees, the drip of the weakest snow reverting to water in the dark.

"In that hospital—I thought—no, I *hoped*—I hoped my granddaughter might haunt us." Patricia shook from head to toe. "Can you believe that? I wished my own desperate, *painful* half existence on a baby. I hate my inability to turn pages or hold my mourning son, my inability to give you a hug. But the worst part is, despite it all? I still wanted that baby to stay. And when she didn't, I had the nerve to feel *disappointed*."

"Your existence is *not* pointless," I whispered. "You told me that. And it really isn't, Patricia. Not to me."

"Thanks for saying so," she said quietly.

"I mean it.

She glanced at me. "You and Sarah—you're some of the worst students I've ever had." She almost laughed. "You don't listen, and you aren't honest, and god knows you don't complete your reading assignments."

"Stick with us, and maybe we'll get better." I shivered in the cold, but the panic was fading, and Patricia was not. She looked at the sky.

"Okay," she said. "I'm done running. Are you?"

"Patricia," I said, when the cold became too much, the quiet too big, "can I tell you about my dad?"

"Only if you want to, dear."

"It's a terrible story," I warned her. "The absolute worst."

"I've rarely met a story that wasn't worth hearing," Patricia said.

I took a deep breath and exhaled the truth.

———

The day was as mundane as any other. It wasn't like Dad was any drunker or angrier than usual. I got home from school and he was already well into his Jack Daniel's. Mom was lying on the couch, treating a black eye with a pack of frozen peas. When I came in, she mumbled something about being too tired to make dinner, and not to bother Dad because he was busy.

What he was busy doing was watching TV in the bedroom. But when he called to me, I knew better than to ignore him. As I passed the couch, Mom grabbed my hand and closed her eyes.

She didn't stop me, and that's one reason I don't love her like I used to.

I could hear cartoons blaring through the door, the sound of crunching chips.

"Hey, beautiful," Dad said when I slid open the door. He was propped up against the pillows in his boxers. The smell of Doritos and alcohol hit my nose. "Come on up here. *Ren & Stimpy*'s on and there are some chips for you."

I was nine, and I knew better than to go near him. I knew better, but I still went near because he was my father. As I inched along the opposite side of the bed that filled the bulk of the room, Dad tilted the bag of Doritos my way. I leaned forward to grab one.

He took hold of my arm and dragged me onto the bed beside him. "Come on, watch cartoons with me. Your mother never watches TV with me."

He didn't touch me right away. But I knew he would. Ever since I'd gotten a little taller in fourth grade, ever since Mom had bought me a trainer bra. I'd cried my eyes out when she made me get one, because I already felt what I was and what I wasn't, even if I couldn't put words to the feeling.

"You're such a pretty girl," Dad said, combing my hair with his fingers.

I was neither. I was a boy and I had a lazy, lazy eye.

I wanted to be sick.

The horrid thing was, I still loved my father. It had never occurred to me not to. I watched a thousand movies on his giant television screen in that tiny room—he'd always spend money on cars or bikes or televisions, but not on clothes or food or school trips. After all, it was his money and he earned it, *goddamnit*. In the movies we watched, fathers loved their daughters, and daughters loved their fathers. My father had two eyes

266

and a nose and a balding hairline and strong arms, and he sometimes laughed or took me for ice cream, or kissed Mom and told her that he loved her.

And if he did the same to me, was that really so bad?

His hand kept stroking my hair, and rested on my shoulder, too. He pulled me close against his arm and kissed me on the forehead.

"You're growing up, baby girl." I could taste the whiskey on his tongue as he pushed his lips against mine. I kept my eyes open and stared at the television over his shoulder. Commercials advertised GigaPets and G.I. Joes, a thousand toys other kids might get for Christmas.

It wasn't the first kiss, but it was the last. Something inspired Dad to put his hand up my shirt, and that invasion, his hand inching toward my chest and its two parts of me I wished didn't exist, was too much. I bit his tongue as hard as I could, until I tasted his blood. He shoved me away, crying out and cursing as he spat.

"You fucking bitch!"

I made it to the living room, where Mom asked, "What's wrong?" before he grabbed me around the middle and threw me against the kitchen counter. Mom screamed and I saw galaxies when he smashed my head against the cupboard.

I woke up in the hospital. Mom was there and so were some police officers. Mom had a cast on her arm. She looked guilty, but she'd also saved me. Even if I couldn't love her anymore, I couldn't hate her, either. She reached for my hand.

"We're moving. And Dad's staying here."

But part of him came with us.

———

After I spoke, the cold really set in. The memory of that night seemed to double in size.

Patricia stayed beside me, close as she was able.

"God, I was so afraid to be out here. I thought he took the night from me." She grimaced, wiping away her tears. "But the moonlight on the snow is still lovely, when you're not alone in it."

"Patricia," I said, "I'm so sorry, Patricia. I'm a liar. I should have told you."

"Told me what?"

"I didn't save Addy. She's not out here in the woods."

"I see. So where is she?"

I saw no hatred in her face.

"Still in the motel, with her killer. She told me to leave without her. I—I didn't save her."

"But you tried, didn't you?"

"I don't know."

She nodded curtly. "So you can try again."

"I was so scared. I . . . ran away."

"By god, if you're *ever* in trouble, run and keep a blade close at hand and fuck the rest. Don't ever stay. Run and run and run. Understand?"

I couldn't answer.

"Dani. Two tragedies are worse than one. It's simple math. Understood?"

She waited for me to find my feet, and we walked home together through the snow.

SWISS ARMY KNIFE

I came through the front door long after midnight, haggard and spent. I was relieved to see Mom still awake, until I noticed that she was on the phone.

"Yeah, I hope we'll see you soon." She hung up and looked at me sheepishly. "Oh, honey. What are you—I thought you were in bed!"

"Who was that?" I already knew.

"We were just catching up, taking care of some financial stuff," she said, defensive. "He asked how you were doing."

I shook my head so hard I thought it might roll off. "No. *No.* He doesn't get to know how I'm doing. Not ever."

"It's not that simple, Dani. He's still your father. He has rights."

"He *molested* me, Mom. Those rights are totally the fuck *gone.*"

She closed her eyes. "He was drunk."

"He was *always* drunk!" There was nothing for me to throw, so I could only shout. "He called me his little angel, and then he put his hands in my *pants.*"

"Daniela! Stop it."

"It's the truth, Mom." My head kept shaking; saying it once meant I could say it a thousand more times. Like Patricia, I was done running. "I can't decide what's worse. Either you don't believe me, or you *do* believe me, and you just don't fucking care."

Mom was close to tears, shivering in her stained work apron. "Look, I'm trying to be understanding, Dani. I'm trying to be better for you. Give me a damn chance."

"Sure you are."

"I am! Do you know what my father would have done to me if I'd told him I wanted to date girls?"

I blinked at her. "You think he would have molested you? Gee, what would *that* be like?"

"Damn it, Dani! Do you *know* what I told your father? I told him to *stop* contacting us, and that we didn't want his child support. I told him we're getting by without him!"

"I want to believe you. But I can't."

How could she be both at once? How could she be a good mother and a horrid one, too? A victim and a hero, damaged and healed? Was everyone in the world just a tragic mess of gray?

"You're not listening," she said. "I'm going to bed."

I couldn't believe I lived in a world where men like my father were allowed to make phone calls and touch their daughters and keep on living just fine, and where people hardly worse than him ended the stories of good people like Patricia.

"If he shows up here, I'm gone," I told her. "I'm gone for good."

"Daniela—"

"*Don't* call me that."

———

I paused to breathe against my bedroom door, then pulled the omnipresent Game Boy from my pocket.

"Seiji's truck didn't steer itself back onto the road, Sarah. You came with us to the hospital, didn't you?"

"Of course." Her usual nightgowned self came into focus before me. "If I'm mad at anyone, it's not Patricia."

"Were you out there with us in the woods, too? Listening?" She looked away. "No."

I didn't know whether to believe her.

"Okay."

"I was busy," she added. "Getting the exorcism kit ready."

I slumped over, exhausted. "The exorcism kit. For *what*, Sarah?"

For once, a chill emanated from her, more winter than summer. "Tell me the truth—what happened to Adelaide?"

"I told you," I said numbly, but Sarah shook her head.

"You told me a lie. If Adelaide and her killer are taken care of, why do I *still* feel sick when I pass that room? Why do I hear her screaming after dark? And why, *Dani*, why can't you look me in the fucking eye when I mention her?"

We locked gazes, seeing each other for the first time in weeks. I felt like I was tiptoeing along a dangerous thread. Even though Patricia and I had walked home together, I couldn't unsee the vision of her jogging a path she'd already jogged too many times, I couldn't see how I was any different.

"Addy's still there, isn't she? You left her. Didn't you?"

"She asked me to."

"Oh? Well, I'm sure that makes you feel better."

"Like keeping secrets from Patricia made you feel better?"

"You still think I was wrong? You think she's okay after all you've put her through?"

"Maybe not, but the truth is better than a lie." I stared at her hard. It astounded me that we could stare at the same image and see something so different—a hero or a victim, a boy you want to bang or a boy you want to be, a favor or a fault.

Sarah's eyes were probably as dead as mine. "What do you think Patricia will say once she realizes? Once she realizes you left Addy in there?"

"I've already told her."

Her face dissipated, even as she tried to hide her hurt. "Oh, because you're buddy-buddy with Patricia now. Right."

"She took it better than you are."

"Gee, how nice for you. Meanwhile, Addy's being tortured four doors down. You could help her, in the way I can't—and you won't. Okay."

"Sarah," I said, drained, ashamed. "What do you want?"

"You know what I want."

I could think of two responses—neither I could face.

"You heard what Patricia said. About her killer?"

"He's still out there." I breathed in slowly. "He visited her every winter, on the path in the woods."

"It's winter now. We could go take care of him. Tonight."

"Sarah . . . I'm so tired."

"You don't even know what tired means," she spat.

"I'm tired of you pretending that you're some selfless ghost-rescuing hero, and I'm a mess and a liar, when really you're just scared, Sarah!"

"Scared?" Her tone was icy.

"Yes! Let's face it; you're fixated on exorcising these *random* killers because you can't face your own! But you know what, it's not that easy. You can't wish monsters away! It doesn't undo what they did. You'll still be dead, won't you?"

Sarah flushed, furious as a flame. "One confession about how your daddy touched you and suddenly you're an *expert* on fear?"

Sarah *had* been in the woods, she *had* been listening, and now her face was twisted with hurt.

"Right. We've established you think I'm terrible. We've outed some of my lies. So answer me this time. One more time. Tell me why you kissed me."

"Don't," she said.

"*Why* did you kiss me, Sarah?"

"Help me exorcise that murderer," she said, standing tall, "and maybe I'll tell you."

BLACK CAT

The cold didn't matter so much as the sheer amount of snow. I pulled on my running shoes as well as my coat. Sarah and I walked together to the other side of town and Holland Park.

"How's your ankle?" Sarah floated above the snow that clung to my feet.

"It's fine," I lied. I readjusted the exorcism bag. It was no longer a fanny pack, but a backpack. Sarah assured me we were better prepared this time.

I should have been afraid. I stumbled on the ice. I was only annoyed at the slush gathering between my toes. Sarah's insubstantial form illuminated the path—she remained to some extent my moon and stars. You can't pick your stars, they've been there so long.

"Should have worn my Docs," I muttered.

"Those big black boots? We had those when I was a kid, but people literally used them for working in mines and whatnot. Who *was* Doctor Marten, even?"

"I don't know. I think it's just the name of the brand."

"Huh." Sarah waited for me to rise and even offered me a hand as I yanked one foot free of the snow. "Does it ever seem strange to you, Dani? The way we all remember the names of random things—boots and toys and TV shows and fictional cookbook writers—but we forget people's names all the damn time. I mean, *all the time*. It's like real people matter less to us."

"I guess I haven't thought about it," I huffed.

"I have," Sarah said. "I've thought about it a whole lot."

———

I didn't recognize Patricia's tree right away, but Sarah did.

"She was right here," she said, "at the base of that pine."

I could barely see the path anymore, so I had to take her word for it. Suddenly it felt foolish to be out there, the two of us alone in the forest, hoping a killer would walk up to us and into our trap. It felt foolish, that is, until Sarah clutched her stomach and hissed through her teeth. The light of her skin dimmed. "Something's coming. Something really rotten."

"You sure?"

She nodded. "Sure as sugar. Get out the salt bomb and a firecracker."

"Salt bomb?" From the backpack I retrieved a cylindrical Black Cat firework and what looked like a huge wine bottle, filled to the brim with road salt. "How did you fill this up on your own?"

She skirted the question. "Levitation and such."

I could only imagine what sort of measured wrath would have allowed a ghost to levitate grains of salt, one by one, into a bottle. If anyone could do that, it was Sarah, whose anger ran in a constant buzz beneath her skin. Maybe I'd gotten that from her, not from my father.

We didn't wait long. Finding him seemed too easy. These

monsters were cocksure and accomplished in violence. They probably felt certain they'd wander around unhindered for eternity, as they'd been so often unhindered in life.

Why would they ever question that?

He materialized on the path like a puddle spreading. He wore a green vest and a turtleneck. Just as the hotel rapist had been faceless, so was he. A similar black tar ran like a fountain from the trunk of his neck, splattering the snow, staining the white an inky black as he walked toward us. He carried a walking stick, but I suspected it wasn't really used for walking.

Patricia had suffered blunt force trauma to her skull and face before she was throttled.

Sarah and I put our hurried plan into motion. I darted behind Patricia's pine tree as Sarah stepped into the path. His pace slowed when he saw her.

The black tar around his mouth parted and revealed a human face beneath, complete with a friendly smile and a grandfatherly beard. "Excuse me, ma'am, can you help me? I'm a little lost."

"He's pretending to ask for *directions*?" It was so simple and so fucking cruel. Most people stop to help the lost. Patricia would have done so, without question. She loved helping people and sharing all kinds of knowledge.

"What a dick," Sarah said under her breath, and then replied in her bubbly voice. "Sure, we can help you. We can help you find your way."

"Really?" He pulled a map from his pocket. The tar closed around his head and dripped onto the paper. He beckoned us closer.

"Ken oo halp meh?" he murmured through the sludge that

filled his expanding mouth. He coughed black taffy, then showed his grainy teeth. "I'm looking for Holland Park."

I gripped the wine bottle full of salt. Sarah grimaced and held her stomach, leaning against the other side of the tree. He approached her calmly. I watched him shift his grip on the walking stick, until he held it like a bat.

I shifted my grip, too, ready to strike.

"I'll give you directions," Sarah said, as he lifted the stick. "*Now!*"

I threw the bottle as hard as I could against the trunk of the tree. Sarah vanished in time to avoid the scalding salt, but Patricia's killer did not. As the glass shattered, he was showered in pink salt crystals. The tar burst from him in splatters and spikes, like he was some sick hybrid of a blister and a puffer fish. One black spike scraped my wrist, leaving a dark welt.

Sarah was already floating high above us, large and vivid.

"The firework!" she shouted. "Before he puts his head back on!"

"Matches?" I cried. It was lumpy, wrapped in duct tape and newspaper.

"There's an electric lighter taped to it! Just toss it and get back!"

I threw the hackneyed bomb at the writhing man.

Sarah snapped her fingers.

———

It was as easy for us to end him as it had been for him to end Patricia, or maybe even easier. I couldn't tell if that was more infuriating or revelatory.

Sarah whooped and screeched as the firework went off in a shower of lights and sizzling flame. The firework sprayed green and then red and finally purple sparks as the newspaper caught fire and swallowed him in its blaze.

It took only a few seconds for him to shrink to black ash and then nothing, as though he were made of tissue paper.

Then there was only the smell of gunpowder and absence.

Sarah touched down, face jubilant and alive. "That's all it took, Dani. Just like that, he's fucking *gone*."

"Is he?" I gasped, eyes streaming. "He is, isn't he?"

"Pink salt and a firework. That's all it took."

"Yeah. Sarah?"

"Dani?"

"Why did you kiss me?"

Sarah looked at me, eyes glittering and alive. "Duh. Because I love you."

I couldn't tell if that confession was hideous or beautiful, a truth or a lie, right or wrong, sickening or justified. I could not tell, and I could not think of how to stop her when she leaned in again.

What if she left me for good?

So I just fell still and let her kiss me again, laughing through her open mouth as some part of my soul left me.

DECEMBER 2002

SEIJI

DUPLO

That week at school I slept through most of my classes, and in the wake of a new self-inflicted haircut and clothes, I began to hear the word "lesbo" on the regular. Given everything else was going crooked, who cared what some breathers said?

Seiji sat with me at lunch and in the hallways. He asked me if I wanted to come over again, whether I wanted to check on Chestnut, the angry calico sprite.

"She's getting fat," he told me. "It's fantastic."

I nodded and did not accept his offer.

He also offered to visit the ghosts and said he could help out in the lobby. He could deliver flowers: poinsettias, violets for decoration. Whatever we wanted.

I nodded and said, "Maybe."

Every time I spoke to him, I thought of everything I wasn't saying. I thought of his father dead in his greenhouse, and my father in the trailer, and the way that telling the truth changed things between people, for better or worse.

Patricia was better, but Sarah was worse. Addy cried in the walls every night.

I didn't know what to do.

"You can tell me anything," Seiji told me.

"I know."

And that was the problem. If I spent too long with Seiji, what else would I tell him? Would I ruin his life by telling him about his father? Would I ruin mine, talking about Sarah and what I was letting her do to me, what I could not seem to refuse?

"You don't want to be around me," Seiji said, finally.

It was three days before our Christmas break, and Rochdale High was celebrating Spirit Week. It was Ugly Sweater Day, but Seiji had missed the memo or gotten it slightly wrong, as usual. His red-and-white-striped cardigan fit him snugly, revealing his firm chest and long torso, making girls whisper about him as he walked by, oblivious.

"It's not . . . that's not exactly it. It's just not a great time."

"Is it about Patricia?"

"Patricia's back to normal, reading up a storm." It was the one healthy glimmer, seeing her hum about the lobby, scheming up little cubbies.

"It's about Sarah."

"No," I said, too quickly.

"Oh. Then is it about your dad?"

His intuition alarmed me. "I haven't said anything about him."

"I know. But I remember when you moved here."

I blinked. "You remember what?"

"I remember that you and your mom left your dad to come here. You were at the Green House at the same time as Aunt Lavonne. I used to see you there when Mom and I visited. We played together in the family room sometimes. Don't you remember?"

I gaped at him. I didn't remember him at all. No wonder Seiji had always been so upset with me. No wonder he'd always tried to confront me with truth.

His face expressed a subtle note of hurt. "You don't remember."

"Wait, Seiji. I don't, and I'm sorry. But yes, I caught Mom talking to my dad." I exhaled. "And . . . I can't sleep lately."

"Bad dreams?"

Addy in the walls, Sarah climbing into bed beside me . . . "Something like that."

"Come to my house. The day before Christmas Eve. Okay?"

I stared at him, looking for any hint of guile. "I might never be able to help your Mom, Seiji."

"That's not why I'm offering."

"Pardon me if I don't believe you."

He stood up abruptly. "I am *not* the one using you."

I wondered what he meant by that. Was he saying I had used him?

Or was he saying someone else was using me?

POWERPOINT

"You haven't been yourself," Patricia told me bluntly. Sarah was in the basement with her projectors and PowerPoints, planning our next big exorcism.

The thing is, neither of us had told Patricia the truth about what we were doing, and what we had already done to her killer.

After being so honest with her, saying nothing felt worse than lying.

I should have questioned why we didn't say anything. I think I knew that regardless of what her killer deserved, Patricia would be livid with us. Patricia wasn't like me or Sarah, not now. Patricia was looking forward, trying to grow instead of decay.

"I've been more myself, honestly," I confessed. "This is me."

She frowned. "Really. In that case, give me a little more *honesty*. Because there's something I need to ask you, Dani. Something serious."

When I looked at her, her expression was troubled. "Have you heard Adelaide crying in the walls?"

"Yes," I admitted. "I have. And I've seen her, too."

She nodded. "My heart aches for her."

"I can't change that," I said. "She told me—I shouldn't have left her. I know that. But she told me to. She didn't want our help."

"She might have wanted help, but some people don't know how to accept it. Sometimes, murderers aside, the haunting comes from inside the house."

"What are you saying?"

"Exorcising my killer—it wouldn't actually improve my unlife, would it? Because no matter how he hurt me, he's not part of my life anymore. It shouldn't matter what happens to him."

"I . . . we're shaped by men like that, though. After my dad, I couldn't . . . after your killer. You said he made you afraid to go out."

"Yes, he did. But if it weren't him, it might have been a dozen others. At a certain point, someone reminded me to go outside anyway. He had no power anymore."

I hated that she was looking at me knowingly, as if I weren't full of bile and lies that she couldn't extricate.

"Patricia," I asked, "have you ever been in love?"

"Oh, gracious. Maybe. I *thought* I was, anyhow."

"What did it feel like?"

"I won't say 'when you know, you know,' because as clichés go that one wasn't true for me. I also think love is probably different for every person who experiences it."

I put my head in my hands. "I'm always so confused."

"My two cents? You might not know when you're in love, but you'll certainly know when you *aren't*. You'll certainly know when something feels wrong to you. Listen to that voice in your head, if you hear it. I'm speaking as a divorcée, here."

Would telling Sarah not to kiss me end our friendship, divorce us, tear us apart forever? And if that happened, who would I become? Who would she?"

"About Addy," I said, "do you think I should try again?

Patricia did not hesitate. "Are you ready for another teacher anecdote?"

I nodded.

"I always let my kids retake their exams. Always. Most of the time they wouldn't take me up on it, but the opportunity was there. Just in case they wanted the help. Just in case they felt willing to push themselves to do better." She shook her head. "This is a terrible allegory for what Addy's going through."

"But keep a door open," I repeated.

"Yes. And if you're ever on the other side of another door— consider going through it when it's kicked open."

The next day, I accepted the invitation to Seiji's place.

TARGET

On December 23, I shoved my half-assed present for Seiji into my backpack, combed my shorn hair, threw on a red department store flannel and a green beanie, and prepared to walk my sorry self to Murphy's Flowers. On my way out, I told Mom I was too busy to bake cookies, but wished her goodbye with hardly any ice in my words. We weren't talking much, but anger was exhausting.

Before I started walking, I popped by the lobby.

Patricia was decorating for the holidays. Sarah had really gotten amazing at levitating things, and she'd managed to string up garlands and lights. Now she stared into the white abyss of a laptop, translucent in the face of it.

"Wanna come to Seiji's with me?" I asked her.

"Honestly, you're *never* gonna convince me to like that guy. Besides, I'm working out a strategy for our next exorcism. It's happening, Dani. You ready?"

I tried to keep my face straight. "Oh? What is it?"

"The O'Connor Petting Zoo. Remember? Seven murders, a hundred years ago?"

"The petting zoo. Really?" She'd worked herself up to tackling the large welt at the base of the map, the place where seven women and a child had been found buried in a field, victims of an unidentified Victorian murderer. "It's the biggest case we're gonna find, so long as we're in Rochdale. Getting this guy'll be a great way to ring in the new year!"

"Yeah."

"It's more important to think of his victims," Patricia trilled. "New roomies."

I wasn't sure we were ready to take in and house eight new ghosts, despite all the beautiful mailbox bedrooms Patricia had created. I didn't say so.

Sarah started rambling about expanding the murder map regionally as well as chronologically. Eventually we'd run out of deaths to avenge in Rochdale, she said, and we'd have to go farther to find ghosts to exorcise.

But there would always be more. There could never be enough cubbies.

I peered at the map with its dozens of remaining local cases. Sarah's old house was still encircled in red. I hadn't asked why; I wasn't sure I ever could.

"You know, there's also the ghost in the flower shop," I suggested. "He needs help."

"That was a suicide. And besides, we aren't taking in men. No chance in hell."

I flinched. "Even if they're victims, too?"

"I get that you're becoming a bleeding heart, but *obviously* we can't let men live here. Men traumatized these women. This is supposed to be a sanctuary."

I wondered whether any woman hated men as blindly as she did. I wondered what Sarah and Patricia would say if I asked them about Seiji's father; would they welcome his big shoulders and sad eyes? We could board him in a different room, one of the empty motel apartments. He *wasn't* a tar-caked monster, but a wounded soul like they were. Certainly he wasn't the only dead guy like that.

"Come back early so we can talk strategy."

"Right," I murmured, and made for the stairs.

Just out of Patricia's sight, Sarah appeared in front of me and kissed me again.

"Merry Christmas, girlfriend."

I tried so hard to smile.

GOLDEN CURRY

Stepping into Murphy's Flowers felt like walking onto the set of some festive commercial. The air was warm and smelled of cinnamon, and small candlelit tables were occupied by snow-sprinkled people in hats and mittens. Candy canes dangled from the rims of flowerpots, and you'd have better luck dodging falling snow than avoiding all the mistletoe. Aunt Lavonne was busy behind the counter, wrapping roses into a bundle for a man in a very nice coat.

The man definitely wasn't from around here, or maybe he was but only came back to visit family at Christmas. An actual Hallmark Movie man. I got in line behind him, trying not to covet his Adam's apple. Maybe one day I could come home looking like that: mature and citified and unmistakably independent, unmistakably myself.

"Coffee or roses?" Aunt Lavonne asked me.

"I'm here to visit Seiji?"

She stared at me for five seconds before realization dawned. "*Dani?* Is that you? My gosh, I didn't recognize you. What's happened to your hair?"

"I buzzed it off." I knew she was privately wondering why I looked like a walking dead boy rather than a living girl. Seiji hadn't come out to his aunt, but her reaction told me an awful lot; until she saw my haircut, she'd probably prayed we were dating.

"Well, welcome! And Merry Christmas! Seiji's waiting for you upstairs."

She sounded jovial. It was grating to suspect—to almost *know*—that this smiling woman in a Santa sweater and crucifix earrings had lied to her nephew about his father's death. It was grating to think I'd met her years ago in a women's shelter, and she'd probably looked nothing like this.

She guided me to a set of stairs just beyond the counter. As I ascended, something savory struck my nostrils, and my stomach screamed.

I hadn't been eating for a while, not really anyhow.

Seiji came to the door after I knocked, wearing a pink floral apron.

"I am so glad you're here," he said, beaming.

My cheeks flushed. "Wow, something smells delicious."

The apartment was very merry, bedecked in classy wreaths and tasteful cards and delicate candles, as if Martha Stewart had been all up in this joint.

Seiji had made Japanese curry, of all things, like he said his father used to. He said you could order packets of the flavoring online, and that maybe it wasn't traditional Christmas food for most people, but it was for his family. He said also that just because he wanted to punch his dad didn't mean he wanted to punch curry.

In the corner there was a small shrine dedicated to his mother. I saw her face for the first time, captured in a small framed photograph. She had Aunt Lavonne's hair and Seiji's sticky-outy ears. Her smile was as sweet as his. She stood proudly beside a counter laden with floral arrangements.

"We'll leave her a bowl of curry, too." He set one in front of her picture and muttered some kind of prayer beneath his breath. I looked away.

The curry was freaking delicious, filled with carrots and potatoes and some sort of fried chicken called katsu that tasted like crispy twice-baked heaven. I ate like a pig, and when it came time for dessert, I discovered a second stomach within me and filled it with three slices of Aunt Lavonne's pecan pie.

After dinner we lounged on a very white sofa and watched "Merry Christmas, Mr. Bean," which turned out to be hilarious in the stupidest way. Chestnut purred on my lap, fat and cuddly after all. I wondered if she was trying to make up for gouging me to pieces the last time we'd seen each other.

"So how goes the ghost world?"

"Oh, I mean, we're planning on rescuing more ghosts soon. Giving them shelter."

"That's amazing. You're amazing."

I wanted to slip between the couch cushions. "Yeah, I guess it's neat."

"You're going to save them." Seiji smiled. "It's more than neat."

I had to change the subject. "Well—you ever heard about the bodies found at the O'Connor Petting Zoo?"

"I thought it was an urban legend. Like the one about the electric hermit who lives in the woods."

"Electric hermit?"

"Yeah, people say there's some kid in the woods who's got X-Men powers. Liz Becker knows him, I think, but she says he's just got extreme allergies."

"That sounds like bullshit. But the O'Connor Petting Zoo isn't bullshit. People really *did* find bodies there. Sarah and I are planning to head over there and see if we can't take care of their murderer."

"What do you mean?"

"Well, exorcise them. Salt and burn them, easy as pie."

"And that actually sends the killers away? For good?"

"We think it might."

"Seems too easy."

I agreed, but would never say so.

"Have any more of them hurt you?" Seiji glanced at my neck. "Or is it one-sided?"

"They've hurt plenty of others," I added, maybe defensively.

Seiji didn't argue, but crept toward the Christmas tree in the corner. It was tasteful like the rest of the apartment, clearly informed by *Better Homes and Gardens*. He pulled a flat, lumpy package out from under the tree and set it on my lap.

"Open mine first." I pulled it from my bag. "Don't expect much. It's a gag gift."

Seiji tore the paper with the reckless abandon of a six-year-old. When he realized what was inside, his careful expression shifted into a big, goofy grin.

"A *matching set*," he announced, holding aloft the larger of two red shirts.

"I told you, it's silly." But Seiji was already pulling the tee over his head. Chestnut didn't seem as pleased when he pulled the tiny matching one over her head and ears, but she tolerated his gentle hands without clawing his eyes out.

He held her up and looked at me. His shirt featured her face, and her shirt featured his, and I had to laugh. Seiji was beaming; Chestnut was scowling as only cats can.

"Actually, I take it back, that's amazing."

Chestnut tolerated her present just long enough for me to snap a picture of the pair with a disposable camera, and then Seiji freed her from her torment and put me back in mine, gesturing at the present on my lap.

"Open it, please."

I felt nervous as I unwrapped the paper. Inside there was a small cardboard box. "If this is a shirt with your face on it, I may lose it," I warned, peeling the box open.

Inside I found a tank top made of beige nylon or spandex, slightly stretchy material. The moment I held it, I knew what it was. I found it suddenly hard to breathe, which seemed ironic.

"I thought beige would be good, in case you want to wear white T-shirts," he said.

I blinked the moisture from my eyes and nodded, clutching the compression chest binder like a talisman. "No more ACE bandages."

When I finally looked up, Seiji's father was there, watching us from across the room. He walked past us toward the stairs, that hangman's rope in his hands again. A moment later, the door eased open and there was a thumping sound on the stairs.

Seiji heard it, too. His dark eyes scanned my face.

"There she goes, right? Mom was just here, wasn't she?"

294

"Seiji," I breathed, setting the binder in my lap. "I have to tell you something."

He waited quietly.

"The ghost in your house isn't your mother."

Seiji frowned. "Oh, but it has to be her. She feels really familiar."

"That's because the ghost is your father."

Seiji closed his mouth and opened it, then closed it again. "No. I told you, my father left. He's not dead. He's gone to Chicago or maybe even back to Kyoto."

"I'm sorry, Seiji, but he's not in Japan. He's here, haunting your greenhouse."

"I'm not great with jokes," he told me, "but I really don't think this is funny."

"Seiji." I put my hands on his shoulders and met his eyes. They seemed so impossibly *open* with his hair pulled back. "I'm not joking. I didn't want to tell you, but I can't keep lying. Your dad—he died here, after your mom died. Downstairs, in Stella's Garden."

"How do you know that?"

"The first time I came here, I saw him. And just now, that was him, too."

He shook his head. "No. If that was true, you would have said so. You would have."

"I didn't want to upset you. I mean, that's awful news to hear."

His laugh was dry. "Even if I believed that—why wouldn't my *aunt* tell me? If my dad's been dead for years, wouldn't *someone* care enough to tell me?"

"I don't know. He . . . Maybe your aunt was too religious to tell you, or too upset, or . . . I don't know."

"What are you saying?"

"Seiji, he killed himself."

He got to his feet slowly. I watched his face do something I hadn't seen before—it crumpled into despair.

"All this time," he asked, "you weren't bullying me again."

"What? No, Seiji—please, talk to your aunt. Ask her!"

He shook his head. "I wanted to believe you. I wanted to think you were my friend. That you didn't hate me anymore. That you liked me, that you understood what it felt like to be a gay loser in Rochdale." He laughed again, as if mocking himself. "That you talked to *ghosts*. Man, I must seem so stupid to you. Simple, stupid Seiji."

"Seiji, I swear—I'm not bullying you. And I *do* see ghosts. I haven't seen your mother. But your father's here, and maybe I can help him instead!"

He closed his eyes. "This is worse than when you framed me."

"*Seiji*—"

He opened the door. "Don't forget your binder."

"Seiji—"

"*Go!*" I'd never heard him shout before.

I walked past him and down the stairs, trembling all over.

In Stella's Garden, Seiji's father dangled from the ceiling, another broken pot at his feet.

"Come with me, if you want," I told his bloated face.

His eyes were pained and aware. He shook his head before fading into nothing.

LISA FRANK (REPRISE)

I went to bed instead of checking in on Sarah, and when I woke in the night, I knew she was there, sitting on my desk.

"How was Seiji's party?"

"You'll be pleased. It went downhill."

"Sorry to hear that," she said softly, "but you know, I'm not surprised."

"You think Seiji's awful," I said, rolling over, putting my back to her. "I get that. But you know what, Sarah? He *never* bullied me. I was wrong, and I treated him like crap for years."

"It's got nothing to do with whether Seiji's awful. It has to do with people being awful in general." She paused. "Sometimes I wonder whether either of us even knows what a good thing is."

I wiped my tears on my pillow.

"I died on my birthday, you know." My eyes shot open—Sarah *never* talked about her death. I watched her drift toward the window. "That used to annoy the hell out of me. I mean, couldn't my killer have waited until I opened my presents? I was supposed to get a hair straightener. Instead I've got eternally frizzy braids."

"I love your braids."

"Well, duh. You love everything about me."

"Not everything." I lifted my face.

"But you do love me, right?" She settled in at the foot of my bed. "You wouldn't have loved me if you'd known me in life. You love me because I haunt you, I *care* about you. Is that a reason to love someone? Just because they don't hit you? I don't know. I don't think so. Speaking for myself."

"Sarah . . ." She was scraping out my rib cage.

"I saw your gift from Seiji. What the hell is it? Some kind of swimsuit?"

"No. It's an FTM binder."

"FTM?"

"Female-to-male. It'll flatten my chest so I'll look more like a boy."

"Why would you want something like that?"

"I think you know why." I was beyond lying. I was tired and reckless. "I *want* to look like a boy, Sarah."

"It's hard being a girl and walking alone at night. I get why you'd want a disguise."

"It's not a disguise, Sarah." I exhaled. "Everything else has been a disguise."

She smiled a little. "Is this about the panda folder? That collection of boys you kept under your bed? I used to think you were in love with them."

"I wasn't in love with them. I wanted to be them."

"So you're a tomboy. A lot of girls are. I used to have scabby knees all the time. So what if you're a little more into it than I was?"

"I'm not a tomboy, Sarah. I'm a boy. An actual boy."

"Boys don't need to bind their chests."

"Some do."

She started to laugh, but stopped when I glared at her. "Gee, and all this time I thought I was living a dangerous lesbian fantasy."

"This isn't a joke, Sarah." I thought of Corina's aunt. "I'm not the only one."

"Well, I don't mean—I mean . . ." She stared at her chipped nail polish, feigning apathy. "I come from a time when people like that are jokes, okay?"

"And I come from a time when ghosts don't exist." I shook my head. "Don't pretend you're behind the times. You're more with it than I've ever been."

"Boys tended to kiss me or kill me." She looked at me, her face twisted. "Dani, I'm not interested in dating a boy."

She was trying to hurt me, but I held steady. Ending this was like drawing poison from a bite. "Good. Because I'm not interested in dating you, either. I never was."

She did not budge, but her eyelids flickered. "Never? Rightbackatcha."

"But—you said—" My stomach dropped to the floor. "Sarah."

She tilted her head. "Aren't we using each other? Isn't that what people do?"

"I don't know." It wasn't like I'd seen relationships to the contrary. I'd only seen my parents, the women at the Green House, my ghostly gang. "I don't know what other people do."

"It's after midnight. If I were alive, I think I'd be so old."

"Happy Birthday, Sarah."

She stood, a moonbeam in the windowless space. "Can I have a present?"

JIM BEAM

I borrowed Mom's truck. She'd fallen asleep sipping eggnog and bourbon on the couch, and it was easy enough to grab her keys. I didn't have a learner's permit, but I knew the basics. When we first moved to Rochdale, Mom told me I needed to know how to get away from danger. She didn't say so, but I think she meant Dad.

I wanted and did not want to think it, but I appreciated the lessons she gave me.

We parked across the road from the O'Connor Petting Zoo, in the snowed-in driveway of some summer home in the woods. Sarah led the way across the vacant road. The zoo was a seasonal attraction, and a yellow sign declared See U Next Sum_er! in peeling letters. The gate at the end of the zoo's long dirt driveway was padlocked shut, but it was easy enough to duck under it on foot.

Sarah waited for me wordlessly on the other side—I guess we weren't talking now. I should have been seething, but mostly I felt tired and cold, and this sort of numb resignation.

It wasn't like I'd truly believed Sarah and I had a healthy

thing going. I wasn't delusional. But her rot was my rot. Having her close—that was our normal for so damn long. And I couldn't tell if she'd been getting sicker, or had been sick all along, and the same went for me, too.

Now, staring at her floating above the long driveway, a pillar of pale in a field of white, I felt like I was seeing her anew. I wondered what it would feel like not to know her. For her to be a ghost to me.

Sarah waved for me to follow her. As always, I did as she asked.

I thought I had some inkling of why my mother had stayed with my father as long as she had.

The air was bitter, maybe only ten degrees with the wind-chill. As we walked the long driveway that was crisscrossed with empty wooden corrals, my breath crystalized on my lips. Christmas lights dotted the roof of the O'Connor farmhouse and barn a few acres away, and smoke spat from a chimney, gray against the starless black night. The snow had been plowed or flattened by tractor tires, and though my toes went numb in my boots, at least they weren't wet. Sarah's toes hung delicately above the tread marks.

When we reached a fork in the driveway, the residence felt too close for comfort. I saw a dog kennel beside the house. Should a farmer appear, angry and gun-toting like some television caricature, all he'd see was one creepy kid trespassing on his property, carrying a shit ton of fireworks and enough salt to fill a small sea.

"Supposedly the bodies were found under the alpaca paddock."

"How are we supposed to find that if the alpacas aren't outside?"

Sarah held her bloody stomach. "We're getting closer."

We took the left fork and made our way toward the barn. We passed a wagon laden with the remainder of pumpkin patch rejects, some frozen and some rotted and caved in. By the glow of Sarah's skin, I thought I spied a folksy-faced scarecrow, his hat frozen to his potato-sack skull.

Sarah flickered in and out of focus as we walked alongside a long wooden fence. "Electric," she observed, as I noticed the silver wires looped along the posts. "Be careful."

I wondered if Sarah felt electricity like living people feel wind.

No matter how close we were, there were always moments of unknowing, a curtain caught between us.

Sarah stopped in front of the third paddock. It looked as empty as the others, but Sarah buckled in half and gasped, vanishing like a popped soap bubble.

"Sarah? Sarah!"

She came back into sight, grimacing. "This is it."

I peered into the darkness. "I don't see anyone."

"No. It's definitely here. I feel like my head's full of aphids."

Seven women and one child, bones a hundred years old.

Sarah put one hand on the electrified wire and held back the current while I clambered over the fence. My battered ankle caught on the top of the fence and I fell onto my hands and knees in the slush, cursing and spitting.

Back by the house, like I'd feared, the dogs heard or smelled me. A cascade of barking cut the night air as I found my feet.

I wondered whether we should run right then, light the fence on fire and flee—

Then I saw them.

I saw *all* of them, standing a few feet away from me in the corral.

Ghosts in old cotton dresses, some in suits torn asunder, some in outfits whole and untouched. I spotted the dead child—he was a boy, and his eyes had been gouged out. None of the dead said a word, but stood statuesque, watching me closely. While they all had bodies, they bore only garish, naked grins. Their faces had been torn away, revealing white bone beneath.

Sarah had been right about the location and the spiritual presence. But she'd been wrong about a lot of other things.

If there was a killer here, I couldn't pick him out from the group.

There were the ghosts of seven women and one child, as predicted. But there were also at least two dozen *more* ghosts, men and women, lining the perimeter of the empty corral. Some had certainly died long after the turn of the century: they wore clothes from the fifties or sixties or eighties. One girl wore a North Face jacket. She might have died last month.

This wasn't just a mass grave. It was a massive one.

"Hi," I said.

NORTH FACE

None of the ghosts responded to my greeting. Sarah leaned against the fence beside me, wincing and bent double.

A dead woman stepped forward. She wore all black, and her hair was tied back in a dark plait. No part of her face remained, but both of her eyes did, floating white orbs in black sockets. She tipped her head and held her arms aloft.

"Welcome, wandering souls. Have you come to abide with us?"

"I'm not—I mean, I'm not dead," I managed.

"Fear not; you shall be one day," she said, not unkindly. "And you are welcome to stay here until that blessed day, if you so choose."

The quiet stillness of the other faceless ghosts chilled me. When she spoke, they did not blink or move. They listened to her with their heads bent, palms together.

"Sarah, we should go."

The gathering watched us, unmoving, beneficent.

"Not yet." Sarah gritted her teeth and addressed the watchful crowd. "We're here to avenge you all." She drew herself up as best she could, staring the half-faced woman in the eyes. "Where is your killer? We'll get rid of him for you."

It was hard to say for sure, given their lack of features and their eerie poses, but uncomfortable glances were exchanged among the gathered dead.

The woman spoke again. "We thank you. But there is no need to avenge us. We have long since forgiven those who ended us."

Sarah's face twisted in disbelief. "*What?* You forgave him?"

"Not him," I repeated. "They said *those. Them.* Sarah, there's no way they were all killed by the same person. They're from different decades."

"It was not one who ended us, but *many* brought us together."

"And together we are one," the others echoed, clapping their hands in unison.

"Holy shit," Sarah uttered in furious disbelief. "It's a *ghost cult.*"

Ludicrous as that sounded, she might have hit the nail on the head.

"We forgave them all," the woman intoned. "Through them, we found each other, and solace in the immortal existence. We are never hungry, we are never alone, we are neither cold nor bruised nor lowly."

"Solace?" Sarah said. "You're standing in an alpaca field, for fuck's sakes!"

"Sarah—stop." Their ghostly bodies pressed closer. "They want to be here."

I felt an electric shock travel up my arm as she swatted away my hand. "No. *No.* Even if they want to be here, I don't care about their forgiveness. So? Where are they? Where are the murderers?"

"They are among us," the woman said, "And they are murderers no more."

In that crowd of faceless people, there was no way of telling which of them had once borne a viscous face of tar. I realized it must have been intentional, and that meant—

"Sarah," I said, "why are *all* their faces gone? *Who* tore them off?"

"We all did," the woman in black declared, "for it was not our place to judge the dead for choices made while living. Here, killers and killed are equals. Here, we are companions."

"Then you're as bad as one another." Sarah's eyes weren't black anymore, but shone as bright as halogen bulbs. Her teeth grew sharper, and light sputtered from her skin in firecracker spikes of red and gold. "Tell me, which of you killed that child, and these women." She snapped her fingers, and the electric fence sparked and popped. The crowd shook at last, broke formation. In a flash of movement, Sarah got her hands on a ghost wearing overalls, lifting him from the ground by the throat. The rabble protested, crying out and closing in.

"Sarah! Stop it!"

Behind me, the dogs were going wild, but the sound seemed like a world away. I only barely registered porch lights turning on.

"Was it this jackass?" Sarah held out her hand and another man, dressed in jeans and flannel, was pulled inexorably toward her grip, yelping as she dragged his neck into her other fist. "Or this one?"

I tried to grab her arm, but it was like trying to hold a hot iron. I passed through her with a yelp, burning welts searing across my palms.

"Tell me!" she demanded. "Are you really going to shelter murderers and rapists?"

"Many brought us together," rasped the first man, as the second gasped in her grip, saying, "and together we are one."

"Do no more harm here, wandering soul," the woman in black intoned. She remained as impassive as the snowbanks, as tranquil as an antique black-and-white photograph. "Leave us be."

"Was it you, then?" Sarah produced a third hand—just as Addy's killer had—and willed the woman in black toward her. The other ghosts cried out as Sarah held her neck, but the woman was stoic like Seiji.

I fell to my knees, placing my scalded hands in the snow, but a great number of ghostly bodies pressed on my shoulders, too, a gentle velvet smothering that left me gasping.

The dead stretched and bent their bodies to wind themselves around Sarah's illuminated figure, separating her from the woman in black. These ghosts became ropes and walls between the two of them. I tried to get up, crying out at the heat, but pushing against the dead was like breathing cotton. I felt so woozy.

And I felt so far from Sarah. She was in another place entirely, glaring at the unreadable face of death.

Then someone dead took my hand.

It was the ghost of the little boy in breeches. "It's all right, ma'am."

"Dani," Sarah growled, eyes flashing. "The fireworks."

"No, Sarah! Let's go, okay?"

"Murderers and rapists, apologists and idiots! They don't get to be left alone! Light them the fuck up, Dani, if you ever cared about me."

My hands began shaking. "If I did that, you'd be gone, too."

"So what? Does that matter?" she cried, eyes desperate as she turned her gaze toward me. "You're outgrowing me, right? So just end it!"

I understood then what she was asking, and why she had seemed so distressed and cruel the past few months. Her reckless behavior, her kisses, her desperate acts of aggression, her meaningless birthdays.

How long had Sarah been looking to die again?

I felt a sob leave my throat and I shook my head. The dead were on all sides of her, their fingers on her skin, their arms around her in knots.

The woman in black reappeared several yards away, alongside a few members of her flock, serene in the face of the swarm.

"Please stop," I begged the woman, scrambling to my feet to fall at hers. "We'll leave. Just let us, okay?"

The woman tilted her blank skull toward me. Beside her, a ghost in track pants and a ghost in bell-bottoms did the same. "*You* may leave, but she is lost. We have found her."

"I found her first!" I declared, as fiercely as I could.

The woman did not flinch. "She does not look found to me."

Sarah screeched and the fence behind me sparked again—I yelled as a jolt of electricity shot through my legs and hands like knives. I couldn't get up.

I saw Sarah's hand emerge from the clouded fog of the dead, and I fumbled for the fireworks at my belt.

I *could* toss them.

I could do as Sarah asked.

The electricity had set the fence posts and a few ghosts alight, and they howled and slapped at their clothes. Sarah's face appeared above the mass of faded and foggy limbs. She held one hand open.

Her expression was angry and—oh god, *terrified?*

"Dani, please." She was crying globs of silver light as her arms and legs were pulled apart. "I'm never going to be better! I'm never going to be good for you! Just do it!"

How long had Sarah seen herself as my poltergeist?

I dropped the unlit fireworks into the snow. "I won't, Sarah. I won't do it."

She looked so crestfallen. The woman in black parted the crowd, who bowed their heads in deference, and bent before kneeling, sobbing Sarah. The woman kissed her on the forehead, then placed pale hands on either side of Sarah's face, caressed her cheeks, and began pulling.

MIRACLE-GRO (REPRISE)

When a ghost in track pants put herself between me and Sarah, I wondered if she'd be the one to take my face. I wondered if that would make it easier to pass as a boy, I wondered if it'd kill me or if it'd be another ugly thing I lived through.

It wasn't until the woman put her back to me that I recognized the shape of her shoulders and the scrunchie in her hair.

"*Patricia?*"

"You really should stay home and read books. Go, Dani. I'll get her out of this."

"Patricia—you're outside—you came with us?"

"I couldn't let the pair of you carry on. This is an intervention." Patricia nodded at the little boy in breeches and flipped on her teacher switch. "You. Young man. What's your name?"

"Alphonse, ma'am."

"Alphonse. You look like a clever boy. Are you?"

"I hope to be, ma'am!" he said, pulling his shoulders straight.

"Alphonse, I need your help. Can you do me the biggest of favors?"

"I can try, miss!"

Patricia jerked her thumb at me. "My friend is alive and in trouble. Can you get him somewhere safe?"

"Okay!" The faceless little boy in breeches squeezed my hand—*actually* squeezed it, as though he were alive and present—

Suddenly I wasn't in the corral, but a hundred meters away, back beside the barn, near the dogs barking in the kennel.

"How the—what did you do?"

"I nudged you, sir."

"What? How?"

Alphonse puffed his chest. I could sense his pride despite his lack of face. "I have been dead and gone a good long while, sir, and I have learned such a lot of wonderful things! I have learned the alphabet, how to tie my laces, and how to whistle!"

"*And teleportation?*"

"*Nudging*, sir."

I clambered to my feet as I heard Sarah scream. My eyes found the sparking alpaca paddock—it was too far away, way too far, but I ran toward it—

"Sir, you *mustn't!*"

The fireworks went off. Not one bundle, but all of them, in a shower of powder and sparks. The exorcism satchel caught fire and I cried out, watching the space go up in flames and bursts of color. A burning fence post had set alight the hay that jutted from the snow, tickling the tall grass and licking it up.

"*Sarah!*" I cried. "Patricia!"

Time didn't stop.

Life wasn't a movie.

But I could see how people felt that way sometimes. The moment of the explosion felt longer than the time it took. And trying to comprehend what had happened would take far longer than that. It was all too much for my mind to absorb.

I felt the needled sting of my hands, the cold in my ears. I smelled smoke and ash and fire. I heard a man hollering, and dogs howling.

Suddenly Alphonse, the little ghost boy, cried, "Sir, you must run! The farmer is most unfriendly and—"

Something heavy and toothy collided with my back, toppling me forward into the snow. I bit my tongue and spat blood. A hound was growling, teeth at my throat, hot drool down my neck. When I tried to roll onto my stomach, he clamped his canines around one of my ears. I yelped as the lobe tore away from the side of my face.

"Goddamn delinquents!" howled a furious voice.

This man wasn't dead. He was worse: living and livid, with a rifle in his arms.

Soon he was on me, pulling his dog back by the scruff and lifting me up by the elbow like I was a rag doll.

"You think you can fucking light my farm on fire, boy? Goddamn delinquent. I should beat the hell outta you!"

Through it all, I found myself laughing. I was *passing*, and I'd still end up dead at the hands of a man. But Sarah was wrong—I never thought being a boy would be safer, being a boy would just be more *me*.

I coughed as the farmer dragged me toward the farmhouse, cussing and threatening murder and the police in equal measure, pondering whether he should give me a black eye or two before the firefighters arrived.

Alphonse scurried around our ankles as the man dragged

me toward the porch. The boy (he was probably a *lad*, I thought deliriously) darted back and forth, apologizing, squeaking that he was sorry, sir, so sorry, but he couldn't nudge me if we were already moving, squeaking that he was rather afraid of dogs, sir.

"It's fine, kid!" I told him. "Just go check on Sarah and Patricia!"

"Yes, sir! Sorry, sir!"

"Talking to yourself, too!" the farmer cried, as I fell into the wet mud of the driveway. "Don't suppose anyone would even miss a rat like you." He looked up at the sound of an engine. "The hell? I didn't order any damn flowers!"

Despite the haze I was in, the farmer's words woke me up. I lifted my bleeding head from the mud, pulled myself free, and kneed him in the groin.

Before I got far he was on me again, pinning my wrists. I wondered if Sarah and Addy had gone through this, if they'd felt as angry and ridiculous as I felt, and how unfair it was that anyone could make you—

There was a swinging *thunk* and the dull thud of impact. The man yelped like one of his dogs and rolled off me, groaning and clutching his skull. A beautiful pair of black eyes looked at me, wide with worry, his hair still pulled back by a festive holiday ribbon.

"I just hit a man over the head. I guess I *am* yakuza now."

"Seiji," I gasped, as he helped me stand. "We have to go back for Sarah and Patricia and the others! Alphonse is a little kid—and some of those women and men aren't monsters. I don't think they are—"

"They're already dead, and we can't go back, unless you want to die in a fire."

"What if I *do* want to?"

"You don't. Besides, how can you say that to me?"

"Seiji—"

"Your tongue is bleeding." He led me to the car. "And your ear's falling off. You are *not* going back there."

"I didn't want to be fucking rescued!" I hollered, and hit him once in the chest. "I'm not some fucking girl in distress!"

"You don't have to be broken to need rescuing, and you don't have to be a girl. Don't be sexist."

Seiji strapped me into his truck. I felt Patricia's hand in mine. "I'm here, hon."

"But Sarah? Where's Sarah?"

She did not answer.

As Seiji pulled away from the barn and the burning field, the pounding in my ears intensified. I peered at Patricia's face, dead but still trying, and Seiji's face, too, alive but still trying. There was nothing else any of us could do.

SARAH (REPRISE)

SOPHIE

I thought I'd wake in a hospital, but I woke someplace warm and familiar. All the rooms inside the Green House were painted a soothing minty green. When I was little, I asked why this was, and one of the staff, a friendly woman named Shanaya, told me that green was a hopeful color, the color of saplings and morning dew.

That bright green didn't soothe me now. It reminded me of Patricia's son and daughter-in-law, longing for a spring their child could never see. Every spring was chased by another winter.

Aching and muddled, I tilted my head on the pillow. The dorms at the shelter usually housed up to three women, with a cot in every corner that didn't have a doorframe. Across the room a recognizable form was tucked under a battered old quilt.

Mom's legs were curled up against her chest, one arm draped over her face. She looked a lot younger when she was sleeping, but even now she was frowning. I wondered who had called her here, and how I'd gotten here, and whether I looked more like her or more like my father today. I wondered whether Mom'd had a moment like mine last night—a striking moment—when she realized she was in love with a bad situation, happily riding a merry-go-round of violence.

I saw Sarah: screaming and calling out, begging to fall off that ride.

"She conked out hours ago." Sophie looked a lot less cheerful than she had at the Thanksgiving party. She was tucked into a chair at my bedside. "We don't usually allow visitors, but Seiji assured us your mom hadn't harmed you. Besides, she's a familiar face around here. We made an exception. Don't report us, now."

"Seiji."

"Yes, he brought you here. Selfless to a fault, that one."

"I've hurt him," I said, swallowing hard. How had he found me? Why had he come after me? Why had he demanded that I save myself?

"He brought some of your things. They're in the nightstand. But now you need to rest, and then we can all work together to come up with a plan."

That sounded like something Sarah would say. I closed my eyes. "A plan."

"Your mother told us this isn't the first time you've turned up bleeding. We operate with confidentiality here, Dani, but I know a pattern when I see one. You don't have to tell us who hurt you—I *wish* you would, but we can't make you. What we *can* do is help you get away from whoever this person is. All right?"

"All right." I couldn't tell her it was ghosts.

318

But maybe it really was one person I needed to escape. Maybe it was Sarah and me, together as one, tied up like we had been for years. Maybe we were sick with each other. I didn't know how either of us would get better, but I was beginning to see the strings.

MOM

The morning passed slowly, but things picked up after Mom woke up, all her hair flattened on one side.

She wouldn't let go of my hand. "I'm gonna start going to a support group here on Thursdays, Dani. And I want you to come with me."

"What?"

"Whatever's going on with you, you can't carry it alone. Sometimes . . . sometimes I get that notion in my head, the idea I can carry everything alone, and I don't think straight, and that's lonely. I *know* I'm not okay. I know I've let terrible things happen to you, and I know I *need* help. But so do you, hon. Say you'll come with me, okay? Please, Dani."

Goddamn it, why was it so hard to be different from her?

"Okay, Mom."

Eventually we left the dorm and made for the lobby, which wasn't as cluttered as the one at the Teepee but was pretty busy and decked out for Christmas. Mom and I played Jenga and euchre with some of the women there, and when my ear and head and bruises began aching, I took some ibuprofen and melatonin and slept most of the afternoon.

Mom had to work that night, but promised to be back as soon as her shift was over. She told me to call her if I needed anything, and that she could call me, too, every half hour, if I wanted.

"I'll be okay, Mom."

"I'll always come back," she said, and kissed me goodbye. "Merry Christmas."

I drew the curtains and shut the door as soon as she left. As darkness encroached on the empty room, I felt too anxious to stay in bed. I paced, desperate for anything to occupy my mind, and remembered Seiji's delivery in the nightstand.

In a box alongside my binder and boots, I found *The Left Hand of Darkness*. I crawled back into bed and peeled open the book, surprised when a red envelope slipped from the pages.

Inside was a schmaltzy Christmas card with a cat on it. Seiji's handwriting was neat and blocky like the rest of him.

> Hey, Dani.
> I'm writing to you because we both know I'm not a great talker and I don't know when I'll see you again. I am pretty good at writing, though.
> I can't imagine how you'll feel when you wake up in the Green House tomorrow, and I'm sorry I won't be there. You should know it's okay to feel whatever you're feeling.
> I asked you why you're always angry, but I have been angry for a long time, too.

I was angry at my mother for dying, which wasn't fair, and I was angry at my father for leaving, and angry at myself for wanting to make out with boys. Now I'm also angry at my aunt for lying to me about Dad.

I confronted Aunt Lavonne in the café. I must have shouted, because a lot of the customers got up and left. She told me the truth, and she told me that Dad's ashes are in the apartment. All that time they've been in one of the flower vases and I never even knew. I don't know if that's more haunting than his haunting.

I don't care if Aunt Lavonne thought it would be too much for me to handle after Mom, and I don't care if she's Christian and thinks people who kill themselves deserve to suffer because that's bullshit. I don't know what to feel about my dad. He's been gone so long, but now it's a different kind of gone.

I came to your place to say sorry. I thought I might find you in the lobby. But when I was there, your ghost friend Patricia got my attention by creaking the doors and fluttering pages, until I figured out she wanted me to go down into the basement.

I'm sorry I told you your friends weren't real, when you're the only real friend I've had. No one's ever bought me a shirt with a cat's face on it before.

Patricia helped me go after you. She was pretty slow at typing, but she showed me the map and where you'd gone and you know the rest. I know you don't want to be rescued because it's a cliché for boys to rescue girls and you aren't a girl. But like I said, boys need rescuers, too.

I think if people cared more about rescuing each other we wouldn't need shelters. We wouldn't need to lie about death and all that.

I wish I could convince you that you aren't as awful as you think you are. I wish I could convince you that even if you've made mistakes, you've done good things, too. I think everyone's like that. All you can do is hope it balances out.

I am not good at ending letters.

Seiji

I read his words several times.
Darkness had fallen, but no one appeared to haunt me.
I was alone, and I really didn't know how to be alone.

———

The morning dawned snowy and bright, another Hallmark Christmas. I celebrated with a dozen other women who weren't exactly strangers. Their expressions were serious, but their kids smiled like any kids would when they received their Toys for Tots.

Maybe some of the smiles were strained, but the space was warm and we made time for charades between rounds of eggnog. I couldn't remember the last time I'd seen Mom talk to anyone outside of work, but she was swapping stories with a woman who'd grown up not far from mom's Ohio hometown.

Rolling Hot Wheels cars on the linoleum with a seven-year-old, I thought that a shelter was not a building so much as a place to belong to. If there was any way to bring that to our lobby, I wanted to try.

APPY

We left the Green House on Boxing Day.

"Don't come back soon," Sophie said. "Unless you're looking for work."

"Do you hire boys here?" I asked.

"We hire people, mostly," Sophie said, smirking. "So sure, we'll hire boys."

Mom didn't comment on that, not even when we were in the car. I'm not sure if she was processing the exchange, ignoring it, or accepting it. It didn't matter. Whatever she decided wouldn't change what I'd decided. It was never going to be easy between us.

———

After Mom went in to work and darkness began sinking through the living room window like mud, I pulled on my coat and stepped outside our crappy apartment. Under the ice, the sidewalk was cracked, paled and broken by years of footsteps.

To my right was the lobby. Maybe Patricia and Sarah were there, but maybe they weren't. Maybe they were faceless in the alpaca field now. Maybe I couldn't expect them to always be there waiting for me.

But to my left, someone else *was* waiting. I couldn't pretend she wasn't anymore.

I walked four doors down to apartment 7 and pushed in the door, ignoring the caution tape and the soot stains.

Fire doesn't just burn and leave a place ashen. It warps plastic into new shapes, it transforms a familiar room into a devastated landscape. Sometimes I thought about kids who grow up to be pyromaniacs, about the boys who set things on fire, and I wondered how much of that started with trying to change the way the world looks.

The roof had collapsed directly over the living room sofa, and pink insulation hung dripping like cartoon cotton candy. Icicles had formed on the roof, and on the lip of the broken coffee table. The walls were marred with arcing swoops of black, hell's graffiti, and the air felt less like it contained oxygen and more like a sulfuric impostor. You'd think a demon had been summoned here, rather than exorcised.

Standing there, I believed Addy's tormentor was gone, at least for the time being. It felt like nothing existed in this place, apart from the door and Addy behind it.

It was still closed, like it had been when she told me to leave her. I expected it to be locked, to be jammed or twisted by the heat, but the plastic-coated plywood eased open, revealing a bedroom spotted in black soot and black mildew.

Addy sat upright in empty space, on a mattress that no longer existed. The ropes were still around her wrists, but she wore them like bangles.

"Hello," she said, as I stepped inside. "I thought I told you not to come back here."

"You did," I said, "but I wasn't sure you meant it."

We didn't mention her hauntings, but I expect we were both thinking of them.

"Maybe I didn't."

"I came to apologize," I told her, before fear could stop me. "For leaving you here with him. No matter what you said, I shouldn't have done that."

"I took care of him," she said simply. "I usually do when he shows up."

"But he keeps showing up?"

"Oh, he always will. Can't change some people, and can't change what's been done," she said. "But I can cope with it."

"Wanna go for a walk, Addy?" I asked her.

"Do you?"

"Yeah, I think so."

Her shoulders trembled as she stood. Her legs seemed wobbly, and instinctively I reached out to help her, but she shook her head. "If you don't mind."

She led the way out of the apartment and onto the sidewalk. Her feet were bare, and under the streetlamps I could see the bruises on her naked skin.

Addy Williams paused to stare at the snow. "It was summer when he picked me up."

She'd re-formed her sheet into a toga, knotted at her shoulder. She looked like a regal ancient queen.

"You know, I have left before. I don't want you to think I haven't, hon. But sometimes . . . well, I end up right back here again. I always end up back here. On occasion, I go looking for trouble, because at least I *know* trouble."

"I don't know how you deal with it all," I told her. "I can't seem to deal with anything at all."

She looked at me, face set. "I come back here, but it's become less and less often. Less and less and less. Lord willing, one day I'll stay gone."

"Are you religious, Addy?"

Her tights were wound into a decorative braid, which she wore as a necklace. "Where I'm from, you don't even *ask* that question."

I wanted to ask her about heaven, about what she thought of her current predicament. But that seemed too big and abstract for the reality where Sarah might have left the world for good.

"It's cold out," she observed. "Cold and dark. Not really a nice night at all."

"Not, not really." I tried to hide my tears.

Addy smiled, like she was caught in a sunbeam. "But not every night's gonna be the same."

PATRICIA

I waited until the next night to visit the lobby. I stood outside the door for minutes or hours, scared to open it. But a little voice called out to me.

"Please come in, sir." The little boy in breeches gestured me inside.

When Patricia appeared behind him and hugged herself at the sight of me, I sniffled all the way to the couch. Little Alphonse sat beside me with his hand on my arm, light as tissue. "It's all right, sir. Tomorrow is a new day!"

I sobbed until I was spent. Patricia waited, quiet and gentle.

"So aren't you going to ask?" Patricia tilted her head toward me.

"I—" I swallowed. "Sarah's . . . Sarah's gone, isn't she?"

I wanted to see Sarah—I always wanted to see her—but I didn't want to chase violent ghosts anymore. Would my last vision of her be that screaming sadness?

There were still things I had to say to her, and things she had to say to me.

Patricia shook her head. "Most of the O'Connor ghosts escaped the fire, apart from the woman in black."

"God rest her," Alphonse said quietly, doffing his cap.

"Sarah, too. I think she got away."

I nearly slid off the couch. "So where is she? Why hasn't she come home?"

Patricia stood up. "There's something you should see."

I followed her down the stairs.

———

"I have been trying to find Sarah. I think she may have returned to her place of death, like I nearly did. Those places have a certain pull for us."

I thought of Addy. "Less and less. Okay. Her old house?"

"Yes." Patricia pulled up Sarah's map. She had been updating it regularly, blacking out the red spots where we'd exorcised or "saved" ghosts. "For a girl who never experienced the wonders of Mavis Beacon, she was so good on a keyboard. Did you know that the spots on her map hyperlink to all her compiled research on each location? If this were a research project from one of my students, I'd give her an A."

Patricia clicked on the grocery store and we were redirected to a folder titled *Malcolm, Tina*. Inside were pictures of a murdered cashier, from her childhood to her Employee of the Month photo. There was a copy of her résumé and evidence she'd once been on the honor roll, the kind of ghostly information that will trail us all to the grave.

"It's so detailed," I whispered, sitting on the floor beside her.

"Yes, it is. She's been incredibly organized. But more than that, she's been incredibly empathetic, Dani. Did you know that she included lists of each person's favorite things, including food they might miss and ask to have on hand when they arrived? She built family trees to see who'd miss them. In my own folder, I found notes on how she could help me reach my family, if I asked."

I pulled my knees in tight. "I had no idea."

"There's something else, Dani. Sarah kept folders on the killers, too, but she kept them separate and password protected, as if she wanted to protect each woman as best she could. I think it is easy to see Sarah as vengeful, but she is so much more than that. We wouldn't have loved her so much if that was all there was to her."

Patricia gave me a moment to my thoughts, then returned to the map. "There's only one location that doesn't link to an external file." I knew the house she'd point at even before the cursor moved.

"That's where I met Sarah. Her old house—our old house."

"At 134 Abbott Row?"

I nodded.

"I thought as much. This is the only address she *hasn't* looked up, according to her search history."

"Well, she already knows what happened there."

"Did Sarah ever tell *you* what happened there, Dani?"

"I promised never to ask. She said she'd leave if I did."

"Usually I would say that was her business. But when Sarah got into my business, I got a new home. Being nosy isn't always a criminal offense. Dani, has Sarah told you anything at all about her killer?"

"No. She wouldn't. Just that one hint, the night we talked about the shelter."

Patricia nodded. "She said she couldn't exorcise her killer, because he's still alive. Did Sarah ever tell you her last name?"

"Never."

"When I checked the real estate records of the house on Abbott, I discovered that two families lived there in the 1970s. The first was a couple with no children, but the second was a family of six—the Zielinskis. The Zielinskis had two daughters and two sons and lived in that house from 1974 to 1979."

"Sarah . . . Zielinski." Knowing her full name made her seem like someone else. "Was there a Sarah Zielinski?"

"There was, according to the 1976 Rochdale High yearbook. Sarah Jean Zielinski, class of 1979. Here's a picture of her as a freshman."

The photo left me breathless. I'd never seen Sarah wear anything but her white nightgown. There she was, long dark hair parted down the center, big goofy smile on her freckled face, wearing a brown tasseled vest and a rainbow-striped shirt.

The living Sarah, the girl I'd never known—she had been there all along, but I hadn't looked for her. Maybe I'd been respecting her wishes, but maybe I'd wanted my Sarah to be the only Sarah that existed. It was either selfish or selfless, but I couldn't pretend Sarah had ever been mine.

"Did you . . . what did her obituary say?"

Patricia whistled, long and soft. "That's the trouble. There wasn't an obituary. In fact, according to the records, Sarah's family reported her missing in 1976."

Patricia showed me the yearbook photo again, but this time it was smaller, a grainy black-and-white image slapped on a MISSING poster.

"The police thought she was a runaway, and the family agreed that was likely. Sarah had a history of running away from home. Eventually the Zielinskis accepted that she wasn't coming back, and moved away without her."

"But she hadn't run away," I whispered. "Oh *god*, she was right there with them, right there in that house. She had to *hear* them giving up on her, packing up and moving on without her. I mean—how could they not have known?" I thought of Sarah under the beds of her brothers or sisters, unseen and alone. "Why wouldn't they have felt her there?"

"Not everyone's like you, Dani. But only Sarah could say if they knew she was there."

I inhaled, covering my dead eye. "Someone in her family might have put her there."

I knew the statistics. I knew what was likely. Long ago, when I first met Sarah, I asked her, didn't I? *Did you know that the majority of murder victims are killed by acquaintances or family members?*

I'd never forget Sarah's answer.

Yeah, I definitely know that.

Maybe I'd guessed it, like she'd guessed the truth about my father's wandering hands. But neither of us chose to breach that delicate silence. "But . . . her body?"

"Sarah Zielinski's body has never been discovered, and that's one reason she's still listed as missing, not deceased. Whoever killed her may be out there growing old, watching football, attending the weddings of their children. Similar evils occur every day. Her body might still be in that house, Dani."

I stood. "I hope the rest of her is, too, so we can bring her home."

SEIJI

Seiji was leaning over the silver table in the storage room, carefully plugging reeds into a rectangular plant pot. The entire counter was lined with minimalist arrangements, single lilies with leaves folded into curves, purple blossoms, and bark.

"Hey, I heard you're in a gang. I've got a few scars now—can I join?"

Seiji stood up and nearly knocked the pot from the table. There wasn't much to catch—just some ribbon grass, but Seiji set each stalk carefully back where it had been. It took more than a minute. Once he was finished, he strode forward and wrapped his big arms around me.

It was the softest bear hug. I hugged him right back.

"How are you?" I asked.

He shrugged and blinked damp eyes.

"Yeah, I second that."

"I've been doing a lot of ikebana."

"I like your arrangements. They seem simple but they're really, really not."

"Oh." Seiji blushed a brilliant red.

"Seiji, do you want me to try talking to your dad?"

He shook his head. "I can't punch him anymore."

"Um . . . what does that mean?"

"I need time to think of what to say to him. I don't want to mess it up."

Over his shoulder, I saw his father's ghost watching the pair of us.

"Sounds like a plan. Seiji, can you help me with something important?"

"I can try."

That was about the best anyone could do.

As we left the back room, he hesitated and glanced at the cluttered shelves.

"Is he here now?" he asked, his voice breaking.

"Yeah, Seiji. He is."

"Don't go anywhere," Seiji commanded of the air. "Don't you *dare*, Dad."

SARAH ZIELINSKI

The house on Abbot had been on the market since we'd left it behind. It was a dump when we moved in, and a dump when we moved out, and even now the house was decorated as though *The Brady Bunch* were still on the air and shag carpets ruled.

I doubted it had ever been stylish, but for me it wasn't so hard to imagine how two bedrooms, a family room, and a basement had housed a family of six. I'd lived in a trailer park for years. Proximity like that was unpleasant, but possible.

Seiji knocked the door in with a single kick. I bit down another yakuza joke as we stepped inside. There was still some neglected furniture in the family room, a table we hadn't bothered moving and a three-legged chair coated in dust. The air smelled of mildew and cold, and rats had made their home in the corners.

"SARAH?" Seiji hollered. "WE'VE COME TO BRING YOU HOME!"

So much for tact or caution. But of course if Sarah were here—and I felt certain she was—all the caution in the world wouldn't make a difference. She would already know we were here.

Maybe bringing Seiji was a mistake, but I didn't want to do this without him. Seiji wasn't here to rescue me if I got into trouble, but as company, as a guarantee of my not having to walk home alone later.

"Where should we start?" Seiji had brought a bag of picks and shovels from the shop.

"The bedroom's where I met her."

"That's where she died, but maybe not where her body was buried," Seiji pointed out. "What if her killer buried her in the woods? In a lake? Or anywhere?"

"I don't have any other ideas."

Seiji nodded. "It won't hurt to make sure."

Oh, it could hurt, but what else could we do.

We began dismantling my old bedroom, prying up the floorboards with a crowbar. Beneath the sordid carpet and wooden planks we found only impenetrable concrete. I mentioned the closet, so Seiji beat through the back of it with the shovel until we could see my mother's old room on the opposite side. When all the floors and closets in the house failed us, we hacked holes in the bathroom walls and pried off the kitchen cupboards. We went outside and searched the side of the house. Seiji kicked in the tiny grate over the crawl space and I crept inside, gasping on cobwebs, discovering dead things that were not Sarah: spiders and rats, mostly.

I emerged empty-handed and coughing, on the brink of tears. "What if she really isn't here?"

Seiji patted me on the back. "A lot of times on TV, it's the backyard."

"The yard is *tiny*." It was past midnight, the air brittle with cold.

"That will make it easier to search."

Seiji kicked at the frozen dirt and found several places where the turf seemed wrong; he said he'd spent enough time around growing things to know when something was amiss. Maybe he was bullshitting me, trying to make our mission seem less futile. We raided the shed and combed the garage, and I imagined I saw her everywhere.

As dawn approached, I collapsed at the foot of the only tree in the backyard (there were no bones beneath it, not that we could find). The roots dug into my tailbone.

"We haven't checked *all* the walls yet. I can tear up the kitchen tiles."

"You don't have to, Seiji."

"I'm going to," he said, and he lumbered back into the house, a shovel in one hand and a hammer in the other.

Would I ever be strong like him? Would I ever be strong in any way at all?

"Aren't you tired, Dani?"

Very slowly, I turned my gaze upward, tracing the tree trunk at my back. I could only see her feet hanging down from a branch yards above my head. I'd know those ten toes anywhere.

"I *am* tired, Sarah. Aren't you?"

"My body's not here, you know," she said. "Don't you think I'd have told you if it was?"

"I don't know, Sarah," I replied. "There's a lot you didn't tell me."

"Rightbackatcha. Maybe you were right about our secrets. You should have told me about your becoming a boy, for instance."

"Damn it, Sarah, I didn't *become* anything."

I heard the leaves rustle. Her voice carried its old sarcasm, but had it always sounded so forced?

"See? I see why you couldn't love me. I'm not a good person."

"You're not a bad one, either. And I really did love you."

"I've hurt you for years." She laughed without humor. "But you couldn't even do me the favor of exorcising me."

"Maybe I'm a bad person, too. I've been too selfish to let you go."

The leaves stilled. "You realize we're in a toxic relationship, right?"

I nodded. "Yeah. But that doesn't mean you should die for it. Again."

"If I were a better person," she said, so quietly she might have been the wind, "if I were better, I'd tell you that I think I'm only here because I'm sapping your life. I'd tell you that you should wash yourself clean of all of us, Dani, and life might go better for you. You might start winning all your races."

"I can't wash away the people I love." It was so hard, trying not to climb up that tree after her, splinters be damned.

"You're fifteen, for Christ's sake. Go make some stupid, petty decisions!"

"Maybe you were angry, Sarah. But even if your intentions were messed up, we have helped a few people." I thought of Seiji's words. "Maybe it equals out."

"I thought that one day I'd feel better. When I met you, I really thought I would." The wind rippled through her shaking feet. "But I bled for a long time, Dani. And I'm stuck in perpetual teen angst. Can you even imagine?"

I laughed. "No, that's gotta be hell for sure."

"I was barely older than you. I'm *still* immature and anxious and that can't change. I died before I knew what to live for. Isn't that the fucking worst?"

"The worst. Sarah?"

"Go ahead," she huffed. "Get it over with."

"Who killed you?"

"Who do you think?"

"Your father." I breathed in memories of alcohol breath and the feel of creeping hands.

"My brother, my uncle, my father. What difference does it make? My whole family covered it up. They all helped bury me, while my mother hid inside." Sarah spoke matter-of-factly, but I heard the branches shudder. "He'd been doing things to me for years. I thought it meant he loved me, but when I got older—I realized . . . I tried to leave."

She ran away more than once.

"I wish you'd left them for good."

"I should have," she said. "So I think I'll leave now."

I could see the bottom of her chin, but not her eyes. "Sarah?"

"I don't want to be like them," she confided. "God, I don't want to love you the wrong way, Dani."

"You wouldn't."

"You and me have been fucked for a long time."

I knew that, but I couldn't imagine anything else.

"I'll miss you," I said finally. "I'll miss you every damn minute."

"You might," she acknowledged. "But you know, minutes all end quickly."

"Sarah, promise me you won't just walk into the sunlight."

It was hard to breathe through my tears. "That you *won't* end it without saying goodbye. Don't exorcise yourself. You're the best friend I've ever had."

"Rightbackatcha." I could feel her grinning, and then Sarah came and sat right before me, same as she ever was. "With the bar set so low, imagine how many better friendships we'll have in the future. I'm over being vicarious, you know?"

"Yeah. Me too."

She whispered in my ear, "Check under the mailbox."

She kissed me once on the head and I wrapped my arms around her, but there was only empty air.

I was still crying when Seiji appeared. "Who were you talking to?"

"Sarah."

"Oh." He glared around the backyard. "HELLO, SARAH! YOU HAVE REALLY UPSET US ALL!"

I tried to breathe. "She's gone, Seiji."

"*Gone*, gone?" He glared at the darkness, as if it had personally knifed her.

"Just gone. Taking a permanent vacation, I think."

"Oh." Seiji pondered this and then leaned over. He stared directly into my eyes. "Is that good or bad?"

"Both, I think. Seiji, have you checked under the mailboxes?"

"No!" He was ready to sprint away, but I caught his arm.

"Don't," I said, standing, looking at the house we'd gutted.

Instead, we paid a visit to the pay phone outside the 7-Eleven between our homes, while wearing Santa hats and sunglasses. We called in an anonymous tip to the Rochdale Police Station. Somehow, in a move that felt so damn *Rochdale*, we got an answering machine. Then again, it was 4:00 a.m., and we were caught in the twilight days between Christmas and New Year's, when nothing felt quite real. Whatever sad sap was on duty was probably out dealing with roadkill cleanup or something.

"The remains of Sarah Zielinski, missing since 1976, can be found beneath the mailboxes at 134 Abbot Row," Seiji said.

"Some dickhead in her family did it!" I added from under his arm.

We hung up.

I watched those hilly shoulders slump. "I could sleep like the dead."

"Was that a joke, Seiji Grayson?"

"I don't know. I'm too tired to know what a joke is."

I looked up at the 7-Eleven sign. Open twenty-four hours, bless them. Open for eternity.

"Wanna get a Slurpee?"

MARCH 2003

DANNY

ME

It was astounding, the difference a few letters could make. When I filed for emancipation from my mother in March, I also filed to change my legal name. I looked at my learner's permit and the official name on it: Daniel Miller.

The emancipation was actually a group decision. Mom and I started going to group therapy at the Green House, where there was an all-honesty policy. During one of our sessions, I admitted that I wasn't a lesbian, cool as lesbians are. I was trans and wanted to make some changes. Mom couldn't ignore what I was saying, not in front of a group of women, several of whom were queer themselves. Maybe to get back at me, or maybe to follow the group's policy, she then admitted that she had been in contact with Dad, and had seriously considered moving back in with him.

"And so I think you're right, Dani," she summarized, while fear built inside me and I crumpled a Styrofoam cup in my hand. "I can't seem to get better, not as quickly as you deserve. And if you're on your own, even if I fail—you'll be okay."

"Mom . . ."

"I mean it. Go make your own choices. You've lived with enough of mine."

So we filed the paperwork. When we were submitting it to the courthouse, I told her I'd probably stick around the apartment even once I was emancipated, so long as Dad wasn't there. We could support each other but also escape each other if we needed to.

Mom liked the idea, or I think she did. It was hard to tell through the sobbing.

I didn't think she would ever have all her shit together, and I likely wouldn't either, even though I had more time to try. At the very least, we were aware of our shit, and aware we might need counseling or medication. Mostly we were aware that we had to keep trying.

We lived together without bickering too much, for once. I wore my binder and told her when school was horrible, and Mom told me whenever she felt tempted to reach out to Dad. Maybe our peace was temporary, but that didn't make it matter less. Maybe the opposite, even.

But not all of me was Mom's business. Mom didn't need to know that I had emailed Corina's aunt Jo about hormone therapy. She didn't need to know I'd be doing my own research on testosterone and packing and my identity. Some things were mine.

I asked Coach Ma if I could return to cross-country on the boys' team the following year. She said, "Sure. We'll need new blood on the JV team. We're booting Charley for harassing his teammates."

I tried not to grin, but I didn't try very hard. I knew it was unkind to gloat, but if you can't gloat at the expense of assholes, what good is victory?

———

"You could have chosen anything," Seiji remarked, when I showed him my learner's permit. We were at the flower shop's café, sipping on hot Assam tea. Aunt Lavonne was around, and she moved like she was constantly apologizing to Seiji, which was awkward, but I suspected they were trying, just like Mom and me. Most people are always trying. "You could have had *any* name."

"What, like Chestnut or Santa or Jerry the Iguana?"

"I'm glad you're still Danny, though."

I snorted. "Why? Easy to remember?"

"You've been you all along." He shrugged. "Makes sense to stay the same."

"You say that like it's a good thing."

"It is." This fucking guy. "Hey. About my dad?"

"Yeah?" The ghost in question was sitting behind us, crying onto his table.

"What if I don't want to do anything about him?" Seiji asked, stirring his tea.

"Oh. Um, I guess that's your choice."

He rested his chin in one hand. "I can't make decisions for him. Whether he goes or stays, I'm his son and I'm sad. But making decisions for him is not my job."

Imagine if Seiji had been my friend for years. Imagine if I'd learned long ago that people could put distance between themselves and trauma. Maybe Sarah and I would have done better with a friend like Seiji.

347

Mr. Nakamura-Grayson stood up and walked into Stella's Garden with the rope in his arms.

Seiji and I both ignored the sound of the breaking pot.

————

The discovery of human remains in Rochdale didn't make national news. Why would it have? How many girls went missing every year? How many had gone missing since Sarah Zielinski vanished in 1976?

Still, Sarah was all the townies could talk about.

It was certainly big news in the lobby at the motel, where we all gathered around to listen to Seiji read the headline and subsequent article. I listened cross-legged on the floor while Addy's floating knitting needles click-clacked beside me.

Patricia shushed some of the children, who didn't understand what the fuss was about. Since the lobby had expanded again, she was happy more often—Alphonse had gone back to the farm to collect any ghosts who were still wandering lost. He brought them back with his sweetness and his nudging.

In addition to two more children found wandering at the petting zoo, there were also some Victorian ladies and gentlemen who were terribly grumpy about the evils of electricity but otherwise seemed kind enough.

Many of the O'Connor ghosts were apologetic, and when asked whether they were murderers, we took them at their word when they denied it. We set up the men in an empty room of the motel, and the women occupied half the mailboxes in the lobby. Sometimes we held gatherings and group therapy sessions; one of the dead women had been an actual psychiatrist in the 1990s. Sometimes the ghosts came and went or had nothing to do with one another.

But given the auspicious news of the day, Patricia and Alphonse had darted around the property until every able ghost was gathered in the lobby. There were fifteen of them living with us now, and many had shrunk down to make way for Seiji, who'd wandered heedless through the crowd to sit atop the check-in counter.

He cleared his throat. "MURDERED, NOT MISSING: Uncovered Body of Teen Girl Missing Since the '70s Implicates Brother."

"God, that's *abysmal* writing," Patricia said, groaning. "Curse the *Rochdale Herald*!"

"The body of Sarah Jean Zielinski of Rochdale was discovered some weeks ago in the yard of her former family home. Zielinski, 16, had been declared missing in 1976, two weeks after she stopped attending school. The teen, who enjoyed chess—"

"Wait, *seriously?*" I said, failing to picture it.

"—and journalism—"

"That's more like it," Patricia said, as we exchanged grins.

"—was first presumed to be a runaway. Now the time for presumption has ended: Sarah Zielinski is in fact dead, and her older brother—"

"Wait," I cried, and Seiji paused.

"Don't bother saying his name!" called Addy.

"Deny him the satisfaction," agreed Valencia, one of the prim older ghosts.

I relayed the message. Seiji nodded. "I'll call him Fuckhead instead."

No one seemed to mind his substitution. One of the old gents said, "Hear, hear!"

Seiji continued, "Fuckhead, now 57, then 19, is suspected to be the primary perpetrator of the crime. According to Zielinski's sister, Ellen Waters, 53, Fuckhead tormented and molested both sisters for years. Waters claims Fuckhead, who was abused himself, became enraged when Zielinski rejected his advances and throttled her in her bed. Waters, then 12, shared a room with her sister and had hid in the closet when she heard their brother approaching. Waters then witnessed the atrocity, but was too frightened to come forward until police contacted her about the body last month. She has since revealed that Fuckhead disposed of his sister with the help of his father and uncle."

Nobody was grinning anymore. The air smelled of empathy and rage. Seiji paused, either sensing this or coping with his own thoughts.

"Zielinski's skeletal remains were discovered upon receiving an anonymous tip. Subsequent DNA evidence, combined with Ellen Waters's testimony, have led to the arrest of family man and meteorologist Fuckhead Fuckington. Neighbors and friends of Fuckhead expressed shock at the news.

"'He's the nicest man ever,' claimed Pam Kletter, his neighbor of five years. He's always waved hello at everyone."

"Neighbors are the absolute worst," observed the elderly ghost of Tina Robins, rolling her eyes. "Busybodies and know-nothings all."

I laughed and relayed this to Seiji.

"I wish I could hear you all," he said wistfully. "And see you too."

"They say they just like to see you smile." That was more what I wanted.

"Don't tell people to smile." But I saw his lips curl behind his fist. I wondered what this must look like to him. I saw a crowd, but he saw only me.

Seiji didn't hesitate, didn't doubt me anymore. I thought his confidence in people like me was as tragic as it was beautiful, his greatest strength and weakness.

"Fuckhead has denied the accusations. He is expected to stand trial this August."

"You know," said Krissie. I didn't know her well yet, but it was hard to miss her dangle earrings and eighties shoulder pads. "I've always been an autumn, myself, but I'm eager to bust out my summer palette."

"Well, there you have it, folks," I said. "Sarah's been solved."

"Well, *she* hasn't," Patricia corrected, "but her murder has."

"People aren't solvable," Krissie said, popping her gum. "But it's a nice idea."

"I have learned how to solve division equations, however!" Alphonse declared, beaming. I had no idea how he already took after Seiji. One of the other faceless O'Connor ghosts ruffled his hair. Finally the dead began to depart, heading back to their private rooms, their cubbies and projects and dreams and unlives.

Addy hung back. "It's going well, now."

"Yeah, somehow."

"We should invite more people here, if they'd like to come. Expand the congregation."

"Addy, please, I know what you mean and I know you're super into churches, but I don't like that word. It's too culty."

"Hear, hear," said a faceless woman before she popped away.

"How you can still be so devout, I don't understand," remarked Tina.

"Because I choose to be," Addy said fiercely, "and no one can tell this girl not to be whatever she wants to be. Not anymore."

"Who are you talking to?" Seiji asked, listening to yet another one-sided conversation.

"Addy. She thinks we should gather more souls."

"*Without* exorcising anyone," she added.

"Without exorcising anyone," I echoed.

Seiji nodded. "Well, it's not as unsafe as it was before."

"How do you mean?"

"I mean, even if I can't see them—aren't there like a dozen women here who'll kick murderer butt if they come knocking?"

"It's not a dozen women." My heart felt full as our gazes locked. He often wore his hair back now, and didn't hide his ruddy cheeks. "Let me walk you home, Seiji."

———

"Do you think Sarah will come back, now that she's been avenged?" Seiji asked.

"Kind of avenged," I amended. "Hopefully, after the trial, she'll actually be avenged."

"Do you think Sarah will come back, now that she's been kind of avenged?"

"I'm not sure. I guess that's up to her, not me."

The snow was finally melting, leaving sad piles of mud behind. It was too dark to be certain, but I thought grass might be poking through the cracks in the sidewalk as we trudged toward Murphy's Flowers. "Maybe she will, but I don't know that this changes anything. I mean, she's still dead, and we still had a really toxic relationship. Sarah doesn't get my being trans. I think she's trying, but she doesn't understand. I'm going to start testosterone soon. If she comes back, she can't pretend it's not happening."

Seiji nodded. "Oh."

"What does that mean?" I demanded, raising an eyebrow.

"It's just, what's not to get?" he asked without guile. "Some people are born with bad eyes, so they wear glasses. Some people are born with funny legs, so they wear splints. And some people are born with, um, endowed torsos, so they wear binders."

I snorted, stepping around a puddle. "God, Seiji, that's such a simple way of looking at it."

"Life is too complicated. I don't want to add to that."

I'd complicated his life, and he'd complicated mine.

"That's true," I admitted. "When you mix everything together, you get gray."

"Or shit brown," he said wisely.

"Speaking of shit." We were outside the shop. Behind the glass, a thousand flowers bloomed. "Are you and your aunt okay now?"

"Not quite." He shrugged. "It's another gray area."

"Right." But maybe, I thought, *maybe*, gray got a bad rap. Maybe gray was beautiful because it was gray, because a lot of lives ended in it, tombstones or ashes. Gray was real, and gray was everywhere and it was ignored like death, but it didn't have to be a bad thing, not if you took ownership of it.

Seiji's eyes were black, not gray, and his lips were pink, but when I leaned up to kiss him, that didn't matter. When he kissed me back, cupping my chin in his hands, I saw every color but mostly violet. Violet and gray were almost the same.

I pulled away, blushing more than he was for once, if our reflections in the window were anything to go by. Two boys kissing and blushing, one searching for the other's eyes, the other staring sheepishly at his feet. "I don't know why I did that."

"Because you like me," Seiji said, still seeking my gaze.

"Damn it, Seiji! But I'm a guy!"

He shrugged. "I mean, I'm a guy, too. I like guys."

"I mean, I'm the kind of guy that probably likes girls!"

"Maybe you like boys, too. Maybe it's another gray area."

"Maybe it is," I agreed, breathing against his neck. "I don't know. I think it's gonna take a long time to figure out. Maybe I *won't* figure it out."

"Well, what's the rush?" Seiji grinned wide. "Not like we're dying."

I punched him on the shoulder, and he laughed, booming, his face alive. If I kissed him again, and then again, no one but the dead saw me do it.

AUTHOR'S NOTE

If you are feeling scared or alone or in need of immediate support, the following lifelines are here to help you.

Trans Lifeline: Staffed by trans people, for trans people.
1-877-565-8860

TrevorLifeline: 24/7 support for LGBTQ+ youth in crisis or in need of connection.
1-866-488-7386

National Suicide Prevention Lifeline
1-800-273-8255

National Domestic Violence Hotline
1-800-799-SAFE